Knight Flyers

Ann McCune

Knight Flyers

Dreamcatcher

['drēmˌkaCHər, 'drēmˌkeCHər]

NOUN

A small hoop containing a horsehair mesh, or a similar construction of string or yarn, decorated with feathers and beads, believed to give its owner good dreams. Dreamcatchers were originally made by Native Americans.

CHAPTER 1

"Was that another moving truck?" I asked, tightening down the drain plug on the oil pan of Billy's truck before pushing my way out from under it. I sat up and watched the semi-truck amble up the mountain towards the Freeman Mansion.

"Looks like it." Billy offered me a hand to help me up.

"I can manage. I wouldn't want you to mess up your manicure." I showed him my oil-covered hands and braced my legs under myself before standing.

"Liz, when are you going to learn to not stick your hand in the oil as it comes out?" He handed me a rag, and I wiped the black sludge off.

"Someday soon, I hope." I put the rag in the trashcan, took a bottle of oil off the shelf, uncapped it, and threw the lid at Billy.

"Hey, watch it! I just got this shirt." He pulled it away from his chest to make sure he didn't get any oil on it.

"How was Denver?" I tipped the bottle into the opening of the oil reservoir and watched the golden liquid leave the bottle.

"Same old, same old. Played so much Call of Duty with my cousins I think I need to start wearing glasses for eyestrain. What did you do?"

"Worked, did homework, tried to figure out what kind of community service I want to do this summer."

"If it wasn't for me you would never have any fun, admit it."

"Oh, Billy the God of Fun. I pledge my allegiance to you," I said, deadpan. "What would we have done if you stayed here for spring break?" He hesitated for a second while I took the empty bottle of oil off the reservoir and threw it in the trash. "Let me guess, play Call of Duty until we passed out from exhaustion?"

"We could have taken the snow machines out, it would have been fun." He stuck his hands in the pocket of his jeans.

"The weather was crap besides I like doing homework." I leaned over the engine of the truck, pulled the dipstick out, cleaned it, then shoved it back into the hole.

"Only because you want to get into the Air Force Academy. Who is that?"

In my hurry to see who he was talking about I pulled the dipstick out too quickly and flung a line of oil across my face. "Crap," I yelled a little too loudly and started to look for another rag.

"Just look." Billy didn't even turn around to see why I was complaining.

I looked out the windows of the garage door and saw a brand-new black suburban parked at the fuel pumps outside. With its tinted windows it reminded me of an FBI vehicle.

"It's a little early for tourists. The road through the Park isn't open yet." I reached for another rag but stopped when the back door opened, and a guy got out to look around. He was tall and beefy, maybe a football player. His hair was light brown and cut short. His jeans hung low on his hips, and I saw a white T-shirt under his black leather jacket. He looked like he should have been in an Abercrombie and Fitch advertisement, not standing at the gas pumps in my little town. He pulled the jacket closer around him, as if he were cold. He turned toward us, and my breath caught. He was gorgeous. He looked to be about my age with a wide strong jaw smooth as a fender with a high-gloss paint job. His nose was a little short and a little wide. His lips made me lick my own in anticipation of how they would feel pressed against mine; they looked soft and pink. I wanted to know what color his eyes were, but it was impossible to tell behind his aviator sunglasses.

He took a step closer to the garage door and bent to look inside. He gave us a little wave, and I waved back then exhaled, remembering to breathe. He wiped his hand down his face, and I remembered I had oil all over mine from the darn dipstick. I felt my cheeks redden and I turned away to wipe the oil off my face.

"What was that about?" Billy asked, looking from me to the guy. "Why are you blushing?"

"I forgot I had oil on my face. I think he's laughing at me." I turned back around and watched him move to the far side of the SUV.

"No, he wasn't laughing, but I am. I don't think I have ever seen you blush before." Billy laughed and walked over to me. "Are you done?"

"With what? Oh, your truck. Yeah, your oil has been changed. Pay up." I shut the hood and held my hand out to Billy, waiting for my payment. I wanted to look over my shoulder at the guy with the suburban, but I didn't need any more grief from Billy.

Billy groaned but handed over the twenty dollars I charged my friends to change their oil. "I wonder if they are the people moving into the Freeman Mansion." I put the money in the pocket of my coveralls and watched as the guy got back in the suburban and pulled onto the road going the same way as the moving trucks had.

"I wouldn't be surprised, it's an expensive vehicle for anyone around here, but I bet they are just passing through. He doesn't look like he belongs in the mountains." Billy opened the door to his truck. "Do you want me to stick around and keep you company?"

"No, I've got homework to do, and you probably do too. Our history paper is due tomorrow." I went over to the garage door opener.

"I know, I have it halfway done. I wasn't a total slacker over break." He stood, waiting to get in his truck.

"See you tomorrow." I hit the button to open the garage door.

"Yeah, see you then." Billy jumped into his truck—he had to jump as it was lifted so high it was the only way he could get in—and fired it up.

An icy wind made me shiver as it blew snow into the garage. Billy pulled the truck out slowly, being careful to clear the door without doing any damage. I pushed the button to lower the door and went to my locker to take my coveralls off. I pulled the twenty out and went into the store. Sundays during mud season were the slowest days at the Twisted Pine Gas N'Go, but I loved it. I could get a lot of homework done, or work on my friends' cars without being disturbed.

At five, I flipped the closed sign on the store and locked up. I walked around the side of the building as snowflakes the size of half dollars swirled around me in the breeze. It was a typical early April storm in the Rocky Mountains, and I was over it. I was ready for warm weather and blue skies.

When I got to the Jeep Wrangler my dad surprised me with on my sixteenth birthday, I was freezing. I wished I would have brought my gloves inside with me instead of leaving them on the passenger seat. I got in and started it up, put my icy gloves on, and pulled my ice scraper off the floor. I cranked up the heat and got out to clean the snow and ice off the windshield. Once my windows were clear, and I got back in, and the heater was blowing warm air. I took my gloves off before putting my seat belt on then pulled out of the parking lot and drove home.

I lived ten miles from the center of Twisted Pines, on the side of Mt. Ersa. My parents' house was typical for the area before the Rocky Mountain National Park opened and vacation rentals started to take over. It was modest, with three bedrooms and two and a half baths. It had one of the best views of Freeman Lake and the town of Twisted Pines at its shores. I loved our house but winding my way up the side of the mountain to get home in the winter often made me wish we would move.

I drove slowly around one of the hairpin turns, covered in ice and snow, when I saw an animal standing in the middle of the road. I hit the brakes hard and the ABS took over making a grinding noise, but not slowing me down. Unfortunately, the moose in front of me had the opposite problem, he didn't want to move. My dad's voice filtered through my thoughts. *Don't swerve to miss an animal, it's better to hit it than to flip.*

CHAPTER 2

The moose's head swung around, and our eyes locked for a split second before I hit him broadside. Time slowed down. He flipped up, landing on the hood then sliding toward me. The weight of the twelve-hundred-pound moose made the metal on the hood groan and deform in protest but didn't slow down his momentum. His antlers slammed into the windshield, shattering it, and came toward me. I put my hands up to protect my face, but it was too late. His antler hit me in the middle of my forehead and I jerked back, some people thought antlers were art, I always thought of them as a weapon. I stomped harder on the brakes, and we finally came to a stop.

He started thrashing his head around, and grunting in a deep baritone, trying to free himself. The hole in the windshield was getting bigger and I shrank back in my seat trying to keep my face as far from the weapon as possible. I'm not sure how, but one second, the antler was a foot from my face, and in the next instant it hit me, hard, across the face. Fireworks exploded before my eyes, a sharp pain blossomed across my face, and I felt blood gushing from a cut near my hairline. I needed to get out of the car. I took my foot off the clutch, stalling the Jeep, and groped for the door handle while trying not to get hit in the head again.

I pulled the handle, and the door opened. I tried to squeeze out, but I was stuck. I couldn't move, and the moose was slowly making a bigger and bigger hole in the windshield. I looked down and realized I still had my seatbelt on. I reached for the buckle and fumbled with the button, my hands shaking so badly I couldn't keep pressure on the button to release myself. I flexed my hand, took a breath, tried not to think about the moose still struggling to free itself, and pushed the button, finally releasing myself from the seat. I slid out as quickly as I could, while trying to stay away from the antlers that were trying to kill me, when something, most likely the antler, hit me on the side of the head and everything went black.

I was walking around Billy's house. It was full of people. He must be having a party, because all my friends were there having a good time, I could smell keg beer, and the sour smell of marijuana. I needed to find Billy, but I couldn't remember why. I went through the kitchen and the living room without finding him. People were staring at me like I had something on my face or I was naked. I looked down and let out a sigh of relief, I had on my usual jeans and hoodie. They were dirty though, caked with something dark, almost rust in color, why would I wear dirty clothes to a party? Yes, I was a tomboy, but even I made sure to wear clean clothes.

I walked upstairs, weaving my way around people, most of them looked at me then whispered to their friend. Even the couples making out stopped what they were doing to gawk at me. When I reached the top of the stairs, I was back in the kitchen. I shook my head confused, how was I back in the kitchen if I had just come up the stairs?

"Liz," I heard Billy yell from somewhere deeper in the house.

"Billy, where are you?" I yelled back, trying to run through the house, but everyone was standing in the way. I zigzagged around them until I broke free from the crowd and yelled for Billy again.

"Liz," he bellowed.

I went to the coat closet under the stairs and pulled the door open. The bare bulb light was on and swaying slightly, causing the light to bounce off the walls in the claustrophobic space. I didn't know if it was the light or the small space, but my stomach rolled and I resisted the urge to throw up. Billy was huddled in the corner with his face buried in his knees. "Billy are you alright?" I bent down in front of him and put my hand on his head.

Moving almost too fast for me to see, Billy grabbed one of my hands and pulled me into the closet while the door slammed closed, locking me in with him. He looked up at me, and I realized it wasn't Billy. Its face was long and hollow, its skin sucked tight to the bones of its face like it was starved. Where its nose should have been, was smooth skin with two slits to breathe through. Where its eyes should have been, were black unseeing holes. I felt like if I looked at them too long they would suck me into their abyss, and I would never escape.

I screamed and tried to pull my arm out of its grip, but it only squeezed harder. I made a fist with my free hand and punched it in the face with every ounce of strength I had. Instead of hurting it and forcing it to let me go, my hand bounced off as if I punched a rubber ball. The monster grabbed my free hand and laughed. I was trapped.

"You can't get away now that I found you, Martröð Veiðimaður," its dry croaking voice said, flashing razor-sharp teeth at me.

"Let me go," I said as tears started to fall down my face. I wanted to kick it, punch it, stab its eyes—even though it had none—but it had my hands in a vicelike grip. It pulled me to the floor and I could not get my legs underneath me to stand. It started to pull me closer to its mouth. When my face was a few inches away, it opened its mouth, giving me an up-close look at its teeth. I screamed again and closed my eyes. How was I going to survive this monster?

Someone pounded on the door startling the monster. I opened my eyes as it loosened its grip, and I pulled my arms away from it and pushed myself back against the door, ready to kick it if it came at me again. "Help." I screamed.

"Watch out I'm going to blow the door open," a male voice I didn't recognize called.

"I have nowhere else to go. I'm on the floor in front of the door and its coming for me again." I braced my hands on the floor, on either side of me, forcing them to take my weight, so I could kick the monster if it came within range.

"He will not save you, Veiðimaður, you are mine." The monster stood; it was impossibly tall and skinny, and Billy's normal T-shirt and jeans were almost falling off its body. It started to walk towards me and I prepared myself to kick it in the knees; it was the only sensitive part I would reach from the floor. I didn't know what scared me more, its unseeing eyes or its sharp teeth. Its arms came down to grab me, and I kicked it hard forcing it to back up a step. The next instant, the door exploded inward, showering me with chunks of wood and splinters.

When I opened my eyes, a hand was being extended down to me. I followed it up his arm to his shoulder, then settled on the guy's face. It was the guy from the gas station in the suburban. Remembering the monster trying to kill me, I tore my gaze away and looked for the monster. It was in a ball on the floor with large chunks of wood sticking out of his back. "You will not escape me forever. I know what you are," said the monster, looking up at with me with a smile that made me shiver.

Still crying, I took my savior's hand and he helped me to my feet. I stepped over what was left of the door, remembering I was still in Billy's house. "Take her," my savior said, his voice was deeper than

I expected.

He gently pushed me toward a woman with long blonde hair pulled back in a high ponytail. She wore a skintight, black, long-sleeved jump suit with a utility belt. She had piercing blue eyes, and her flawless complexion made her look like she should be a model for Covergirl.

She put her hands on my shoulders and looked into my eyes. "You're dreaming. You have to wake up or you're going to die."

What? I'm dreaming? I thought to myself. I didn't remember going to bed. What had I been doing before the party? I was in my Jeep driving home from work.

"I'm not dreaming, I'm unconscious." This was the most bizarre dream I had ever had.

"Crap," the woman said, taking me by the hand and leading me into the corner of the room. "Base, this is Heather, do you copy?" she asked, talking into a mic on her wrist. She went quiet for a minute. "We have an unconscious civilian trapped by a mare." Turning to me, she asked, "Do you know where you are?"

"I'm on County Road 35 just past the McFisk place. I hit a moose."

"Did you copy that base?" She waited again. She looked at me and smiled. "Okay, paramedics and the sheriff are on their way. Now, we just have to keep you safe until they get there."

A loud thud pulled my attention to the closet I had been trapped in. A second later, an ear-splitting scream erupted from the room, and I put my fingers in my ears to block it out.

I moved to get closer to the closet, wanting to make sure the guy who saved me was okay, but Heather put her arm up, blocking my way before I could get past her.

"Where are you going?" she asked, putting her other hand on her hip.

"I want to make sure your friend is alright." I looked at her then the closet.

"He's fine. The scream you heard was the mare dying. He will be out in a second."

True to her word the guy came out of the closet covered in a gel-like substance, reminding me of the slime that covers fish, only it was neon green. "What's all over him?"

"It's what's left of the mare he killed. Don't get too close, it smells horrible."

The guy walked over to us looking concerned. "Why is she still here? Didn't you tell her to wake up?" he asked, wiping the slime off his face with his hand. Even covered with slime, he was still the best-looking guy I had seen up close in my life. I looked into his eyes, they were the palest blue, like ice when it freezes smooth in a pond.

"She was in a car accident and was knocked unconscious. I notified base, help is on the way."

"This is the most messed up dream I have ever I had," I heard myself saying, unable to take my eyes off the guy.

"Don't worry, princess, you won't remember a thing." He smiled, showing off his dimples and straight, white teeth.

"Don't call me princess." I was anything but a princess, much to my mother's dismay.

"Then what should I call you?" He took a step closer.

"Elizabeth, my friends call me Liz." My cheeks started to burn but I didn't back down. "What do you go by? Dickhead?"

"Only my friends get to call me Dickhead. You can call me Shawn." He took another step closer and I could smell the slime dripping off him. Heather was right, the smell was somewhere between day-old fish guts, and a bloated dead cow right after it popped.

I tried to take a step back to find some clean air, but they had me in the corner and I ran into the wall. With nowhere to go, I took a breath and my stomach revolted. I bent over, grabbed my knees, and threw up everything in my stomach. What a nightmare, first I'm attacked by a monster then I throw up on the shoes of the hottest guy I had ever seen. *Wait, I'm dreaming, how could I throw up in my dream?*

"Way to go, Dickhead." Heather pulled my hair out of my face. "Now her car is going to be covered in vomit."

"Not the Jeep," I murmured, feeling dizzy after emptying my stomach.

"It is probably totaled if she hit a moose," Shawn said.

I tried to focus on him, but I couldn't. My head was spinning, and I couldn't make it stop long enough to see him clearly.

"They're waking her up," I heard Heather say as I closed my eyes hoping the spinning would stop. I forced myself to open my eyes, but my eyelids felt like they weighed as much as a bulldozer. "What's happening to me?"

"Don't worry, princess, they're waking you up. You won't remember any of this."

I tried to say, *don't call me princess,* but darkness enveloped me, and I was floating away.

CHAPTER 3

I was lying on something hard. It kept jostling forward and backward then it would shake like I was on a rolling bed going over a bump. I wanted everything to stop. I wanted to wake up and open my eyes, but they were so heavy. My head felt like it was splitting inch by inch and I wondered what would happen if it broke in half. I heard people murmuring and a woman crying. It was a familiar sound. I knew who was crying. Mom.

I forced my eyes open. "Mom," I whispered. "It's okay, I'm right here."

She jerked her head toward me and squeezed my hand. "Elizabeth, can you hear me?"

"Yes, Mom, I'm okay." There was something sticking in my nose, and I tried to bring my hand up to my face, but I couldn't move it. I struggled for a second before I realized I was tied down. "Where are we?"

"In an ambulance on the way to the hospital in Spruce. Do you remember what happened?"

I thought about it for a second. The only thing running through my mind was the messed-up dream I had with the guy. I thought harder. "There was a moose in the road, it wouldn't move out of the way." I thought of the sickening thud as the front of my Jeep hit it, then the shattering glass as his antlers came through the windshield. "I did what Dad said. I didn't swerve to miss it. His antler came in through the windshield and hit me a couple of times."

"That's right, honey. You have a pretty big cut on the side of your head, and they think you have a concussion."

"Maybe that's why I remember my dream." When I closed my eyes all I saw were Shawn's blue eyes. "They said I wouldn't remember it, but I do."

"What are you talking about?"

"I had a dream and there were these people, they saved me from a monster, Mom."

"Just rest, sweetie, we'll be at the hospital before you know it. Dad is right behind us."

I was poked and prodded by a doctor and nurse when we arrived at the hospital. My head was stitched and CAT-scanned. I had a minor concussion, but they still wanted to me to spend the next two nights in the hospital.

When I asked my dad how bad the Jeep was, he shook his head and turned away, making me cry. I had it for almost a year and it was dead. When I asked about the moose, he told me it was still alive when the sheriff got there but had three broken legs, and the sheriff had to put him down.

Part of me was sad the moose suffered for so long, but I put my hand to my head, feeling the jagged line of stitches and thought about my Jeep, maybe he deserved it for hanging out on the icy road.

I spent the next day and night in the hospital. They thought I would be fine but my dad, the doctor, insisted they keep me for observation. I spent most of the time sleeping and being woken up by either my mom or the nurses to make sure I wasn't dead. All I wanted to do was go home and sleep in my own bed.

The next morning, I went into the bathroom to brush my teeth and take a shower. When I looked in the mirror I was horrified by what I saw. My normal ivory skin tone was now more like black and purple. Those darn antlers did a number on my face. I could only open my left eye partway because the skin around it was completely black and swollen. A blood vessel in my eye had burst resulting in the worst bloodshot green eye I had ever seen. There was a dark bruise under my right eye, and my jaw. My lower lip was a lovely shade of purple.

I was missing a chunk of my long blond hair where they had to shave it to clean and stitch up my head. I managed to get the blood and vomit out of my hair and wash my face without getting the stitches wet.

After my careful shower, I got dressed in a comfortable pair of lounge pants, and my favorite Denver Broncos hoodie. Once I was dressed, my mom had finished my discharge paperwork, and they forced me to ride in a wheelchair to get to my dad's four-door Dodge truck. It was cold but clear when we made it outside, and I wondered where my sunglasses were as I squinted in the light.

"Can we at least go by my Jeep, so I can get my backpack?" I asked, turning to look at my mom, who forced me to ride in front. She thought I might get car sick sitting in the back.

"No, Billy is going to pick it up after school. You are taking a brain break today," Mom said from the backseat, and Dad nodded his head in agreement.

"But I'll get behind if I don't work on some stuff today."

"Your mother is right. You need to take it easy. You have a concussion; your brain needs to heal. Overworking it isn't going to solve any problems."

"At least I have my computer," I mumbled to myself.

"Nope. You have two options today. Trashy television or sleep."

"Seriously? You guys are not being fair about this."

"Sweetheart, you were in a major accident. You need to rest, not worrying about school or getting into the Air Force Academy for at least the rest of today." Mom leaned forward and put her hand on my shoulder.

"You guys are so unfair." I slumped in my seat, closed my eyes, and pretended to sleep the rest of the way home.

After Mom tucked me in on the couch with an extra dreamcatcher hanging over it, she gave me the remote control and went into the kitchen to make lunch. Dad went back to work at the clinic and I was stuck with crappy daytime television to keep me company. I found an old *X-Files* marathon to watch, but I couldn't stay awake for long.

I dreamt of the monster from my dream. I was standing on the dock at the lake. It was a beautiful summer day. The sun was out, and the air was warm. I was wearing my favorite cargo shorts and white tank top. I was waiting for Billy to come pick me up on his dad's boat. I heard something growl and turned around to see the monster racing up the dock. I backpedaled until I reached the end of the dock because I didn't want to jump in the water. I didn't know why, but my gut told me I may not make it out if I went in, so I bent my knees and readied myself to fight the monster. When it was ten feet from me, it jumped, and I lowered myself even further to prepare for impact, closing my eyes tightly. Only the impact never came. I opened my eyes. The monster was flat on its back staring up at the sky.

"You think you're safe Veiðimaður? You will not always have your protection, and when you don't... you will be mine," its scratchy voice said before laughing at the sky. "Yes, you will be mine."

All I could do was stare at the monster. How had it ended up on its back? I held my hand up and waved it through the air. There was nothing there, but something had stopped the monster from getting me. I felt a hand on my shoulder and I jerked.

"Stay away from me," I yelled, waking up on the couch and looking around.

"I love you too," Billy said, walking around the couch to stand in front of me with a bouquet of flowers and a bunch of balloons telling me to 'get well soon.' He sat them on the coffee table and took a step back. "Wow, you look like you got into a fight with a moose."

"Ha-ha, I did get into a fight with a moose, smartass. At least I survived. Thanks for the flowers."

Billy sat on the coffee table facing me. "But you had help, I heard the Jeep isn't going to make it and you're welcome for the flowers."

"My poor Jeep, it was the best car I ever had."

"It was the only car you've ever had." Billy crossed his arms over his chest.

"That doesn't mean it wasn't the best." I sat up and leaned against the armrest of the couch.

"You had insurance, you'll find another Jeep. I hope you feel better then you look." He grimaced.

"Thanks, Billy. Yeah, I'm feeling good, just tired. My mom thinks I'm going to die in my sleep and comes in every hour to wake me up and check on me."

"I'll be sure to thank her. I don't want you to die either." He patted the top of my head.

I pulled away from him as pain radiated from my head down my neck. "Ow, watch it. Just because you can't see a bruise doesn't mean it doesn't hurt."

"Sorry, I thought you were tougher." Billy sounded like he was being mean, but he was looking at me like I was a dog in an ASPCA commercial.

"I'll be okay. Are you going to give me a ride to school tomorrow, or am I going to have to take the bus?"

"Are you sure you want to go to school with the way you look?

Everyone is going to make fun of you."

"Thanks for making me feel even more self-conscious than I already do, ass. I'm sure you will be there to protect me if someone makes fun of me tomorrow."

"You know I will." He smiled shyly, which was unlike him. "So, tell me what happened. Your mom and dad glazed over it for me, but I want to know what you remember."

I spent the next twenty minutes telling Billy everything I remembered about the moose, and its collision with the Jeep, before my mom came in.

"Billy, I hate to chase you off, but Liz needs to rest," Mom said, handing me a soda.

"Rest would be nice," I said, looking at her instead of Billy.

"Okay, I'll pick you up tomorrow morning." Billy stood to leave.

"Thanks for coming over to check on me."

"No problem, I know you would do the same for me," he said, walking toward the front door.

Mom put the Sprite down then followed Billy out. She came back soon after and sat on the coffee table. "He was really worried about you." She pushed a piece of hair back from my face.

"I know. I don't think I could ask for a better best friend." I shrugged.

"Be careful, Lizzy. You are both getting older, and I have a feeling he wants more than only being your best friend."

"What are you trying to say, Mom? Nothing is going to come between me and Billy, we've been friends for too long."

"He has had a crush on you since you were in kindergarten, and I don't think you feel the same way about him. Just treat him carefully."

"What? Billy has a crush on me? Thanks for trying to cheer me up, Mom, but there's no way Billy wants me to be his girlfriend. You should hear how he talks about other girls. Plus, if he did, he would've told me. We have always talked about everything."

"Just think about it and be careful with him. I don't want the two of you to get into a friendship-ending fight."

"You can't be right, but I'll be careful, Mom," I said as she got up and went back into the kitchen.

After eating dinner with Mom and Dad I went to my room and went back to sleep, hoping my mom would let me sleep through the night.

I was at school, walking into my history class. I kept my eye out for the monster who was making itself at home in my dreams, but the only person in the room was Shawn, who was standing at the whiteboard board.

"How are you?" he asked, staring at the board.

"I'll survive," I said, taking a seat at a desk in the front row with a hinged top. "Thank you for saving me from the monster."

"You're welcome." He turned and approached my desk. He put his hands on the sides of it and leaned in. "It sounds like you're lucky to be alive."

"That is what everyone keeps telling me. If I'd had my seat any closer to the windshield, I probably wouldn't be here right now."

"I'm glad you made it. I would like to meet you in person at some point." He leaned closer and his breath on my cheek made me shiver.

"Me too, but how? You're just a dream. You were passing through town when I saw you at the gas station, right?"

"Were you checking me out?" He laughed, not answering my question, and taking a step backwards.

"No," I drew the word out while I was coming up with an excuse. "You were too far away to check out. I couldn't see much."

"I could see you with oil all over your face." He laughed again.

"Were you checking me out?" I couldn't believe I asked, but this was a dream. I could do whatever I wanted.

"From what I could see through the windows of the garage, I liked what I saw." He licked his lips and his eyes became hooded.

"You're kind of an ass." I wanted to get up and put some space between us, because even though he was an ass, his plump lips looked soft, and I wanted to know how they would taste.

"But I'm an ass who saved you from the goblin last night."

"Why did you call it a goblin?"

"I don't know. What would you call it?"

"A monster."

"Well, I'm pretty sure it was a goblin, and I saved you from it. Do I get a reward?" He leaned in so close our noses almost touched.

His lips were so close to mine and I ached to press mine against his to see if they were as soft as they looked, but his snarky attitude stopped me. "What do you want?" I asked, unable to stop myself from licking my lips.

"Oh, I think you know." He moved into me to kiss me, and as much as it pained me, I pulled up the hinged top of the desk and he groaned when his face met the desk instead of my lips.

I scrambled to my feet and ran for the door. "You're nice to look at and all, but you need to work on your manners." The bell started to ring, but it wasn't the short burst of sound it normally was. This was louder and didn't stop. Finally, I figured out it was my alarm clock, time to get up.

CHAPTER 4

I hit the off button on my alarm and forced myself to get out of bed. My whole body hurt, partly from lying around for the past two days, partly from the fight with the moose.

I took a shower, being careful not to get my stitches wet. My face was a dark rainbow of black and blue, but the swelling around my eye was better. I could almost open it all the way. I got dressed in my most comfortable, non-stained jeans, and a vintage AC/DC T-shirt. I finished the look off with a hoodie, with a Jeep logo.

"Morning, Mom," I said when I entered the kitchen. I grabbed a cup of coffee then went and sat at the bar.

"Morning, dear, I have your lunch ready and here is your breakfast." She turned and put a plate with an egg burrito in front of me on the counter. "Are you sure you want to go to school today?"

"Yes, I don't want to get any more behind then I already am." I picked up the stuffed tortilla and brought it to my mouth. Pain radiated through my jaw when I chewed, but the melding of eggs, cheese, and ham was worth the pain.

"Hello?" Billy called from the hallway.

"Hey, Billy," I said, before taking another bite.

"I stopped at your Jeep and picked up your backpack last night." Billy put it on the ground at my feet.

"Why didn't you bring it in last night?" I gave him an evil eye.

"Your mom told me not to." He took the stool next to me at the bar.

"You didn't need to worry about homework last night," Mom said as she washed the skillet she used to make breakfast.

"You guys are such a pain," I said under my breath.

"What was that, sweetheart?" Mom asked, looking up at me.

"Nothing, Mom." I rolled my eyes.

She picked up my now empty plate and took it to the sink. "If today gets to be too much, call me and I'll come get you," Mom said as we headed to the door.

"I will, but it will be fine, Mom." I gave her a hug, before Billy and I went out the front door to his truck. The sun was coming up over the mountains and it looked like it was going to be a clear day, but it was still cold.

Once we were on the road, I started thinking about what people were going to say when they saw my multicolored face, and partially shaved head. "Everyone at school is going to want to know what happened, and I'm not really ready to talk about it."

"Everyone already knows what happened. You know how the rumor mill works. The EMTs told their kids and they told everyone." Billy looked at me from the corner of his eye. "Don't worry, it wasn't your fault. Everyone will be glad you're back."

"I know it wasn't my fault, but you know how I hate attention." My pulse quickened as we came closer to the spot where the moose had clobbered me. I looked over to Billy, he was driving safely and looking around to make sure nothing was going to jump in front of us. When we reached the spot where I hit the moose there was no sign of the accident, the snow must have covered it all up.

"Where's the moose?" Usually animals hit by cars were pulled to the side of the road and left there until spring. "Mom told me they had to put it down, but don't they usually leave it on the side of the road?"

"The game warden took it. Since it was a bull he didn't want anyone to cut his antlers off. He was going to see if the meat was still good. If it is, he's going to donate it to the food bank." Billy sounded serious, which didn't happen very often.

"Well, at least some good will come of it. I should get to keep the antlers after what he did to my Jeep."

"I'll tell him next time I see him. He will probably say you were poaching since you hit it out of season and without a license."

I laughed. "He's such a hard-ass. Did I miss anything at school?"

"We have a bunch of new kids. They all moved here during spring break. I guess their parents are part of Knight Inc, the cyber security firm, who moved into the Freeman Mansion."

"How many new kids are we talking about?" I pulled my eyebrows together.

"Four so far. Two in our class, one sophomore, and one freshman. It sounds like there may be more by fall."

"Wow, when was the last time we had a new kid? Have you met any of them yet?"

"Yeah, I have a couple classes with Shawn and one with Jo. They sat with us at lunch yesterday. You'll like them. Actually, Shawn is the guy you saw at the gas station on Sunday."

"What?" I tensed, every muscle in my body locked and pain radiated from my neck into my head. I was going to have to see the guy I had been dreaming about? "Do I have any classes with him?"

"Yeah, he's in our history class. Why are you so worried?" Billy gave me a sideways glance as we pulled onto the highway.

"I made a fool of myself the first time I saw him." I was scrambling for an excuse; I didn't want to tell Billy about the dreams. "I hate not making a good first impression."

"He's pretty chill, and I doubt he could see you through the glare on the garage door. I bet he won't even know you're the same person, especially with the bruises." We pulled into the parking lot of the high school and I forced myself to take a deep breath.

Billy was right, I had nothing to worry about. When he saw me, I was covered in oil and wearing my coveralls. There was no way he would recognize me as the same person.

The day crawled by, my head hurt, and it was hard to concentrate. I wanted to go home and take a nap, but I wasn't going to let the pain get me anymore behind in my school work than I already was. When lunch came around, the entire school had seen the damage the moose had done.

I went to my table in the cafeteria only to find the guy from my dreams sitting in my spot and the new girl sitting across from him. I wanted to turn around and find a closet to eat in, but Billy had already seen me. Frustrated, I went to the end of the table and sat. I didn't know how to act around a guy I had never met in real life but who was starring in my dreams.

"There you are," Billy said. "Where have you been?"

"Mrs. Webber wanted to make sure I was doing okay. Why is everyone acting so overprotective?" I opened my lunch bag and pulled out the sandwich and apple my mom packed.

"Because hitting a moose and getting an antler to the head is a big deal," Tommy said, before taking a bite of his pizza.

"Plus, look at you," Sam said, holding up his hands. "You look like you got your ass kicked."

"Thank you for making me feel so much better, Sam. Do you

think I don't know how bad I look? I wish I could wave a magic wand and make the bruises go away, but I can't." I blew out a breath and took a bite of my sandwich.

"Guys. Leave her alone. You know she hates attention," Billy said, browbeating the guys. "Hey, have you met Jo and Shawn yet?"

"No," I had forgotten that Billy told me his name on the way to school that morning and remembering while being introduced to him was not what I needed. "Hi, I'm Elizabeth, but you can call me Liz." I nodded my head to Shawn.

"Nice to meet you," he nodded back with a knowing grin on his face. "I'm Shawn."

"You too." I almost said, *but your friends call you Dickhead, right?* but I held my tongue. It was only a few dreams, right? "You must be Jo." I shifted my gaze to the girl sitting across from Shawn.

"Yeah, nice to meet you. Billy told us all about you, sorry about the moose." She nodded giving me a smile.

"Thanks." I smiled, then went back to my lunch. If they were going to sit with us I hoped she wasn't like Tracy; obsessed with hair, makeup, and clothes.

I didn't have a lot of girlfriends because most of the girls at school were very girly-girl and I was not. There were a few girls who sat with us at lunch, and I considered them friends, but I usually ended up hanging out with the guys. They were a lot less drama than girls.

I tuned everyone out as they started talking about car accidents they had been in. I just wanted the day to be over already. When I was done eating, I got up to leave.

"Liz, where are you going?" Billy asked, giving me a confused look.

"I want to get to class early, I have a bunch of work to catch up on." I crinkled my paper bag and took a step back.

"I'm sure Mr. Pearson won't mind. Stay and hang out." I watched Jo glare at him and wondered what that was about.

"We can hang out when I'm caught up with all my homework. I'll see you in history." I left the cafeteria, throwing my trash away at the door.

I was pulling my coveralls on when I felt someone come up behind me. I turned and almost ran into a chest. I took a step back and looked up. Shawn was standing there with his coveralls already on looking at me expectantly.

"Can I do something for you, Shawn?" I crossed my arms over my chest. I didn't want to treat him like the jerk like he was in my dreams, but the dreams were so real it was hard not to.

"Yeah, I noticed you were really quiet at lunch. Are you alright?"

"I would be if people stopped asking me if was alright. My head hurts, I totaled my Jeep, and everyone wants to know if I'm alright. I'm not alright, but there isn't anything you or anyone else can do to make me feel better right now." Why was I being so mean to him? "Look I'm sorry, it's been a crappy day and..." I almost said, *you were a jerk in my dream last night*, but I caught myself. "I want everyone to stop treating me like a cripple."

"Give them till the end of the week, then they will be used to it." He gave me the bright smile I remembered from my dreams and I could not stop my cringe. "Did I say something wrong?"

"This is going to sound crazy, but I keep having these dreams about you," I said, feeling my face turn red. I hoped the bruises covered the blush, because I didn't think I had ever blushed harder.

His face went slack with disbelief, before he smiled again. "You dreamed of me before we met?"

"I saw you getting gas on Sunday, I work there."

"I must have made quite an impression at the gas station,

huh?" He wiggled his eyebrows at me.

"No, I have no idea why I dreamed of you. Maybe I'm psychic since you are acting just like you did in my dream." I turned and went over to the motor I was overhauling. I put on a pair of disposable gloves and got to work.

He followed me laughing. "How is a guy supposed to act when a girl he just met says she been dreaming about him?"

"I don't know. I've never told anyone about my dreams before, but I would think a sensible person wouldn't make a big deal about it."

"I don't mean to make a big deal about it. It's flattering." He held his hands up. "Will you tell me what you dreamed?"

I looked over at him. His unblinking stare told me he was starting to take me seriously, almost like he was worried. "Fine, the first one was when I was knocked unconscious by the moose. It was super realistic, there was a monster or a goblin trying to eat me, suck me dry or something. You busted the door down and killed it. There was a woman there too, I have no idea who she was, but you saved me, then gloated about it. You smelled disgusting." I watched his face as I talked, it went from smug, to concerned, to horrified before he hid it behind an obviously fake smile.

"Then, last night we were in a classroom and you were being a cocky ass, trying to get me to kiss you in appreciation for saving me from the goblin, or whatever was trying to kill me the night I hit the moose." His eyes were huge once I finished telling him about the dream.

He opened his mouth to say something, but Mr. Pearson called us to the front of the shop to start class.

I listened and tried to take notes, but Shawn was distracting me. He kept staring at me, but whenever I looked over to him he would look away. I almost regretted telling him about the dream, but at least he was leaving me alone.

After class, I went back to my locker and got my history book out, wondering where Shawn had gone. I figured he would want to talk to me again, but he was nowhere around when I left the shop.

When I got to history, Billy was sitting in his normal seat, and I took my seat next to him. "How's it going?"

"I'll be happy when this day is over." I opened my history book to review what I missed the day before.

"Do you want to go home? We can leave now." Billy looked concerned.

"No, I want everyone to stop treating me like I'm dying and need to be coddled." I blew out a breath and looked at the ceiling. "Can you just treat me like you normally do?"

"I'll try, but you look like you are in a lot of pain." His eyes were doing that sad ASPCA thing again.

I rolled my eyes just as Shawn walked into the room. He took a seat in the front row almost as far away from us as he could get. Had I done something to make him mad?

"Shawn," Billy called. "Why don't you sit over here with us?"

"I need to sit closer to the white board to see," Shawn said, turning to look at Billy.

"Alright," Billy said, looking confused. He turned to me. "He sat back here with me yesterday and was reading the board just fine."

"I don't know, maybe he lost a contact or something." I had a feeling it had something to with what I told him about my dreams.

After class, Billy and I watched Shawn practically run out of the room. We went to Billy's locker first, and he grabbed his bag and coat then we went to mine where I did the same. As we walked out the front of the school we watched Shawn get into a brand-new, lifted, matt-black Jeep Rubicon and start it up.

"Wow, nice car," I said, trying not to drool.

"Yeah, he said his dad bought it for him because he needed a four-wheel drive up here. I wish my dad would buy me a brand-new truck because we lived up here." Billy unlocked the passenger-side door of his truck and opened it for me.

I grabbed the chicken bar and pulled myself up into the seat. "Yeah, no kidding. I wonder if my parents will even let me get another car after what happened."

Billy shut the door, went around to the driver-side door, and got in. "They will. How else will you get to work?"

"Oh crap, I need to call Bob. I was supposed to work this afternoon." I was so mad my phone didn't survive the accident, there wasn't a lot of cell phone service in Twisted Pines, but I felt lost without it.

"Don't worry, your mom called him. You have the week off. Sorry about your phone." He pulled out of the parking lot and turned towards Twisted Pines' only tow yard and auto body shop.

"Man, this day isn't getting any better," I mumbled to myself as we sped down the road.

CHAPTER 5

"Can you fix it, Phil?" I asked, looking at the squashed front end of my Jeep. The radiator was sitting ninety degrees from where it should have been, both fenders were dented, the hood was caved in from the weight of the moose, and the windshield was gone. The dash looked like someone had fun with a razor blade. There was dried blood and vomit all over the seat and floor, and there was a chunk missing from the steering wheel. I took a step back and put my hands to my midsection.

"Your insurance adjuster was here this morning. He is going to total it. I'm sorry, Liz, I know you loved your Jeep." Phil put a reassuring hand on my shoulder. I fought back tears; it was stupid to cry over a car, but I loved it. "Do you want to get your stuff out?"

"Why don't you give us a few minutes?" Billy asked, pulling me into his arms. I fell into him and let the tears fall, oblivious to Phil walking away. When I was finally done crying, I pulled back from Billy.

"Let's put him to bed." I went to the driver-side door and yanked it open.

"I can do it if you want." Billy put a hand on my lower back and tried to steer me away from what was left of my Jeep.

"No, I got it. I just didn't realize how bad it was. I was really lucky."

"Now do you understand why everyone is so concerned?"
He put his hands on his hips.

"Yeah, I get it now." I took a deep breath and started going through the glove box. Billy and I pulled my stuff out and put everything in trash bags since everything needed to be cleaned or thrown out. It was too cold to go through everything in the tow yard, it could wait until I got home. As we pulled out of the parking lot, I waved goodbye to my Jeep. It had a good life, now it was time for it to go to Jeep heaven.

"Just put the bags on the floor," I said to Billy, dropping the bag I was carrying in front of the work bench. "I need to make some room on the bench for us to work."

"Okay. I'll go get the last bag while you make room." He dropped the bag next to me and left. I started moving boxes of Christmas decorations off the work bench and pushed them onto the third shelf against the wall, my dad had forgotten to put them away after Christmas. I had them all up except for one. Something was already on the shelf, but I couldn't see what it was. I got the stepladder from the other side of the room and set it up. I was about to start climbing up when Billy came back with the last bag.

"Hey, what are you doing?" he asked, dropping the bag, and pulling me away from the ladder. "Girls with concussions are not allowed on ladders."

"Fine," I wasn't in the mood to argue with him. "I can't get this last box up there; something's in the way."

"I'll check it out." Billy climbed the ladder and pulled out a small tin box, about fourteen inches around and six inches tall. "It looks like more Christmas decorations. It must have fallen out of the box." He handed it to me, and I ran my hands over the dusty lid.

"I've never seen this before. It looks old." The Santa on the cover was dressed in blue instead of red and some of the paint had chipped off. I put it on the bench and picked up the last box. "Here, since you are already up there, can you put this on the shelf?"

"Yeah," Billy said, taking the box from me, and sliding it into place. "What do you want to do with the tin?"

"I'll ask my mom about it later. Let's go through this stuff, so we can go in and get warm." I pushed the tin aside and pulled one of the bags onto the work bench.

We spent an hour going through the bags making three piles: the trash pile, keep pile, and needed cleaning pile. When we were done, the only thing left on the work bench was the tin. "Are you coming in or heading home?" I asked, ready to get inside and make some hot chocolate. My fingers hurt with cold and my nose was running.

"I better head home, I need to get my chores done then start on homework." Billy walked toward the side door on the garage. "I'll see you tomorrow morning."

"Thanks for your help with everything. See you tomorrow." I picked up my backpack and the tin, then went up to my room.

I didn't have a huge bedroom, but it was all I needed. I painted the walls dark-gray the year before, then covered it with posters of military planes and Jeeps. I had a full-size bed with a wrought iron headboard pushed up against the wall with a fluffy, white, down comforter on top of it and a dreamcatcher hanging above it on the wall. I had a white desk in front of a large window where I could see town and the lake beyond during the day. My matching dresser was against the wall opposite the bed. My small closet was filled with various stages of jeans, from newish, to ripped, to covered in oil, along with my hoodies, and T-shirts. I had a Jack and Jill bathroom, but since it connected to the guest bedroom, I didn't really have to share it.

I set the tin on my desk then took a shower. I felt like I was covered in blood and vomit, even though my hands were clean.

When I felt clean again, I put on my sweat pants and a T-shirt before grabbing my backpack and sitting down at my desk. I was about to pull out my math book when I saw the tin. Abandoning my homework, I opened it and looked inside. There were pictures, a stone with something etched on it strung with a leather thong, and a journal. It must have been my mom's when she was a teenager, but I only found her in one of the pictures. She was standing with a man I had never seen before, wearing white and holding a bouquet of daisies. The man was in a white suit, with a white tie. He had blond hair, the opposite of my mother, and dazzling green eyes that shone like highly polished emeralds. I looked up and caught my reflection in the window, then looked back down at the man.

I turned the photo over and almost dropped it. Written in my mom's perfect handwriting was *Victor and Sandy 1999*. It was my mom and biological father's wedding picture. I looked at the other pictures, this was my father's stuff. Now that I knew what he looked like I found him easily in each picture. A tear streaked down my cheek, I would never get to meet the man who helped make me. I was lucky to have Burt, he treated me like his own daughter, and he was my dad every way that mattered, but occasionally, I would wonder what my biological father was like. I couldn't talk to my mom about it because every time I tried, she would end up crying and I would feel guilty for causing it.

I pulled the journal out. It was nothing more than a hard-cover notebook with the word, *Journal*, written on the outside. Would I be intruding on his privacy if I looked at it? He was dead, but why else would my mom have kept it, if not to give it to me? I opened the cover and dropped it on my desk like it had just burst into flames.

On the inside cover were the words, *Property of Victor*

Robinson, and next to that was a drawing of the goblin who had been showing up in my dreams. I wanted to cry out, to tell someone that something was after me, maybe it was the same something that killed my father.

I shook my head, he died of elevation sickness, there was no way the goblin killed him, besides it was just a dream. I was about to turn the next page when I heard the garage door open and looked at the clock. *Crap,* I thought to myself, *it's already six and I haven't gotten any homework done.*

"Liz?" Mom called. "Where are you?"

"In my room, I'll be right down." I put everything back in the tin, closed the lid, and shoved it under my bed. I didn't know if Mom would be happy I found it or not but for the time being, I was going to keep it a secret. I went downstairs and followed my nose to the kitchen.

"You brought Chinese?" I asked, rushing over to her to take the bags from her arms.

"I didn't feel like cooking tonight. I hope it's alright." She took her coat off and hung it on a peg before prying her boots off.

"I never say no to Chinese." I put the bags on the counter, opened the first one and pulled out a square box of rice.

"Here, I will do this, you go set the table." Mom pushed me out of the way to stop me from eating straight out of the containers.

I went to the cabinet and pulled out the plates then went back to the bag and found the chopsticks. I took them into the dining room and set the table. When I was done, Dad was in the mudroom taking his coat off.

We sat at the table and ate in silence for a few minutes before I remembered my poor Jeep. "Billy and I cleaned out the Jeep today."

"Did Phil tell you it was totaled?" Dad asked, using his chopsticks to pick up a piece of chicken.

"Yeah, seeing it made me realize why everyone is freaking out about how I'm doing. I was really lucky," I said, around a mouthful of chicken chow mein.

"Yes, you were." Mom was trying to hide how upset she still was about the accident, but I could see the worry in her eyes.

"Have you thought about what kind of car you want to replace it with?" Dad asked.

"I don't need to think about it. I want another Wrangler."

"Are you sure you wouldn't like a Subaru? They're the safest car on the market." Dad looked down at his plate and grabbed a chunk of rice with his chopsticks.

"I hate Subarus, and you know it." I put my chopsticks down. "The Wrangler protected me just fine, a Subaru wouldn't have changed what happened."

"I know, but Wranglers like to flip. We just want you to be safe," Mom said.

"I am safe. I did everything I was supposed to do when I saw him. I'll drive safe no matter what kind of vehicle I have, but I will not be a Subaru driver." I got up from the table and picked up my plate. "I'm not hungry anymore. I'm going upstairs to do my homework."

"Elizabeth don't be like this," Dad called. I ignored him and threw away what was left of my food, rinsed my plate, and put it in the dishwasher, then I stomped up the stairs to my room.

I took my pack off the bed and pulled my books out. I looked out the dark window, fuming. I would walk before I would drive a Subaru. I couldn't believe they wanted me to get a hippy car. The accident wasn't my fault.

I took a deep breath and opened my math book. Homework was the last thing I wanted to do, but I could not afford to get more behind than I already was.

CHAPTER 6

I was in a small fiberglass fishing boat on the Freeman Lake. It was summer, and the sun was out. It was too bright to be out there without my sunglasses. I felt on top of my head for them, but they weren't there. I would have to go back to shore for them.

I went to the small motor at the aft of the boat and pulled the starter string. The motor started for a second then died. I tried again, and nothing happened. I found the primer bulb, squeezed it a few times and pulled, still nothing.

"You know this is a dream, right? Your mind must not want you to start the engine since it won't start," a voice said from behind me. I jumped so high I was surprised I didn't fall out of the boat.

I spun around to find Shawn sitting backward on the wood bench seat at the bow. He had one foot propped on the seat in front of him, and his arms were crossed over his chest. He was wearing a red tank top, khaki cargo shorts, and flip flops. The sun was behind him making his hair glow with golden highlights. I let out a relieved breath, it wasn't the goblin from my nightmare.

"What are you doing here? Can't I dream in peace?" I didn't mean it, I wanted to ask him why he got mad earlier in the day.

"Hey, it's your dream. You tell me why I'm here." He crossed his arms over his chest.

"Alright, why did you start acting all weird today?" I sat on the seat next to the motor.

"Because you remembered your dreams about me. You aren't supposed to be able to. No one remembers their dreams when we are in them. How are you able to?" He put his foot down and leaned forward resting his forearms on his thighs.

"I have no idea. I have always been able to remember my dreams, ever since I was a little kid. Maybe I'm just special. Why do you care?" I crossed my arms over my chest, feeling like he was making fun of me.

"I want to protect you." He pulled his eyebrows together and frowned.

"Why?" He barely knew me. What made me so special?

"I like you." He wouldn't bring his eyes up to meet mine.

"You like me?" My mouth dropped open, a guy had never told me they *liked* me before.

"Well, I think I do. I don't know you very well, but I get a pretty good feeling about you." He stared at his foot like he had never seen it before.

"I know what you mean, I feel the same way about you." I felt myself blush, and I stared at the bottom of the boat. "Except when you are being a dickhead."

"Are you always this honest?" He smirked.

"About stuff like this? No, but this is a dream." I released my arms and folded my fingers together.

"Really? So, what else do you like about me?" he asked, as an alarm started to beep from somewhere across the lake.

"You don't want to know," I said, looking around. "I think that's my alarm clock. Guess I'll see you around."

"Timing is everything," he replied and disappeared.

I rolled over and turned my alarm off. Another strange dream. How was I supposed to see this guy every day and dream of him every night? It wasn't fair. He was nicer in my dream this time. Maybe it was because I actually met him and talked to him face-to-face. There was something different about him but I couldn't put my finger on what it was. Why was I drawn to him? Was it because he was a good-looking guy I hadn't known for my entire life, or was it just because of who he was?

I forced myself to stop thinking about him and rolled out of bed to get ready for the day. After I showered, I looked in the mirror and had to take a step back. The black and blue marks were fading, but they were replaced by a yellowy-green color. I opened the drawer holding the makeup Mom had bought me for Christmas then closed it. I didn't think I could cover up the rainbow of colors on my face without a Hollywood makeup artist. Plus, everyone saw me the day before with the bruises, so if I showed up with a bunch of makeup covering them, they would know I was being self-conscious about it.

Mom was waiting for me with my lunch, and an egg and cheese sandwich. "Thanks, Mom," I said, grabbing a mug from the cabinet, and filling it with coffee.

"How did you sleep?" She leaned back against the bar and crossed her arms over her chest.

I walked around and sat on the other side of it. "Good, weird dreams though. Ever since the accident I have been having weird dreams, but I feel rested." I took a bite of the sandwich and chewed slowly. She made the best egg sandwiches. When I opened my eyes, she was staring past me, frowning.

"What's wrong?" I asked, putting my sandwich back on the plate.

"Your biological father always talked about dreams, how you have to pay attention to them. He was always worried about my dreams, like he was afraid something was going to happen to me in them." She wiped a tear from her cheek. "Then he had to go and die in his sleep, like so many others in Twisted Pines."

"I'm sorry, Mom. Don't worry, they aren't nightmares." I got up from the bar and wrapped my arms around her.

"Stupid man. He refused to sleep with a dreamcatcher over his head. He thought if he could defeat the monsters plaguing his dreams he could save everyone in town from them." She wiped at her eye. "Then he had to go and die." She lapsed into silence then pulled away from me. She had never told me about his dreams before, and I wondered if, somehow, the same goblin that was stalking my dreams was the one who my bio-dad dreamed of.

The coroner said he died of an altitude induced heart attack. They had just moved to Twisted Pines from California and going from sea level to over eight thousand feet puts a lot of strain on the heart. It takes time to adapt. They had only been in town for a few weeks and Mom was six months pregnant.

Mom met Burt before I was born. He was the doctor who she was seeing for prenatal checkups. He helped her through her grief, then give birth to me, somewhere in there they fell in love and got married. He was the only father I had ever known. I could tell she loved my dad and I loved him too, but she still got upset whenever she talked about my biological father.

The goblin in my dream had called me Martröð Veiðimaður and said he would find me again. I needed to find out what Martröð Veiðimaður meant, it was important for some reason. I looked at my watch and sighed. Billy would be there shortly, and I wanted to finish eating before he arrived. There was a loud knock on the front door before it opened, and Billy yelled out a greeting, breaking the silence between us.

"We're in the kitchen," I said, before going back to my breakfast.

"Good morning," Billy said, coming in going over to the cabinet to get a mug then pouring himself some coffee.

"Good morning, Billy, help yourself," Mom said in a short, clipped voice before and leaving the room.

"Thanks," Billy called after her. He raised his eyebrows at me while taking a sip of the hot coffee. "Was it something I said?"

"No, she started talking about my bio-dad. You know how she gets." I took a sip of my coffee.

"I'm sorry." Billy took another sip of his coffee. "Your face is turning into a rainbow. Is there a pot of gold at the end of it?"

"Ass, just what a girl wants to hear about her appearance." I rolled my eyes, finished my coffee, and took my dishes to the sink. I rinsed them and put them in the dishwasher.

"Since when do you care about how you look?" Billy asked, following me with his eyes as I moved around the kitchen

"Since my face is more black, blue, and green, than it is pink and flesh-colored." I went over to the mudroom, took my Carhartt jacket off its peg, put it on, then went to the counter and put my lunch in my backpack. "Are you ready?" I asked, slinging the strap over my shoulder.

"Your carriage awaits, my rainbow girl." Billy twirled his arm and bowed toward the door.

"You are in fine form this morning." I led the way out of the house. "Bye, Mom, love you," I called, before I shut the front door behind us.

Billy and I were quiet on the way to school, both stuck in our own thoughts. I hadn't seen my mom cry over my bio-dad in years. I wondered why telling her about my dreams made her think about him. *Crap*, I thought to myself. *How was I going to look at Shawn in the eye after last night's dream?* He already knew I dreamed about him, as long as he didn't ask me what I dreamed about it would be okay. I just needed to remember to avoid the topic and it wouldn't be a big deal. They were just dreams after all.

CHAPTER 7

We arrived at school later than I would have liked and had to hurry to our lockers to make it to class on time.

I didn't need to worry about talking to Shawn until lunch, since we never crossed paths, and I was starting to ignore the pitiful looks I was getting from people staring at the bruises on my face.

When I walked into the cafeteria Shawn and Jo were the only ones sitting at our table. I wanted to turn around and wait for Billy in the hallway, but they had already seen me. *I could do this. Just act like nothing has changed since yesterday.* I straightened my back, pulled my chin up, and walked over to the table with a fake smile plastered on my face.

"Hi, how are you guys?" I asked, sitting down, and putting my bag on the table.

"Just another day at school," Jo said, rolling her eyes, and opening a fun-size size bag of chips. "Is it June yet?"

"I wish," I said, giving her a genuine smile now.

"This school isn't so bad, at least we don't have to walk through metal detectors," Shawn added, taking a bite out of his sandwich.

"No joke. It could be much worse," Jo said, eating a chip from her bag.

"Where were you guys before you moved here?" I asked.

"New York City," Jo said, around a mouthful. "Jon made us go to public school for the life lesson."

"Who's Jon?" I asked, looking at them baffled.

"My dad, he's in charge of our branch of Knights Inc.," Shawn said, taking a sip from his soda. "We didn't know how long we were staying. It was pointless to spend the money on a private school when there was a chance we wouldn't be there for the whole year."

"Oh." I had no idea what it would be like to move around so much.

"Hello, all," Tommy said, sitting down next to Jo, while Tracy sat next to him.

"How is your day going, rainbow girl?" Billy asked, sitting down next to me.

I punched him in the arm and everyone laughed. "Don't call me that." I looked at everyone at the table making it clear if anyone else started calling me rainbow girl there would be hell to pay.

"When did you become such a princess?" Tommy asked, looking confused.

"Don't call her princess," Shawn said, before his eyes bulged and his mouth hung open. It looked like someone had kicked him between the legs.

I wanted to say something, but all I could do was stare at him, stunned. There was no way for him to know I hated to be called a princess unless he was in my dream too. Had he really killed the goblin? What if he wasn't a figment of my imagination? I felt my face flush and hoped the bruises would hide it from the rest of the guys.

"Why not? She's acting like one," Tommy said.

"She hates being called a princess." Shawn dropped his eyes to the table and didn't look up. His expression went from anger to disbelief. He stood abruptly, gathered what was left of his lunch, and walked away.

I watched him leave, too dumbstruck to say anything. I looked at Jo and she shrugged her shoulders. Something was going on, but I didn't think she knew what it was. "Jo?" I asked softly.

She picked up her lunch and stood. "I better go talk to him. Sorry, everyone, I don't know what his problem is."

Everyone else at the table looked at each other confused.

I moved to get up. "Hey, I'm sorry. You know I don't think of you as a princess," Tommy said.

"Yeah, don't get all mad and storm off," Billy said, recovering from the moment, and putting a hand on my shoulder.

I relaxed and sat back down. There was no need to cause a bigger scene than Shawn already had. My next class was with him, I would talk to him then.

"So, prom is in a few weeks, are you going?" Tracy asked me.

I did a double take. Tracy and I weren't what I called 'friends.' She sat with us because she and Tommy had been together since a fated New Year's Eve kiss. I didn't mind her, but we had never had girl talk before. I wasn't sure I knew how.

"I haven't really thought about it." There were so many things going through my mind it took me a minute to understand what she was saying. "Don't I need a date?"

"No one's asked you yet?" She arched an eyebrow and quickly looked at Billy then back at me.

"No, but I'm not really a *prom* person." I had never even thought about going to prom. It wasn't something that sounded like fun for numerous reasons: I would have to wear a dress, do something crazy with my hair, wear makeup, and dance. I could work on almost any motorized vehicle, but I could *not* dance.

"I bet someone will. Maybe we could go to Denver and go dress shopping this weekend."

"I don't have a car to drive," I mumbled, dress shopping sounded worse than wearing one.

"My mom is going to let me borrow hers. Well, let me know if you want to. A few of the other girls are planning to go too. I better get to class." She got up, taking her trash with her.

"Yeah, I'll let you know," I said, shocked for the second time in the past ten minutes.

The bell rang, and I robotically got up and threw my trash away before mindlessly walking to shop class, thinking about what Shawn had said. The only way he could know about the princess thing was if he was in my dream. How could that be possible? People couldn't share dreams, could they?

I had to confront him about it, and I planned to before class started, but he wasn't there. I went to my locker and put my coveralls on then went to my station, thinking I would corner him during class. I watched students file in, but Shawn never showed. Where the heck was he? Was he avoiding me?

I made it through class, barely getting anything done, but at least I had shown up. I couldn't stop thinking about Shawn and how he knew what I dreamed about. Not showing up was as good as admitting he was somehow entering my dreams. Did I really want to know we had been sharing dreams, though? Dreams were supposed to be private, thinking about him being in mine made me blush, again.

When I made it to history I sat next to Billy like I weighed a thousand pounds and my legs could not bear the weight any longer.

"What's wrong?" Billy asked, turning to look at me. "Are you feeling sick? Do you want me to take you home?"

"Stop asking me that, I'm fine." I opened my history book but kept my eye on the door waiting for Shawn to come in. He never did.

After school, Billy and I walked to his truck, and I looked over at Shawn's Rubicon. He was sitting in the car with the music blaring. "Billy, give me a second." Not waiting for a response, I walked over and knocked on Shawn's window.

Shawn jumped, looked at me, and shook his head. I made the universal motion for 'roll down your window.'

"We need to talk," I said, folding my arms in front of my chest.

"What do we need to talk about?" he asked, raising his eyebrows like he had no clue, but I noticed his grip on the steering wheel tighten.

"You know what? How do you know about my dreams?" His avoidance was making me angry, and I didn't get angry off very often.

"I'm sorry, I have no idea what you are talking about. Look, the rest of the crew is on their way over here so can you please let it go?" He pushed the button to roll up the window, ending the conversation almost before it begun.

I turned around and looked behind me. Jo, another girl, and a boy were walking toward us. "This isn't over," I yelled at the window then walked over to Billy's truck.

"What was that about?" he asked once I was in and buckled up.

"I just needed to talk to him about something we went over in shop class," I said, lying. Billy didn't need to know Shawn was starring in my dreams.

"Okay, did you find out where he was during history?" Billy turned out of the parking lot and drove toward my house.

"No, I forgot to ask him." I looked out the window. Shawn was hiding something, and I needed to find out what.

"What are you doing this weekend?" Billy asked, changing the subject.

"Hopefully, I'll be Jeep shopping with my dad. First, I have to convince him to let me get another Jeep, not a Subaru."

"You're kidding?" Billy asked, squishing his face together like he took a bite out of a lemon.

"No, I got into a fight with him last night about it. I would rather walk than drive a Subaru."

"Yeah, you want another Wrangler?" He sounded bummed about it.

"Of course. I loved mine. I just need to convince my parents they aren't a death trap."

"How are you going to do that?" Billy asked as he pulled into my driveway.

"I don't know, but I'll figure something out. What are you doing this weekend?" I asked, picking up my backpack, and setting it in my lap.

"We are taking our end-of-the-season snow-machine trip. Do you want to come?"

"There is no way my parents would let me go. I'm already hurt, and they're worried I'll get hurt again just walking down the stairs. I better go get started on my homework. See you tomorrow morning?" I asked, opening the door.

"Yes, your chauffeur will be here tomorrow to pick you up. You need to find a ride home from school though. We're leaving right after to get our sleds ready."

"Thank you, but I will be docking your pay for not being at my beck and call."

"What pay?" Billy asked, laughing.

"See you tomorrow." I stuck my tongue out at him, shut the door, and walked to the door to the mudroom, digging my keys out on the way.

I went up to my room and grabbed my laptop, then went back downstairs and set myself up at the dining room table. I needed to work on my homework and start looking for a new jeep, but the words from the goblin had been running through my mind all day. I pulled up my favorite search engine and stared at the blank search box. I had no idea how to spell what the goblin had called me. I knew it wasn't English, but from there I knew nothing. It didn't sound like any language I had ever heard before. I started typing, taking an educated guess. Martro Veioimaour, was the best I could do, and it auto-corrected to metro Vilamoura. I was pretty sure the goblin was not asking me how to get to Vilamoura by bus. All the other websites I found wanted to translate it from Spanish to English. It wasn't Spanish, I could tell by the accent. I didn't know how to explain it, but it wasn't a romantic language. With no idea where else to find the answers I needed, I gave up and started looking for a new Jeep.

After a few minutes my Facebook chimed with a friend request. Surprised, I clicked on it. It was from Shawn Ericson. What was with this guy? Curious, I accepted his friendship then went back to Jeep shopping. I was looking at one that looked just like my old one only a year newer, blue instead of red, and it was located in Spruce, when a message from Shawn popped up.

Hi, thanks for accepting my request. Sorry I was a dickhead today.

I read the message shaking my head. **You seem to be good at being a dickhead. No wonder it's what your friends call you. Why didn't you want to talk to me?**

I waited for him to respond for a minute. When he didn't, I went back to Jeep shopping. Ten minutes later a new message popped up.

It's complicated. It is supposed to be a secret. I couldn't tell you while Jo was there. I would've gotten in big trouble.

So, tell me now. I typed back.

No someone may be monitoring my computer. I can't risk it, maybe I can later.

I wondered what he meant by later, like tomorrow or in my dreams. It didn't matter, he was being weird, and I had better things to do.

Then you are an idiot telling me about some big secret you want to tell me but can't because they might be monitoring you. This sounds like some big joke to make a fool out of me. When you want to be honest let me know.

I closed the chat window and the lid on my computer. I didn't want to think about him anymore. I got my homework out and got to work.

Mom came home a little while later, changed her clothes, and went into the kitchen to start dinner.

I heard the door to the garage close and the telltale sounds of my dad taking his boots off. "Hey, Dad," I called.

"Hi, honey, how was your day?" He sat across from me at the dining room table.

"It was alright, just another day at school. Hey, I have been looking at cars and I want to show you this." I opened my computer and brought up the Jeep I had been looking for.

"But, sweetheart, Subarus are so much safer," he said as soon as he saw the Jeep on the screen.

"Dad, getting a Jeep makes more sense. With the money I'm getting from the insurance company I could get this Jeep or this Subaru." I clicked over to the ugliest car I had ever seen to show him the picture of the Subaru. "The Jeep is five years newer and has half the miles of the Subaru. I already know how to work on Jeeps, whereas I would be clueless with a Subaru. If it broke down I would have to pay someone to fix it instead of doing it myself. Plus, it's older with higher mileage and would be more likely to break down than the Jeep. Shouldn't we buy American whenever we can?" I held my breath knowing half of what I said was fluff.

"Okay, sweetie, we will go look at Jeeps on Saturday, but if you get in another accident you are getting a Subaru."

"Thanks, Dad." I jumped up from my seat, went around the table and gave him a hug.

"Dinner's ready," Mom called from the kitchen. I went to help her bring it out and spent the rest of the evening with them trying not to think about Shawn.

I went upstairs to my room around ten, but the last thing I wanted to do was go to sleep. I didn't want to see Shawn or the goblin in my dreams. I stayed up late reading and trying not to think about him. Unfortunately, sleep got the better of me and I fell asleep with the lights on and the book on my chest.

CHAPTER 8

I was in a room with white walls and ceiling. There were no doors, windows, or furniture in the room. I walked over to the wall and touched it. It was soft. *Seriously? I was in a padded room? Maybe I was going insane,* I thought to myself.

"You aren't going insane," Shawn said from behind me, making me jump.

I whirled around and looked at him. "You can read minds now?" I asked, folding my arms across my chest.

"No." He walked around me, looking me up and down as if trying to memorize the way I looked. I double-checked I had clothes on and let out a breath when I saw my jeans and T-shirt. "I thought the same thing when I came here for the first time." After he walked around me, he backed up and leaned against the wall. "It's safe to talk in here. No one can eavesdrop on us."

"This is a dream, isn't it obvious no one can eavesdrop on us. This isn't even a real conversation, it's a dream," I said, going to the wall farthest away from him and sitting down. "Why do I keep dreaming of you?"

"Because I'm invading your dreams. How else would I know you hate being called princess?" He sat across from me and brought his knees up to his chest. He wrapped his arms around them and laced his hands together where they met.

"How?" I rubbed my temples and laid my head on my knees, looking away from him.

"It's a gift. You have it too. No one has ever remembered a dream I entered before, and you remember them all." His voice was calm and serious, so unlike Shawn from school or my other dreams.

"Why couldn't you talk about it at school today? Why do you think I'm going to believe you in a dream?"

"I messed up, like I said on Facebook. If anyone finds out that you remember your dreams my dad will make me stay away from you. I want to protect you from the mares, if word gets out, you'll be on your own when you have a nightmare." He got back to his feet and stood over me.

"What are 'mares?' Why should I believe you?"

"Mares are goblins, who are between dimensions. They feed on people's souls via their fear. They aren't in our dimension, so the only way they can eat is by creating nightmares and feeding on the fear the nightmares create. If one gets to you, it won't stop until you die of fright." He paced back and forth across the room, running his hands through his hair. "I shouldn't be telling you this but since one already tried to get you, I think you have a right to know."

"That is a pretty good story, but again, why should I believe you? I could be just dreaming all this." I laced my fingers together and rested them on my head. Why were my dreams always so messed up?

"Because it's the truth, and you're like me, at least a little. You shouldn't be able to remember your dreams when I am in them."

"Do you know how creepy that sounds?" I shivered. "Like you are giving me a date-rape drug, so I won't remember what you did to me in my dreams."

"You had to take it there." He shook his head. "I would never do something so horrible to someone. We have a code to live by."

"Does it cover stalking my dreams?" I asked. He was being honest for a change, but I was having a hard time not poking him.

"No, and I'm glad. I like hanging out in your dreams." He stopped pacing and looked down at me.

"It's better than the alternative," I said more to myself than to him.

"What do you mean?" he asked, pulling his eyebrows together in confusion.

"Ever since the accident, I either dream of you or the goblin. You are much better then he is." I ran my hand through my hair and stared at the floor.

"Another one found you already?"

"No, it was the same one."

"I killed that one, he can't be stalking you."

"Well, unless he has a twin, it's the same goblin."

"Do you have any weird marks or burns?" he asked, sitting down across from me, and taking my hand again.

"No, just the bruises and the stitches from the moose." Part of me wanted to pull my hand out of his, he was stalking my dreams, if I believed him, but the other part of me was savoring the feel of his touch.

"That's good but tell me about your dreams when he is there."

"Well, in the last one, I was on the dock and it was summer. I was waiting for Billy to pick me up in his dad's boat, and the goblin came running toward me on the dock like he was going to tackle me. Before he reached me though he ran into an invisible wall and fell flat on his back. It was pretty funny."

Shawn let out a breath and looked at the ceiling. "Thank God, it sounds like you have some kind of protection."

"Why are you so concerned? This is just a dream. You aren't really here." I leveraged myself up the wall and got to my feet.

"I am, and I'll prove it to you tomorrow." He turned toward me and licked his lips.

"How? If you can't risk your crew hearing you and word getting back to your dad how will you prove it to me?"

"I am going to ask you how you liked the padded room." He stood and walked over to me. "I promise, I'm telling you the truth."

"What are you?" He took my hand and squeezed it. Goosebumps broke out on my arm when we touched, and I felt myself blush.

"I'm Martröð Veiðimaður, or a Knight Flyer, we protect people from the Mares, or goblins, as you called them."

Wasn't that what the goblin had called me? "Wait say that again."

"Say what?"

"What are you?" I asked, I didn't even want to try to repeat what he had called himself.

"You mean Martröð Veiðimaður?" He opened his mouth to answer but shut it and put his finger to his ear. "Crap, I have to go. I'll see you tomorrow, right?" Before I could say anything, he closed the distance between us and kissed me for the briefest moment. I wanted to kiss him back, but he was gone.

CHAPTER 9

The next morning, I was up and ready for school an hour early. Part of me wanted to find Shawn and find out if he was really invading my dreams but the other part remembered everything I said to him on the boat. The last thing I wanted to do was find out it was true. He knew about the princess thing, and he didn't comment about my dickhead remark. Was it possible? How did he learn to enter people's dreams? If he was saving people from the *mares*, how did he know they needed saving? I had so many questions I wanted to ask him, but I didn't know when we would be alone for me to ask.

I was downstairs before either of my parents and I decided to make breakfast. It would give me something to do other than think about Shawn. "I made pancakes," I said to my dad when he poked his head in the kitchen. I set a plate piled high with them on the bar and set the butter and syrup next to his plate.

"Wow why are you up so early?" he asked, taking a seat, and digging into the food.

"Just woke up early." I would never admit I was up early because of a boy.

"Are you going to hang out with the guys tonight?"

"No, they're getting their sleds ready for tomorrow. They are going on their annual end-of-the-season winter camping trip this weekend." I went with them the year before, it wasn't fun. I ended up being cold, wet, and soggy the entire time.

"You don't want to go?" He looked up from the table while I flipped more hotcakes on the griddle.

"No, last year sucked, and I have a great excuse not to go this year." I pointed to the stitches in my head. "I told Billy there was no way you would let me go."

"You're right." Dad laughed. "The last thing you need to do is play around on a snow machine, your head needs time to heal."

"I would rather go Jeep shopping tomorrow anyway. I'm going to have to take the bus home today though." I made an ugly face and went back to the stove.

"It will be fun." He scraped his plate with his fork to pick up the last traces of syrup and pancake crumbs.

"When was the last time you took a bus home, filled with kids?" The noise was bad enough, but my stop was the last one on the route, it would take over an hour to get home.

"I never did, except field trips. My house was right next to the school. You'll survive." He got up with his plate and took it to the sink. "Thank you for making breakfast. I have to go. I'll see you tonight, sweetheart." He kissed the top of my head and went into the mudroom.

Mom came in a little while later and I gave her a plate covered with food. We ate together until I heard the front door open, and Billy came in. I put my plate in the sink, grabbed my bag, and we left for school.

"You're bubbly this morning," Billy said as he drove.

"I think I'm feeling better. I have a ton of energy today," I said, looking out the window, excited and nervous to see Shawn. "Are you excited for your trip?"

"Yeah, it will be fun. I wish you were coming though. You always keep us from doing something stupid."

"You could stop them too, you know." Remembering a hillside, they looked at for an hour trying to decide if they could run straight up it on their sleds. I finally talked them out of it with threats of Flight-For-Life, and the beatings their mothers would give them.

"They don't listen to me like they do you. Hey, have you thought about prom?" His sudden change of subject had me whipping my head around to look at him.

"Not really, I mean it's not really my kind of thing you know?" *Please don't ask me to go with you*, I thought. If I was going to go to prom I wanted to go with someone who I didn't think of as a brother.

"Yeah, I think Tommy is going to ask Tracy in some elaborate way at lunch today." He was twitching in his seat.

"I don't understand why people are doing these elaborate things just to ask someone to prom. It's not like he's asking her to marry him or something."

"I don't get it either." Billy was looking more and more nervous.

I had a bad feeling about this. *Oh no*, I thought. *Was he going to ask me?* "I think it falls into the whole fairytale princess thing. A grand gesture and they will live happily ever after." We were pulling into the parking lot. I had two choices, I could change the subject, or jump out of the moving truck. Jumping was starting to sound good when I saw Shawn and Jo walking toward the front entrance of the school. "There's Shawn, I hope he shows up for class today we have a test."

"We have a test today?" Billy slammed his hand on the steering wheel. "I thought it was next week."

It worked. I blew out a breath. "Is it next week? I can't remember, maybe you're right." Billy parked the car and I opened the door as soon as were stopped.

"Don't mess with me, Liz. When's the test?" He got out, slamming his door.

"I can't remember now. I'll have to look at my notebook." I started walking toward the school, not waiting for him.

"Let's go check now. If we have a test, I'm going to have to cram between classes." He hurried to keep up with me.

I was pretty sure we didn't have a test, but then I started second-guessing myself. If we had a test I was screwed too.

We got to my locker and I pulled out my notebook. I turned to the last page and smiled up at him. "The test is next week."

"Thank God." Billy blew out an audible breath and ran his hand through his hair. "Don't scare me like that."

"I'm sorry, I couldn't remember, concussion brain." The warning bell rang. "Look I have to get to class, I'll see you at lunch okay?"

"Yeah, see you then." He turned and started walking to his locker.

At least I had stopped him from asking me to prom, if that was even what he was going to do. I didn't want to have to tell him no. Maybe my mom was right, maybe Billy had a crush on me. I shook my head, grabbed my math book, and closed my locker. Talking to Shawn was going to have to wait.

The day dragged. I tried to pay attention in my classes, but I found myself looking at the clock more often than the teacher. When the bell for lunch finally rang, I all but ran to my locker to get my lunch then forced myself to walk to the cafeteria.

I was so anxious to talk to Shawn I was the first person of our group to get to the there. I took my normal seat and took my lunch out but didn't start eating. Tracy sat across from me and I held in a sigh. I was hoping Shawn would sit there. I tried to use the Jedi mind trick on her to make her move, but my Midi-Chlorian count must not have been high enough for it to work.

Billy sat next to me and it took everything I had not to yell at him. Tommy sat next to Tracy and everyone started talking about their plans for the weekend.

"I think we need to try and get to the summit of Wolfhead," Billy said before eating a chip.

"You can't get to the top of Wolfhead and back in two days," Tommy said, around a mouth full of food. "I think we should try Rattlesnake Canyon."

"We've never tried it, and it's not too far away." Billy leaned back from the table and thought about it. "Let's see what Sam thinks, if he's in then I am too."

"What are you doing this weekend, Liz?" Tracy asked, clearly upset that Tommy was going to be gone all weekend.

"Car shopping with my dad tomorrow, studying on Sunday. What about you?" I took a bite of my sandwich and looked around the room for Shawn.

"Dress shopping and homework." She ate a mouthful of her salad. "What kind of car are you going to get?"

"If everything goes to plan I will have another Wrangler before the weekend is over."

"You're so lucky. I hate driving the minivan."

I couldn't blame her; the minivan was boring, and it wasn't very good in the snow. I was about to commiserate with her when Jo took a seat next to Tracy.

"Hey, where's Shawn?" I asked, feeling like an idiot. "I mean hi, how are you?" Billy looked over at me with his eyebrows raised in question.

"I'm good thanks," she said with half a laugh. "He's making up work for missing class yesterday. I don't know what his problem was. He was fine one minute then pissed at the world the next."

"Have you two been together long?" I didn't think they were boyfriend/girlfriend, but you never could tell.

She laughed. "He's not my boyfriend; he's more like a brother than anything. We've known each other for too long." She glanced at Billy for a second before looking back at me.

I smiled and felt instant relief. It was nice knowing they weren't together. "I know what you mean." I looked to the other side of me where Billy had gone back to talking to Tommy and Sam about their trip.

"Really?" she asked, looking confused. "I thought you two were together too."

"No," I said, a little too loudly and everyone at the table stopped talking and looked at me. I ducked my head as I felt my cheeks start to burn.

"No what?" Billy asked, looking concerned.

"None of your business," Jo said, winking at me. "Just girl talk."

"I didn't think Liz was capable of having girl talk," Tracy chimed in, looking interested. "I thought all she liked to talk about was engines and hunting."

"Maybe she just needed the right girl to talk to," Jo said, sticking up for me.

"I'm right here." I looked from Jo to Tracy. "I am a female, Tracy. I like to talk about engines and hunting more than my beauty regime, but I'm capable of talking about other things."

"Sorry," Tracy said, and turned back to Tommy.

I looked at Jo and rolled my eyes. "Well I'm going to take off. See you later, Jo."

"Yeah, see you."

I threw my trash away then made my way to my locker. Tracy could be such a jerk sometimes. I had girl talk with her yesterday, about prom. At least I knew Jo wasn't Shawn's girlfriend, not that I cared. I rounded the corner to the hallway my locker was in and found Shawn leaning against it. I couldn't stop the smile that crossed my lips.

"Hi," I said as I approached him. Butterflies erupted in my stomach when I realized he was waiting for me.

"Hey." He pushed off the locker and moved a few feet away, allowing me to open it.

"Missed you at lunch." I twirled the combination on the locker and looked at him from the corner of my eye.

"Yeah, I had to make up for missing history yesterday." He stuck his hands in his pockets and rocked back on his heels.

I wanted to ask him about my dream, but I was chicken. What if it was all just a dream? I opened my locker. "So . . ." I trailed off. I had no idea what to say.

"What are you doing this weekend?" he asked.

"Not a lot. I'm going Jeep shopping with my dad tomorrow. The guys are going on a snow-machining trip, and until I get a new car I can't go back to work. Why?" I closed my locker and we started to walk to auto-shop.

"Do you want to go out tonight?" His hands were still in his pockets and he was looking at the floor.

"Like on a date?" I put my hands in my pockets and felt my face turn beet red.

"Yeah, I promise it will be more entertaining than the padded room."

I stopped in my tracks with my mouth hanging open. "It wasn't just a dream?"

"It was a dream, but I was there too." He looked at me through hooded eyes with a smile playing on his lips. "They all were."

I hid my face in my hands and groaned. I didn't know if I had ever been more embarrassed. "That's an invasion of my privacy you know."

"I couldn't help myself. You intrigued me after our first meeting."

"I thought you were a jerk." I smiled and brought my hands down to look at him.

"I was being a jerk. It was the first time I got to save someone and I was feeling cocky. When I found you in the classroom I thought you wouldn't remember me and I wanted to know what it would be like to kiss you."

"Well, I'm still alive, so I guess you did a good job. Who was the girl with you the first night?" I remembered her trying to get me to wake up.

"My sister, Heather, she's my partner sometimes. We should probably get to class," he said as the warning bell rang.

"Are you going to tell me what being a Martröð Veiðimaður means?" I asked, as we started walking again.

"If you go out with me tonight I will." Our hands brushed each other as we walked. I blushed at the thought of holding his hand and walking down the hall for everyone to see. I sighed, we hadn't even gone out yet and I was acting like all the girls I made fun of. Maybe I was missing something.

"I'll have to check with my parents, but I don't see why they wouldn't let me. What do you want to do?"

"You will just have to wait and see," he said.

"Hi, you're Shawn, right?" a high-pitched voice called, and we both turned around. Tiffany, a senior, with bleached hair, a push-up bra, and a shirt at least two sizes too small was almost running toward us.

"Yeah," Shawn said, glancing at her then looking back at me.

"Hi, I'm Tiffany. I'm sorry I haven't had a chance to introduce myself yet. You are kind of hard to track down." She stuck her hand out and Shawn shook it briefly then pulled his hand away from hers.

"Nice to meet you." He looked down the hall that was slowly emptying of people. "Sorry, but we need to go, or we'll be late for class." Shawn took my hand and pulled me down the hall.

"Okay, well, see you around," she called from behind us.

"That was weird," Shawn said, still pulling me along.

"Tiffany thinks she's god's gift to man. Watch out or she will sink her claws into you then there will be no escape until she has sucked you dry." I giggled at the thought of Tiffany and Shawn together.

"I would believe it. Besides why would I want her when you're right here?" He stopped, pulled me into his arms, and he was kissing me. My lips tingled with the feeling of his soft, full lips pressed against mine. It was over as quickly as it started, but when he pulled away, my chest was tight, and it was hard to breathe.

"Why did you do that?" I asked, when I was finally able to breathe.

"I wanted to see if it was as good as it was in your dream." He bumped my shoulder.

"The real thing was better." I felt my cheeks heat up as the words left my mouth.

"I thought so too." He opened the door to the shop and held it for me.

I could have stood next to Shawn for the rest of the day and not minded, but Mr. Pearson had us working on our engines throughout class and Shawn's station was on the opposite side of the room from mine. I tried to get my work done, but I couldn't keep my eyes off him for long.

"Liz? Are you alright?" Mr. Pearson asked, dragging me out of a daydream starring Shawn.

"What? Yes, sorry just can't seem to keep my mind on my work today." I bent over the engine and picked up where I left off.

"Are you sure?"

"Yes, I'm sorry, I will get this done."

"Okay but take it easy if you need to." He turned and went to the next station.

I looked over at Shawn to see him quietly laughing at me. I shook my head and forced myself to get to work. I finished my assignment and changed out of my coveralls right before the bell rang. Shawn walked with me to my locker to get my history book, then we went to his locker, so he could get his book.

I sat in my normal seat and Shawn took the one on my right leaving Billy's seat for him. When Billy came into the room he saw me and smiled then he saw Shawn and his smile faded.

"Hey," I said, as he took his seat.

"Hey, how's it going?"

"Alright, I am ready for this week to be over. Are you ready for your trip?"

"I will be, but I have a feeling it's going to be a long night. Oh, hey, Shawn." Billy finally acknowledged him after getting his books out of his bag.

"Hey, Billy." I saw him smirk out of the corner of his eye and I wondered what it was about.

"I'm sure you guys are going to have a great time," I said as Mr. Anderson started class and we all settled in to hear him talk about Western Civilization's royal dynasties.

I had the same problem in History as I had in shop class. I kept sneaking glances at Shawn and ignoring almost everything Mr. Anderson said. Every time Shawn caught me he would wink, and I would blush. The bell finally rang, and I closed my book.

"Are you alright?" Billy asked.

"Yeah, why wouldn't I be?" I asked, trying not to blush.

"You keep turning red and closing your eyes. Do you have a

fever? Do you need to go see your dad?" He looked concerned.

"I'm fine, I promise. Have a good time this weekend, please be careful," I said, getting up from my desk and walking toward the door.

"Are you sure? Maybe I should give you a ride home after all," he said, from behind me.

"You need a ride home? I have room, then I'll know where to pick you up later," Shawn said, standing up from his desk.

"What do you mean when he picks you up later?" Billy asked as we walked out the door and into the hallway filling with students ready to escape for the weekend.

"We're going out tonight." I was embarrassed, but I told myself not to be. So what if I had never been on a date before?

"Hey, my locker is that way." Shawn pointed in the opposite direction of mine. "I'll meet you at my car in ten minutes?" he said, making it a question.

"Sounds good. Thanks, Shawn." I continued down the hall, dodging around people in my path. Billy kept up with me instead of going to his locker, which was closer to Shawn's than mine.

"Were you going to tell me?" Billy asked.

"I'm sure I would've told you eventually. What's the big deal?"

"You barely know this guy and you're going out on a date with him, by yourself." Billy stopped at my locker and waited while I opened it.

"You sound like my dad, Billy. Look everyone knows where he lives. If anything happens you can go all Frankenstein's villagers on the mansion and torch it." I opened my locker and started loading books into my bag.

"I'm just worried about you is all. You've had a tough week."

"Hey, I'll be fine. You're the one who needs to be careful. You guys tend to get out of control. Promise me you won't do anything stupid."

"I promise, but the same goes for you. Keep your goals in mind. I don't want you to end up seventeen and pregnant or anything."

My face turned bright red, I turned and punched him in the arm. "I can't believe you just said that." I shrugged my coat on and closed my locker.

"I'm sorry, but keep it in mind," Billy said, walking with me up the hall.

"I'm done talking to you now. Have a good weekend. I'll call you if I need a ride on Monday." I walked away before he could say anything else.

I couldn't believe how overprotective he was being. Why was it any of his business if I went out on a date? *Crap,* I thought to myself when it dawned on me Mom was right, *Billy has a crush on me.*

CHAPTER 10

I went outside and made my way to Shawn's Rubicon. Jo and the other two kids he always gave a ride to were waiting by it. I walked over to them wondering where Shawn was.

"Hey, Shawn said he could give me a ride home," I said to the group, feeling awkward.

"Who are you?" The girl leaning against the car asked, frowning.

"I'm Liz, I have a couple of classes with Shawn. Who are you?"

"Mary," she said, standing up and walking to the other side of the car.

"I'm Jeff," the boy said, bobbing his head at me.

"Nice to meet you." I nodded at him.

"You too. Don't mind Mary she gets jealous of any girl Shawn talks to," he said, lowering his voice.

"Oh, are they . . ." I trailed off hoping he wasn't dating the girl since he had kissed me in the hallway and asked me out. If he had a girlfriend I was going to be pissed.

"What? No." Jeff laughed. "She has a crush on him."

At least he wasn't cheating on his real girlfriend with me, I blew out a breath. "Thanks for the heads-up." I turned and looked at the front of the school. "Where's Shawn?"

"Who knows, but he better hurry, I have stuff to do," Jo said, looking at her watch. "What are you doing this weekend?"

"Umm, well I think Shawn and I are going out tonight. Tomorrow I'm going car shopping with my dad. I hate not having a car."

"I know what you mean. My parents won't let me get a car in case we move again. It's expensive to move cars across the country."

"Do you think you will be moving again soon?" I asked, praying she would say no. It would be just my luck, actually have a date with a guy I liked and have him move away before I could get to know him. Plus, I didn't understand why they moved to Twisted Pines in the first place.

"My dad said you never know, but we all like it here so far. Hopefully, we will get to stay awhile."

Shawn and Billy walked out of the front door, looking everywhere but at each other, and neither of them looked happy. I wondered if I was going to have to talk to Billy about staying out of my love life. Billy stomped off to his truck without giving me a backward glance. Shawn hit the unlock button on his key fob and Mary came around to the front passenger side. She almost had the door open when Shawn said in a low angry voice. "Mary, get in the back. Liz is sitting in front. You can have her seat after we drop her off."

Mary crossed her arms in front of her chest and huffed, but when Shawn leveled a stare at her she stomped to the back door and got in after Jeff. Jo rolled her eyes and got into the backseat.

"Are you okay?"

"I'm fine. Just had words with your boyfriend," Shawn said,

crossing his arms over his chest.

"Who, Billy?" I was going to kill him, Billy was going to be a dead man when I got my hands on him.

"Who else would it be? Or should I ask how many boyfriends you have?" He leaned forward into my personal space.

"Billy is not my boyfriend. I don't have a boyfriend. I don't know what he told you, but he is nothing but a friend."

"I didn't think so either, but the way he talked, it was like you were already married."

"What did he say? Billy and I are not involved. He's my best friend, that's all." I crossed my arms over my chest.

"Then why did he tell me to cancel our date and stay away from you?" His eyebrows came together and the frown he was wearing deepened.

"I don't know, but I will have words with him. He doesn't get to tell me what I can and can't do." I held my hands out to him. "I really want to go out with you tonight, but if you are going to believe what other people say about me without listening to my side, then you are not the person I thought you were."

"I'm sorry, Billy made me really mad. He knew exactly what to say to make me doubt you. I want to go out with you too."

"I'm sorry too. I don't know what has gotten into him lately."

He relaxed and gave me a small smile. "Okay, let's get you home so you can get ready for your big date." He winked at me and opened my door.

"Thanks." I breathed a sigh of relief and got into the Jeep.

"What was that about?" Jo asked, while Shawn walked around to his side of the car.

"Billy is being an overprotective ass." I looked at my bruises in the side-view mirror. My first date and I was going to be covered in bruises, great.

Shawn opened his door and jumped in. "Let's get home." He started the car and classic rock-and-roll poured out of the stereo.

"You like Guns N' Roses?" I asked, over Axel singing about his sweet child.

"Yeah, classic eighties band. Don't tell me you don't like them?" He gave me a sideways glance as he backed out of the parking spot then put the Jeep into drive.

"They're great, you just don't look like the type is all." I looked down at his automatic transmission and shook my head.

"What's wrong?" He must have seen me shake my head.

"That's too bad." I shook my head again.

"What?" He touched my arm, forcing me to meet his eyes.

"You have an automatic transmission. They're for babies. I don't know if I can go out with a guy who doesn't drive a stick shift."

"My dad bought it, not me, I didn't have a choice." He slapped the steering wheel.

"Hey, can you turn it down? We can't hear what you guys are saying," Mary asked, acting like a sweet little girl instead of the hell spawn I first met.

"That's the point, munchkin," Shawn said, looking at her through the rearview mirror.

"Don't call me munchkin," she yelled.

"Okay, I'll give you a pass on the transmission this time." I smiled and winked at him.

"Oh, thank you, princess. How will I ever repay you for giving me a pass?"

"I'm sure you'll think of something, now shut up and drive," I said, laughing.

We did not talk on the way to my house other than me giving him directions. The music was too good and too loud to have a conversation. I loved it. The only radio station we had in town was country. I could not even stream music because cell phone service was so spotty. All I had was my digital music library, and I hadn't updated it in months.

"This is it," I said, pointing to my driveway. He pulled in and turned the music down.

"Nice house," he said, bending a bit in his seat to get a better look at it through the windshield.

"Not as nice as yours I'm sure, but I can't complain." I got out of the car.

"Can I pick you up around seven?" he asked, staring intently at the gear shift.

"Alright. Are we going to dinner or should I eat before you get here?" I stood in the open door aware of Mary standing behind me waiting to claim her seat.

"We're going to dinner." He leaned against the steering wheel to see me better and the horn went off making him jump in his seat.

I laughed and watched as he turned red for a change. "See you around seven then." I backed away from the door and Mary practically pushed me out of the way to get her seat.

"Nice to meet you, Mary," I said, as she slammed the door in my face and stuck her tongue out at me.

The music came back up before I reached the door to the house, and I smiled. *At least he has good taste in music*, I thought pulling my keys out and unlocking the door

I went into the kitchen and grabbed the cordless phone, since I lost my phone in the accident, and dialed Billy's number. If he was at Tommy's house, he would have service. The phone rang and rang, but eventually went to voicemail. I hung up and called him again, again it went to voicemail. I dialed one more time, if he didn't answer I was going to leave him one hell of a message.

"What?" he barked into the phone.

"Don't you ever tell anyone to stay away from me unless I give you permission," I yelled into the phone.

"He told you I talked to him?" Billy sounded mad. "Dick move."

"He gave me a ride home, what did you think was going to happen?" I started pacing around the room.

"I thought he would be a man and do as I asked."

"What gives you the right to tell me who I can and can't date?"

"Liz, I care about your wellbeing." He hesitated for a second. "Nobody knows this guy."

"There's only one way to change that." I stomped around the room.

"I agree but going out on a date with him by yourself is not the way to get to know him."

"I've had enough of you. You have no say in what I do with my life. Mind your own business." I hung up the phone and continued my pacing. I didn't understand what his problem was. He needed to grow up. I wasn't his to boss around.

I looked at the clock, I had a few hours before Shawn was coming over to pick me up and at least a half-hour before my mom got home from work. My dad's hours varied depending on how busy the clinic was. I still had to ask them if I could go, but I didn't see why they wouldn't let me. Billy's actions were making me think everyone hated Shawn just because he was new in town.

I went up to my room and unloaded my backpack on my desk. Normally, if I wasn't doing anything with Billy I would get my homework done so I could hang out the rest of the weekend, but my mind was buzzing.

I lay down on my bed and stared at the ceiling hardly

believing I had a real date. Wait, I had a date, what was I supposed to wear on a date? Panicked, I jumped up and ran to my closet. I started going through every piece of clothing I had. Hoodie, hoodie, hoodie, T-shirt, T-shirt, T-shirt, jeans with little holes, jeans with big holes, jeans with oil stains, comfy jeans three sizes too big, I had nothing even kind of date worthy. I went to my dresser and did the same thing. I had nothing to wear. What was I going to do? I didn't have a car to run to Spruce and visit the one women's boutique within a hundred miles. I had no idea what I was going to do.

A knock at my door startled me. "Come in," I went back to my closet and stared at my boring wardrobe.

"Are you alright?" Mom asked, coming into my room, and looking at the clothes I scattered all over the floor.

"No," I said, as a tear leaked out. I crossed my arms over my chest.

"Sweetheart, what's wrong?" She moved toward me to give me a hug.

"I have a date tonight and I have nothing to wear." I ran my finger under my eye to wipe away the tears.

Mom gave me a confused look. "I'm sure Billy won't care what you have on."

"Billy? What I wear on my date with Shawn is none of Billy's business."

"I'm lost, Liz. You are going on a date with a boy named Shawn?"

"Sorry, it's been a long day." I turned to her. "Shawn Ericson lives in the mansion. He asked me out today and I said yes. Then Billy told him to stay away from me. I yelled at Billy to mind his own business. Anyway, I'm mad at him and all I have in my closet are T-shirts and hoodies. Aren't you supposed to dress up for a date?" I was rambling but hopefully she understood what I was saying. I didn't want to go through it again.

"First, were you going ask us if you could go out tonight?" Mom's voice was tight. I didn't know if she was mad or trying not to laugh at me.

"Yes, but then I realized I needed something to wear and here I am freaking out." I let my arms fall and balled my hands into fists.

"Good, just making sure. Now let's think about this, where do you think he will take you?" Mom took my hand forced my fingers to relax.

"He said dinner, I don't know after that." I squeezed her hand.

"You've eaten at all the restaurants in Twisted Pine, what do most people wear to dinner?" She pried my hand out of hers and shook it to get the feeling back.

"I don't know, nothing special I guess. I'm sorry, I'm really nervous." I shook my hand again.

"If you don't want to wear a hoodie, I'm sure I have something you can borrow. Why don't we go into my room and see if we can find a sweater to go with your jeans?"

CHAPTER 11

We went into my parents' bedroom and went through Mom's closet. When my dad got home I was dressed in my favorite pair of jeans, a formfitting, bright blue, V-neck sweater of my mom's, and her low-heeled bootees. She tried to get me to put some makeup on, but I didn't see the point, the bruises were almost gone, and Shawn already knew I had them. I did take the braid out of my hair and let my soft, blond waves fall almost to my waist.

When I was done getting ready, Mom and I went back downstairs to find Dad sitting in front of the television watching hockey with a beer in his hand.

"Liz, what are you wearing?" He looked up from the television with a shocked look on his face.

"Burt," Mom said sharply. "Liz is going on her first date tonight." She sat on the armrest of the recliner and put her arm around him.

"Billy finally asked you out?" he asked, with a knowing smile.

"Why does everyone assume its Billy? I would never go on a date with Billy. It would be like going on a date with your sister, Dad." I threw my arms up in the air. "I'm going out with Shawn Ericson, he is one of the new kids who started this week."

Dad's face went from a sly grin to a tight-lipped frown. "Did you think about asking us before you accepted?"

"I asked Mom when she got home. What's the big deal?"

"We don't know this boy. He could be bad news. We just want to make sure you're safe," Mom said, before Dad could open his mouth.

"What time is he coming?" Dad asked, getting up from his chair and finishing his beer.

"He's kind of shy, I'm supposed to meet him at the end of the street." I was torturing my parents, but they were making way too big of a deal over this.

"What?" my dad yelled. "Over my dead body, are you going out with this boy."

"Dad calm down, I'm kidding, he will be here around seven." I laughed, and Mom gave me a dirty look.

"I don't know, we don't know anything about this boy, Sandy. I need a beer." He started toward the kitchen and I rolled my eyes at Mom. She shrugged in response and we followed him into the kitchen.

"Dad, I know how to take care of myself and he's going to come in and meet you and Mom." I followed behind him.

"Burt, this is her first date. She's seventeen, it's time," Mom said from behind me.

"Didn't we say she wasn't allowed to date until she was twenty-one?" Dad opened the refrigerator and stared at the contents.

"You said that the day she was born. You know we can't stop this." Mom went behind him and put her hand on his back and rubbed it in circles. "If we let her go now we won't have to worry about her sneaking around to see this boy." I heard her whisper.

"Fine, but if I don't like him when he comes to pick her up she isn't going." He grabbed another beer from the fridge and closed the door.

"Thanks, Dad," I went up to him and kissed his cheek.

"You promise not to get pregnant?" He went to a drawer and took out a bottle opener.

"Why does everyone keep asking me that?" I ran my fingers through my hair, took a handful and pulled it in frustration. "I just met the guy. I'm not going to go there with him."

"Who else asked you?" Mom asked, at the same time Dad asked, "Is that a promise?"

"Yes, I will not get pregnant tonight and Billy." I sat on one of the kitchen stools and lay my head on the table.

"It will be okay, sweetheart," Mom said, putting her hand on my back this time, and rubbing it.

Dad put his beer on the bar and walked away. "Where are you going?" I asked. I had a bad feeling about this.

"I just remembered, I forgot to clean my gun after elk season. Now seems like a good time."

"You've got to be kidding me." I sat up and looked at my mom. "Please, stop him."

"Honey, there are a few things in this world no wife can stop from happening. Your father being overprotective is one of those things." She gave me an, *I'm sorry but there is nothing I can do* smile and got up to start making dinner.

Dad came back a few minutes later with his gun case and the cleaning kit. I looked at the clock it was six forty-five. There was no way he was going to finish before Shawn showed up.

I wandered around the house, giddy with excitement and nervousness. I checked my hair too many times for me to be comfortable with and kept looking in the full-length mirror to make sure nothing was out of place. At seven o'clock I camped out on the stairs and stared at the front door.

"Liz, can you please come in here?" my dad called.

I went into the dining room to find newspaper spread over the table, and Dad's rifle completely taken apart. The barrel was pointed at the wall and he was rubbing solvent on the bolt. "What's up, Dad?"

"Sit down. Watch and learn." He put the bolt down and took the rod from the cleaning kit. He threaded a small square piece of cotton through the metal loop on the end then he covered it in the solution and stuck it down the barrel of the gun.

"I know how to clean a gun, Dad. You taught me before I got my hunter's safety card." I rested my elbows on the table and rested my head in my hand.

"I'm not talking about cleaning a gun. I'm talking about waiting for your date." He pulled the rod back out of the barrel, the square was still white.

"Did you even get a shot off last season? I can't remember," I said, raising my eyebrows.

"There is a freezer full of meat that says I did and you can never be too sure." He winked at me and ran the rod back down the barrel. The doorbell rang, and I shot to my feet ready to run to the door. "Sit your butt back down, your mom can answer the door. Always make a boy wait a minute, dear," Dad said, sounding unconcerned.

I grunted and slouched down in my chair, this was almost as bad as Billy telling Shawn to stay away from me. I heard Mom answer the door, then an exchange of muffled words. I made myself sit up as footsteps came our way.

Mom came in with Shawn behind her. "Liz, your date is here," she practically sang, and I felt my face heat. I stood and went to Shawn. He was wearing an unzipped forest-green down coat. Under that he had a cream button-down shirt tucked into dark blue jeans that weren't too tight, but not too loose. His short, dark blond hair was combed to the side, and the smile on his face made me want to drool.

"Mom, Dad this is Shawn Ericson. Shawn, these are my parents Sandy and Burt Lawson," I said, praying my dad would not embarrass me by saying something stupid like, *don't get my daughter pregnant.*

"Nice to meet you Mr. & Mrs. Lawson." Shawn extended his hand to my dad, saw the gun on the table, almost pulled his hand back, but thought better of it and kept it out waiting for my dad to take it.

"It's actually Dr. Lawson, and I would shake your hand, but I'm covered in cleaning solution." Dad indicated the small bottle sitting on the table.

"Okay," Shawn mumbled and put his hands in his pockets. I didn't think any of us knew what to do next, we all just stood there silently for a second. My parents had never had a boy pick up their daughter for a date and they were clueless about what we were supposed to do.

"Sandy, why don't you get Shawn a beer?" Dad asked, folding his arms across his chest.

What was he doing? I thought to myself. Shawn's eye widened and took a step back.

"No thank you, sir. I would never drink before getting in a car." Shawn blew out a breath and looked at me like he was rethinking asking me out.

"Right answer." Dad started to put the rifle back together without looking up. "Where are you two going tonight?"

"Well, I'm new in town, but I heard The Diner has pretty good food. Then depending on what Liz wants to do, I was thinking of bowling." I wondered how he knew exactly the right thing to say to my dad.

"What time are you going to have her home?" The gun was back together, and he checked the smoothness of the action as he opened and closed the bolt a few times.

"She never told me what her curfew was, but I would say no later than eleven. If that's okay with you, sir."

"I think that's reasonable, Shawn. You two go and have fun," Mom said, holding her arm out toward the front door.

I jumped to my feet gave my dad a peck on the cheek. "Thanks, Dad. We'll be good."

"You better be, or I'll get the STD poster out again," he mumbled, slumping in his chair.

"Thanks, Mom." I followed Shawn to the front door.

"Have a good time but be careful." She stopped at the hall closet and pulled out my down coat for me.

"We will, have fun dealing with Dad." I pulled the coat on and Shawn opened the door for me. Once we were outside I stopped and took a deep cleansing breath. "I'm so sorry, my parents are not used to me dating," I said as he moved to stand next to me.

"The rifle was definitely a first for me." Shawn laughed. "Come on let's go before he decides he needs some target practice."

"Good idea." We walked to his Jeep, and he opened my door for me. My butterflies were still in full swing, but I remembered to hit the unlock button on the door handle to make sure his door was unlocked. He opened the door with a small grin on his face and got in.

CHAPTER 12

"What kind of music do you like?" Shawn asked, starting the Jeep, and turning the radio on.

"Anything but country and I can deal." I never understood country music and I never would.

He smiled hitting a button on the stereo. "That's a relief. You didn't look like someone who listened to country, but when it's all you have up here you can never tell." A classic Green Day song came on the radio and I mentally started singing it in my head. "I had to beg my dad to let me keep the satellite radio subscription when it expired." Shawn turned the music up.

"You have satellite radio? I'm so jealous. All I have are the MP3s I downloaded on my phone. And my phone was smashed by the moose."

"I've been there. When I was twelve, we lived in this tiny town in Minnesota and they only had one radio station. I was going insane. I begged my dad for the satellite radio when we moved here because of that experience. So, is dinner at The Diner is okay with you?" He sounded nervous.

"Sure, their food is really good. You'll like it."

"Good," he let out an audible breath as he drove down the road. "Tell me about the poster your dad was talking about."

"Oh my God, pray you never have to see it." The images flashed in my mind and my stomach turned over.

"Why?" he asked, looking at me from the corner of his eye.

"It has these disgusting photos of STDs." My stomach turned thinking about it.

"Like people's private parts?" He almost choked on his words.

"Yes, it is the grossest thing I have ever seen." I blinked and shook my head, trying to get the pictures out of my mind.

"I'll try and make sure I never have to see it."

When we reached the part in the road where I met the moose my knuckles tightened on the door handle and I looked frantically around.

"Are you alright?" Shawn asked, looking over at me.

"Keep your eyes on the road this is where I hit the moose," I barked. I hadn't been on this road in the dark since the accident.

"Sorry, yeah, help me keep a look out." Shawn turned his head back to look at the road.

"I'm just paranoid. I don't ever want to go through that again." I looked down at my shaking hands.

"I bet it was terrifying. I've never even seen a moose, but I'm sure I would be just as freaked out after going through what you did."

We came to the end of the dirt road and he turned onto the highway heading toward downtown. I looked out the window and stared at the half moon rising over the lake.

"So, what do you do for fun up here?" Shawn broke the silence.

"This time of year, there isn't a lot. The snow is melting so the snow machining isn't very good. The boys are going to spend half their trip trying to figure out how to stay in the snow. At the same time there is still too much snow to go four wheeling and the ice on the lake is too thin to go ice fishing. Bowling, and hanging out is all there is. After the ice on the lake breaks up we hang out at the lake or on the boat most of the time. I like to go hiking off the beaten path and camping. It probably sounds kind of boring to you."

He shook his head. "I love being in the mountains with clean air and animals to look at. I'm really looking forward to this summer. I can't wait to be in the mountains instead of breathing in the smog of a big city."

I smiled, that was something we had in common. Most of the girls at school would jump at any chance they could get to get out of town and hang out in Denver. I hated it, there was just too much concrete and asphalt for me.

"Whose boat do you go out on?" Shawn stopped in the middle of the road, put the Jeep into reverse and started to parallel park. He made it look easy.

"My parents have a sail boat they keep in the marina and Billy's dad has a power boat we wakeboard on." He put the Jeep in park and turned to look at me. "How are you so good at parallel parking? It takes me fifteen minutes to get it almost right."

"I learned to drive in the city. You had to parallel park or you didn't pass the driver's test. I'll teach you sometime if you want." He smiled and turned the engine off. "Shall we?"

"Yeah, I'm starving." I opened my door and stepped out onto the icy road forgetting I had my mom's boots on. I slipped but caught myself on the door and pulled myself up.

"Be careful, it's icy," Shawn called and came around to my side and offered me his hand.

"I know, I forgot I had these stupid boots on." I regained my balance and closed the door. I looked at his offered hand and took it turning tomato red in the process.

"Why did you wear them if you knew it would be icy?" he asked, as I teetered onto the icy sidewalk, it wasn't much better than the road.

"Aren't you supposed to dress up for a date?" I asked and regretted it immediately. "I mean, I wanted to wear something different than I do at school."

"I forgot to tell you at your house, your dad was scaring me. You look beautiful."

I stopped walking and he stopped next to me. "Wow, thanks. You look nice too," I said in a small voice. No one other than my family had ever called me beautiful before.

When we reached the door to the diner I reached for the door, but he stopped me with a hand and opened it for me. "Thanks," I said, going through the door, and trying not to blush.

"Wow," Shawn said, taking in the 1950s' décor. The Twisted Pines Diner originally opened in the 1950s. Until the national park opened it had been everyone's favorite greasy spoon that barely broke even. With the opening of the national park the owners had been able to remodel the inside but keep the same vibe. The walls were decorated with records and photographs of stars from the era. The floor was covered in black and white checkered linoleum. There was a long black and silver Formica counter with chrome accented stools covered in red vinyl. Booths lined the exterior wall with vinyl and chrome to match the stools at the counter. There was a miniature jukebox at every table with menus and a napkin dispenser.

It was busy for a Friday night during mud season, over half the booths were full and there were a few people sitting at the counter. As soon as we were in the door, all conversation stopped, and everyone turned to stare at us. It wasn't unusual for people to stop mid-sentence to see who was coming in during mud season, but normally the conversation only paused for a second before it resumed. Tonight, everyone stared at us without resuming their conversations. The only noise was coming from the jukebox playing *In*

I groaned when I saw Tiffany walking toward us, I completely forgot her grandparents owned the restaurant and she worked there.

"You guys can sit wherever," she said, batting her eyes at Shawn before delivering the plates she was holding to the booth by the door.

"Thanks," Shawn said, taking my hand, and leading us to a booth at the back of the room.

Everyone we walked by started whispering low to each other as we passed. What was the big deal? Couldn't a girl go out on a date with the new kid in town? When we got to our booth I took my coat off and hung it on the coat rack at the end of the booth and Shawn did the same. We sat across from each other and everyone finally started talking normally again.

"Was that weird or was it me?" he asked, in a low voice.

"What's the big deal?" I asked, agreeing with him. "I want to stand up and tell them all to mind their own business." Everyone in town knew me, either because my dad was one of two doctors in town, or because they all came into the Gas N'Go at some point. It didn't matter, I was allowed to go out on a date and not have people whispering about me behind my back. Then it dawned on me. "You know it's probably because of the bruises from the accident, but still, can't they mind their own business?" I pulled menus from behind the miniature jukebox and handed one to Shawn.

He took the menu and opened it. "So, what's good here?"

"Everything, but their burgers are to die for," I said, reading the menu even though I had it memorized. "Their shakes are good too."

We were quiet while Shawn read the menu. Tiffany came over after a few minutes with two glasses of water. "What can I get you?" she asked Shawn, not even giving me a glance.

"You go first," Shawn said, meeting my eyes, and ignoring Tiffany.

"I'll have the ultimate burger, medium, with fries, and a strawberry shake." I closed my menu and put it back behind the jukebox.

"Really? You're going to eat all that? Aren't you on a date?"
Tiffany asked, her eyebrows so high they disappeared behind her
bangs.

I felt myself blush. What was I supposed to order on a date?
Was there some unknown menu I needed to order from?

"I like a woman who knows how to eat," Shawn said, closing
his menu. "I'll have the same only I would like a chocolate shake
instead of strawberry."

Tiffany shook her head then wrote it down. "I'll have that
right up." She turned and walked away, putting a little more sway in
her hips than the occasion called for.

"Don't let her get to you. I hate women who can't be
themselves on a date." Shawn smiled and took a sip of his water.

"I'm sorry, I've never been on a date before. I have no idea
what I'm doing." I put my elbows on the table and covered my hands
with my face.

"Don't worry about it. I think you're doing great." His voice
was upbeat and reassuring.

"How do you figure?" I asked, bringing my hands down and
resting them on the table.

"I'm having fun. Are you?" He gave me one of his dazzling
smiles that made his eyes crinkle at the corners.

"If I could get over being embarrassed about everything I do
I would be." I half-laughed.

"You're overthinking it. We are just hanging out, having a
good time, and getting to know each other." He leaned back in his
seat and rested his folded hands on the table.

I took a deep breath and let it out. "Okay, I can do this," I
said, more to myself than to Shawn.

"Are you ready for the history test next week?" he asked.

"I think so, but I'll do some cramming this weekend." I didn't want to talk about school, I wanted to find out more about dreams.

"Yeah, me too but, maybe we could study together on Sunday if your dad doesn't shoot me when I bring you home." He half-laughed and drummed his hands on the table.

"He won't shoot you." I laughed. "Unless I ask him to."

"Really? Remind me to stay on your good side." He laughed back.

"How are you able to do it?" I looked around the diner. Everyone had gone back to their conversations. "Invade my dreams." I didn't know how to talk about it with him. I wasn't sure what to ask so I started with the biggest question.

Shawn looked around making sure no one was in earshot. "I'm a Knight Flyer, like I told you, it's a gift I was born with. The people in my family and others are the protectors of dreams."

"So, can Jo, Jeff, and Mary do it too?"

"They can, but they're still in training. Jo should be finishing in the next few months." He was looking everywhere but at me as he spoke.

"What's wrong? Do you not want to talk about it?"

"I do. I want to tell you everything, but if my dad finds out he'll kill me."

"I don't want you to get in trouble, but why you did move here? Twisted Pines is just another small mountain town."

"I have no idea why we moved here. He doesn't think I am worthy of the information, but I'm happy we did." He reached across the table and took my hand.

"Me too," I said just as Tiffany arrived with our food.

"Can I get you anything else?" she asked Shawn, it looked like she undid a few of the buttons on her shirt and she pushed her chest out in Shawn's direction.

"Do you need anything?" he asked, moving around Tiffany's breasts to see me.

"No, I'm good." I pulled a napkin out of the dispenser and unfolded it on my lap.

"I think we're good." Shawn didn't take his eyes off me.

"Just give me a shout if you need anything." She straightened, gave me a dirty look, and walked away.

"She likes you," I said, grabbing the catsup off the table, and putting some on my burger.

"What makes you say that?" he asked, taking the catsup from me when I offered it to him.

"Are you telling me you didn't notice her boobs in your face? Besides, she couldn't take her eyes off you, and she asked you all the questions. It was like I wasn't even here." I picked up my burger and took a bite.

"Well, too bad for her I only have eyes for you." He picked up his burger and took a bite.

I almost choked on the food in my mouth. Was he for real? I felt myself blush for what felt like the hundredth time in the past hour. "Umm, thanks?" I wasn't sure how to respond.

He took a bite of his burger and gave me a closed-lipped smile. I smiled back. "How do you fight the mares?" I asked around a bite, keeping my voice low.

He looked around before he started to talk. "Any way I can, when you're dreaming, if you have control, you can manipulate it. So, if you need a gun, and can think about everything you need to make a gun work, you can manifest one in your dream. If you are good you can create anything you need."

"So, if the goblin comes back I can just think of a gun and shoot him? Isn't that what you did in my dream the night we met?" I asked, taking a bite. I wanted to know how to fight the goblin in case he was able to get through my barrier.

"Theoretically, yes, the mare I killed in your dream should have been sent back to hell. I don't know if it's the same one coming after you now or a different one. We don't understand everything about them. We can't exactly capture one and make him tell us his secrets." He sucked on the straw in his milkshake.

"So, what do I do if he gets through my barrier and you're not around?" I asked, finishing the last bite of my burger, and sucking on my milkshake.

"Run, hide, if that doesn't work you will have to try and kill him. Are you familiar with any weapons?"

"I'm good with guns, and a few knives but nothing too big."

"Good, then think of a gun and shoot it until it stops or one of us comes to help you." He sucked on his straw until his shake made a slurping noise.

"I think I can do that. Thanks, Shawn."

"You're right that was one of the best burgers I've ever had," he said, changing the subject. He leaned back in his seat when he was done.

"I'm glad you liked it," I said, leaning back, and smiling. Tiffany brought the bill over and I went to take it, but Shawn beat me to it.

"I'm the one who asked you out, this is my treat." He pulled his wallet out after reviewing the bill.

"Thank you." I was feeling shy, I forgot we were on a date. If this was how all dates went, I didn't understand why it was such a big deal. It felt like I was just hanging out with one of the guys. Was there supposed to be a difference when you were out on a date with a guy instead of just hanging out?

He put some cash on the table. "Are you ready?" he asked, moving to get out of the booth.

"Yeah, I just need to go to the bathroom. I'll be right back," I said, sliding out of the booth.

"Okay, I'll wait here."

I got up and walked quickly to the bathroom, glad we were sitting towards the back of the restaurant, I didn't have to walk by anyone I knew.

As I was washing my hands I looked in the mirror. The bruises were finally fading, and the yellow and green were almost gone as well. I would be so happy when I could look in the mirror and see my old unbruised face looking back at me. My hair was starting to grow back where they had shaved it, but it was going to take forever for it to catch up with the rest. At least it was shaved on the side of my head, so I could cover it up with the hair above. I smiled at myself, making sure there wasn't any food in my teeth then exited the bathroom.

Tiffany was standing by our booth, leaning toward Shawn when I came out. I didn't know why I agreed to go on a date with him. How could I compete with a girl like her? She was pretty and a senior. From what I had heard she had a lot more experience in the boyfriend department than I did, but no matter what I was feeling about the date, what right did she have to hit on him? I really wanted to punch her in the face, but then I would be banned from the diner, and would starve to death. I walked over to them and shoved my hands in my pockets to keep myself from involuntarily hitting her.

"Tiffany, shouldn't you get back to work?" I asked, standing behind her.

She looked over her shoulder at me and rolled her eyes. "I was off ten minutes ago. I was just asking Shawn if he wanted to go to a senior party with me later."

"And I was telling her that I'm not a senior and I'm with you, so she should go and have fun." Shawn rolled his eyes and shook his head.

"Well, if you change your mind here's my number." She slid a folded piece of paper toward him and took a step back.

"Don't worry, I won't." He stood leaving the paper with her phone number on the table and moved to the other side of the booth. He took my coat off the hook and held it for me to put on. I had never had anyone help me put my coat on before, it was weird.

Tiffany flung her hair out of her face and stomped off to the back room.

"Thanks, sorry she's such a bitch," I said, turning to him, and watching as he put his coat on.

"It's okay, every school has a girl who thinks she can have whoever she wants." He zipped his coat up and we walked to the door. He held it open for me and I waited for him on the other side. He took my hand in his and we walked back to his Jeep. It was a cold night. The stars were out, and the moon was casting its eerie glow over town. It reminded me of the opening credits for a horror movie.

Shawn stopped abruptly, I was jerked back and almost ran into his chest before he caught me. I looked up to apologize, but before I could form the words his lips landed on mine. I instinctively kissed him back as sparks zinged through my body and my arms went around him. After a moment, I pulled back, blushing, and looked around, maybe the moonlight didn't remind me of a horror story, but one of those romance movies on the Hallmark channel instead.

"Wow," I mumbled, looking everywhere but at him.

"No kidding." He took my hand again and we walked to his Jeep.

CHAPTER 13

We went through the doors of the bowling alley and were immediately surrounded by the sounds of balls rolling down the lanes, colliding with pins, and pins falling to the wood floor. We went to the counter and rented shoes. I paid for the first game without Shawn catching on until it was too late. He went to the snack bar and got us drinks while I started looking for my favorite ball.

There were a lot of kids from school there, I said hi to a few of them before finding the eight-pound, lime-green ball I loved to use. I went to our lane, put my ball in the return slot and sat in one of the chairs to change my shoes. I had never been so happy to put on ugly bowling shoes as I was then. My feet were killing me from wearing my mom's heels.

Shawn put the drinks on the table, sat next me, pulled his shoes off, and went to work putting the bowling shoes on.

"Why do you think they make bowling shoes the ugliest shoes known to man?" he asked, tying his laces.

"I think it's so you are less likely to steal them, or if you do they will be able to find you by the color." I laughed and went to the computer to enter our names.

"So, what are we playing for?" Shawn asked when the pins finished resetting indicating a new game was ready to go.

"Who said we were playing for anything?" I loved a good challenge, but he could be part of the three hundred club for all I knew.

"I did. Hmm, let's see." He picked up his ball, lined up with the arrows in the floor, took two steps forward, brought his arm back, and hurled the ball down the alley toward the pins. I watched as all the pins fell with a crash. "How about, if I win you go to prom with me."

I wanted to go out with him again, but prom? I didn't even know if I wanted to go. "I don't know, prom isn't really my thing." I asked as he waited for his ball to be return, so he could throw his second shot. "You will have to give me something really good in return."

He picked his ball up when it came out and lined up again. I wasn't sure if he was ignoring me or concentrating on the pins at the other end of the alley. He took three steps then launched the ball over the oil wood. He waited and watched as the ball tore down the lane hitting the front pin at the perfect angel forcing all the pins to fall down.

I went to give him a high five, but before I knew what was happening he was pulling me into his arms and squeezing me tight.

"I need a hug when I get a strike. You're my good luck charm." He whispered in my ear before letting go.

Blushing and speechless I picked up my ball, found my spot on the floor, lined up and threw the ball at the pins. I hit the center pin at the perfect angle and the domino effect knocked all the pins down. I put my hands in the air in victory as I waited for my ball to come back and the pins to reset. My second throw was just as good as my first and I walked back to the chairs with my hands in the air again. Shawn pulled me into another hug and swung me around so fast my feet left the ground.

"Shawn, put me down. You're crazy." My arms were locked tight around him. I didn't really want to let him go.

After swinging me around a few more times he put me down and I looked around. Almost everyone in the alley had stopped what they were doing to watch us. *It was going to be a pain dating in this town,* I thought to myself feeling my cheeks redden. "As I was saying, what do I get if I win?"

"What do you want?" he asked, taking his ball, and getting ready to throw it.

I thought about it. What did I want from him? Well I wouldn't mind another kiss, but I could do better. Before I could answer him, his ball rolled down the alley hitting half the pins and he turned with a frown on his face. "You can't get them all every time," I said, giving him a smile. "If I win, I get to drive your Jeep when the ground is ready for some real four-wheeling."

He looked at the floor then back to me, from the look he was giving me he didn't let anyone drive his Jeep. "Deal." He blew out a breath as his ball came back through the receiver. He picked it up, lined up, and threw the ball. It arched over to the far side of the lane, almost falling in the gutter before it turned and hit the remaining pins.

I gave him a high five for the spare. "You only get a hug for strikes," I said, passing him by and picking up my ball.

I lined up and was just about to let go of the ball when Shawn yelled, "Miss it," but it was too late, the ball left my fingers and raced down the wood hitting the front pin straight on, and only knocking the pins in the middle down. Now I was stuck with a split.

"Do you really want to play dirty?" I asked, walking back to the receiver, and waiting for my ball to come back.

"What do you mean play dirty? I didn't say anything." He looked around frantically then pointed at the group next to us. "It was them."

"Right." I picked my ball up and went back to the line. I rolled the ball down the lane as close to the gutter as I could, hoping it wouldn't fall in. I held my breath until it hit the outside edge of the pin. It whipped across the lane and hit the other two pins. I jumped up and down. "Do I get extra points for that?"

"No way." He laughed and gave me a high five before picking his ball up.

"What do you do for fun when you aren't betting on bowling?" I asked, sitting down in my chair, and watching him line up.

"Fun? I play some video games, but I like to be outside. I love to trail run, mountain bike, and swim. I don't get much free time though." He rolled the ball down the lane and did a fist pump when he threw a strike. He waited for his ball to come back and threw the ball a second time hitting half the pins.

I got up to give him his hug. "How come?"

He let go of me and took a seat. "If I'm not at school or studying, I'm training."

"Training?" I asked, not understanding as I picked up my ball and lined up.

"Yeah, for my job."

I threw my ball toward the pins, but his comment caught me off guard and my ball went straight into the gutter. I forgot he wasn't a typical guy.

"Hey, what happened?" he asked, watching my ball roll down the gutter.

"I just forgot you're not a typical teenager." I put my hands on my hips and blew out a breath.

"I am, I just have this other thing I'm part of." His voice was low, and he stared at the ground as he spoke, almost like he was ashamed of what he did.

"We don't have to talk about it if it upsets you," I said.

"I want you to know, but let's talk about it later. I don't want to talk about work anymore. It might distract me from beating you." I picked up my ball as he took my seat to watch.

"Deal." I looked at the pins at the end of the alley. "Now I'm really behind." I rolled the ball down the lane and this time bowled a spare.

We continued playing and flirting. I was having a great time. Shawn was easy to talk to, and the nervousness that plagued me from the beginning of the night had completely disappeared. I won the first game by a few points and he immediately called for two out of three.

Shawn ended up winning the second round by the same margin. He looked at his watch and sighed. "We better go. I don't want to get you home late on our first date."

I looked at my watch. We had a half hour before I needed to be home. I wasn't ready for the night to end, but I didn't want to test my parents. "Okay, but, what do we do about the bet?" I pulled my bowling shoes off and forced my feet into the heels.

"We will have to postpone it." With an evil grin on his face he sat next to me and started to change his shoes. "But, if I were you, I would make sure you have a dress for prom."

"Really?" I blushed, hiding my face behind my hair as I zipped my boot up. "If I win the bet what would I need a dress for? I'd hate to waste the money."

"I think you'll need it, no matter what." With his shoes on he retrieved our balls and put them away.

I stood, still blushing. Was he so sure I would agree to go with him? Who was I kidding? I was secretly hoping he would ask me. With both my boots on, I picked up our bowling shoes and took them to the counter.

"Hi, Carol," I said, to one of the owners. She was in her late sixties, with long silver hair falling around her shoulders. I put our shoes on the counter and gave her a smile.

"Hi, Liz, did you and your date have a good time?" she asked, taking our shoes, and setting them on the counter against the wall.

"Yeah, it was really fun," I said as my face heated up with a blush again.

"He's a tall drink of water. Where did you find him?" she asked, wiggling her eyebrows at me.

"What?" I didn't understand what she meant. "He's new in town."

"Oh, is he living up in the mansion?"

"Yep." Shawn came up beside me and put his arm around my shoulder. "Shawn, this is Carol, one of the owners, Carol, this is Shawn Ericson."

"Nice to meet you, Shawn," she cooed, giving him a good once-over.

"You too," he said, shuffling from foot to foot.

"Carol, we better get home before I break curfew. We will see you around." I took Shawn's hand and pulled him toward the door.

"Drive safe, sweetie. Shawn, I'm sure we will see each other again soon."

"Was she hitting on me?" he asked, as we walked toward the door.

"I think she was just flirting, she's been married for fifty years." I laughed at his discomfort.

"I feel dirty, I need a shower. I don't think I have ever been checked out so blatantly by a woman that old."

"I'm sure you have. They just weren't as in your face about it." I giggled.

"Please stop, I don't know how much more I can take."

Shawn opened the door to his Jeep for me, I climbed in then put my seat belt on while he walked around to his side. He got in, started the Jeep, and put his seatbelt on before putting it into drive and pulling out of the parking lot.

"That was really fun. Thank you," I said, looking out the window as we drove through town.

"It was. Thanks for going out with me." He took my hand, laced his fingers with mine, squeezed them then rested our clasped hands on my leg.

Butterflies erupted in my stomach again and I squeezed back. "What are you doing for the rest of the weekend?" I asked, trying to keep the conversation going.

"I'm on duty tonight and I have training for most of the day tomorrow. Sunday I'm studying with a beautiful girl. What are you doing?"

"Going car shopping with my dad tomorrow since mine was totaled. Then studying on Sunday with some guy. He seems nice, but I'm not sure if he's my type."

"Really, why isn't he your type?" he asked, not believing a word I said and squeezing my hand.

"That's easy, I've never had a type." I smirked and squeezed his hand back. When we pulled off the paved road I let go of his hand. "Will you please put both hands on the wheel?" I was acting neurotic. I needed to get over my fear of hitting another moose, but I could not seem to get a grip on my anxiety.

"Sure, I get it." He put his hand on the steering wheel.

I let out a breath at his understanding. I was afraid a moose was going to jump out in front us at any moment. Sensing my paranoia, we drove in silence until we pulled into the driveway of my house. "Sorry, I need to get over this."

He put the Jeep in park. "It's alright, I would probably be the same way if I went through what you did."

"Thank you for understanding." I undid my seat belt and opened the door.

"What are you doing?" I asked, watching him open his door while I was halfway out of the Jeep.

"Walking you to the door. It's what dates are supposed to do I think."

"Oh, alright," I got out and closed the door, feeling myself blush, again.

He came around to my side of the Jeep, took my hand, and walked me to the door. "I had a really nice time. Will I see you later?" I asked, thinking about my dreams.

"I had a good time too and I want to see you again, but I'm not sure about later tonight. I'm on duty so I'll probably be out hunting mares."

"Oh, alright." I smiled, trying to hide my disappointment.

"If I get done early, I'll find you." He squeezed my hand.

"Okay, if I don't see you, give me a call me tomorrow, and we can set up a time to study on Sunday."

We arrived at the front door, and he turned to me. "I will be in touch one way or another." He leaned down and kissed me. Lightning shot through my veins, and I wrapped my arms around his neck and ran my hand through his hair. He pulled away with a smile on his face.

"We have an audience," he said, looking over my shoulder at the windows.

I took a step back feeling like I was going to explode from embarrassment. I turned and saw my parents watching us from the bay window next to the front door. I gave them a weak wave.

I turned back to Shawn. "I'll talk to you later." I turned went inside.

"That was quite a kiss," Mom said as soon as I closed the door behind me.

"Can't you mind your own business?" I asked, not really mad, but not thrilled they had been watching.

"You are our business," Dad said, following me to the closet. I took off my coat and hung it up.

"Did you have a good time?" Mom asked, trailing behind me as I went into the kitchen.

"Yeah, I really did. We ate at The Diner, then went to the bowling alley and played a few games. He's really fun."

"Good, did he ask you to prom yet?" Mom sat at the bar watching me as I went to the cabinet and got a glass out.

"No, but I think he might." I grinned at her and went to the sink to fill up the glass with water.

"So, car shopping this weekend, dress shopping next weekend?" Mom drummed her fingers on the counter, thinking. "It will be a week before prom so maybe we can get your hair and nails done too."

I stood across from her with the bar between us and gulped the water. "He didn't buy you anything to drink?" Dad asked, accusingly when he walked into the kitchen.

"Yes, he did. I'm just thirsty tonight." I shot an evil glance to my dad. "What is wrong with him?" I asked Mom.

He folded his arms across his chest. "I just have a bad feeling about him."

"Well, get over it. He was nothing but a gentleman tonight." I put my glass in the sink.

"We'll see." He ran a hand through his hair and let out a breath. "Are we still looking at those Jeeps tomorrow?"

"Yes, I hate not having a car and I'm sure Bob wants me back at work on Monday."

"Good, I'm going to bed."

"Night, Dad." He left the room and I blew out a breath. "I hope he gets over this."

"He will sweetheart. He has never wanted you to grow up. To him it feels like yesterday you were going to your first day of school." Mom patted my hand before following him upstairs. I finished my water, turned out the lights and went to bed.

CHAPTER 14

I was driving around in my old Jeep, listening to the radio, the top was off, and the sun was out. I thought I was going home, but I drove past my driveway. It was almost like I was being pulled somewhere. I parked at a pull out just past my house. I got out and followed my favorite hiking trail for about a mile before I realized something was different. Instead of staying on the trail, something pulled me off the main trail and onto a two-track I never noticed before. I wanted to stop, but I continued, as if I had no control over where my legs took me.

The trail led me deep into the forest of twisted pines. It twisted and turned, leading me around the trees that stopped the trail from continuing in a straight line. It felt like they were trying to stop me from going any further.

I shivered and looked around for the goblin who had been haunting my dreams, but I was alone. Completely alone, the normal sounds of the forest: birds chirping, squirrels threatening me when I got too close to their nests, weren't there. It was like all the animals just disappeared.

I finally found my way through the trees and emerged in a small clearing on the side of the hill. It was weird, there were no trees or saplings, and the grass was short and yellow. I would have thought it was autumn except the few Aspen trees on the edge of the clearing had green leaves. Right in the middle of the clearing there was an old mineshaft.

My legs continued to carry me forward, even though I knew there was something wrong with this place. I tried to stop, but I had no control over what my body was doing. I closed my eyes and concentrated on stopping. When my legs finally stopped I was about twenty yards from the opening of the shaft. It was calling to me with a dark, sinister, all-encompassing power. I didn't want to move closer, but I lost control of my feet again and started to move closer to the opening. When I was a few feet from it, I peered into the darkness. It was the darkest thing I had ever seen, like there was nothing in the hole to reflect the light. A chill shook me, and as I looked into the abyss, it felt like this was where true evil was born. I wanted to run home but my body refused to obey my mind. My legs dragged me closer to the opening, and I started to make out cobwebs and darker things I could not put a name to scurrying around in the dark.

"There you are, Elizabeth Robinson," the scratchy voice said from behind me. I forced myself to spin around as my heart rate picked up. "Welcome to my home. I didn't think I would find you here."

"Leave me alone," I said through gritted teeth.

"Now, what fun would that be? You are the last piece of the puzzle. Once I have you, we will move to your plane and eat until my hunger is finally sated." He took a step closer to me and reached a hand out as if to caress my cheek, but the force field stopped him. "Damn you and your protection," he bellowed.

I took a step to the side. I didn't like being between him and the opening to the shaft. "Why do you think sucking my soul out will help you change planes?" I asked, thankful for my protection but ready to leave the clearing.

"Because when I sucked the soul of your father, he gave me

more power than I had ever had, and you are stronger than he was." The goblin laughed, and I started to shake.

"You killed my father?" I asked, my voice trembling from fear and anger. He was the reason why I had never met my bio-dad.

"Yes, he thought he could close the gate and send us back to our dimension for good. The silly man had no idea who he was going up against." The goblin walked around me, looking for a weakness in my protection.

"You bastard," I yelled, and remembering what Shawn had told me about thinking of a gun.

I closed my eyes and thought about the .30-06 my dad was cleaning when Shawn came to pick me up for our date. It had a wooden stock, stained so black I could barely see the grain in the wood. It was bolt action with a scope, and the magazine held three rounds plus one in the chamber. It was heavy, and the shoulder strap always dug in when I was hiking with it. When I opened my eyes, it was in my hands and I brought it to my shoulder and took aim at the goblin.

"You can't kill me, silly girl. Your weapons are useless. I may leave for a time, but I will come back for you."

Ignoring him, I pulled the trigger, but it was too late; he disappeared. I screamed in frustration and dropped the gun. I turned, ready to hike out of the clearing, but my body had other ideas as it started to back toward the opening of the shaft. I knew going down there would mean the end of me. I couldn't let it happen. I turned to face the abyss and forced myself to my knees, refusing to go any further. The top half of my body was forced forward and my hands shot out to save me from a face full of dirt. Wind began blowing through the opening and into my face, bringing with it voices. I couldn't understand what they were saying, but it was important, I felt it in my gut. I needed to understand whatever they were trying to tell me.

"What? I can't understand what you are saying," I yelled into the opening. The wind picked up and the voices became louder.

They were all saying the same thing, but it was so disjointed I couldn't figure it out. I closed my eyes and tried to find one voice to concentrate on. "Help us." I finally made out.

I stood and backed up a step, the force pulling me into the opening was gone. "How?" I called back, not wanting to venture into the darkness.

They all started speaking at once again, and I couldn't understand them. I closed my eyes again and listened hard. "You have to close the gate."

"How? Where is it?" I asked as the wind picked up, I had to lean into it to keep my footing.

They started talking again but the wind was becoming too much, all I could hear was the wind blowing across my ears. Without warning, a gust picked me up off the ground and flung me through the air away from the mineshaft. Terrified I would be impaled on a tree, I closed my eyes and reminded myself it was just a dream.

The wind stopped, and I felt my legs connect with the ground. I opened my eyes and found myself in Shawn's padded room. I was shaking uncontrollably, my heart was racing, and I was cold, so cold. I looked around, I was alone. I sat against the wall and brought my knees up to my chest, wrapped my arms around them, and rested my head on my knees. *Just breathe*, I thought to myself. It was just a dream, nothing bad could happen to me in a dream.

Something brushed my arm, and I jumped, jerking my head up, ready to fight. Shawn was standing there looking confused. "Are you alright? What are you doing here?"

"I had a weird dream, I was trying to get out of it. I thought of a safe place and I ended up here." I stood, and realized I was trembling.

"Was something chasing you?" he asked, looking me over.

"No, but the goblin showed up. He said he killed my dad. He said I was the last piece of the puzzle, he thinks if he can suck out my soul he can come through to our plane. I tried to shoot him, but he disappeared before I got the shot off.

"Then there was this mineshaft opening, and it was dark. I don't mean just no light dark, but the feeling emanating from it was dark. Then these voices started calling for me to help them. When I asked them how, the wind picked up and blew me through the air. The next thing I knew, I was here."

"That's an odd dream. You're shaking come here." Shawn pulled me into his arms. "You're alright, everything is fine."

I closed my eyes and wrapped my arms around him, steadying myself in his embrace. "Thanks. Are you going to get in trouble for being here?"

"No, I'm done for the night. Is there anything I can do?" He pulled back to look at me.

"Just stay with me. I don't want to be alone right now." I rested my head on his shoulder, breathed in the smell of him, and finally started to relax.

I don't know how long we stood there wrapped in each other's arms but when my alarm started to go off I was calm, and the shaking had stopped.

CHAPTER 15

Saturday ended up being a great day even after the nightmare from the night before. Dad and I went to Spruce, I got a new cell phone and a bright blue Jeep Wrangler. It was a couple of years newer than my old one and had an aftermarket stereo with satellite radio. I was going to have to dig into my savings to pay for the radio, but it would be worth it. Shawn and I texted each other while I had service, I think he was worried about me.

When we got home from car shopping I worked on my homework and watched a movie with my parents. Shawn was on duty again that night and I was terrified of going to sleep. I finished my homework but didn't want to study for my history test since I was going to study with Shawn the next day. I was looking for a book to read when I remembered my bio-dad's journal.

I pulled it out of the drawer in my night stand and took it to my desk. I took a deep breath then opened it.

January 5, 1998

It was a long night, but I managed to save five souls and kill four of the goblins feeding off them. I'm going to find a way to send the goblins back to wherever they came from for good. I asked Jon to help me with my research, but he wants no part of it and I don't understand why.

I would love to retire from this life and live like a normal person. Go on a date, have children, and not worry about producing more Knights, but I will not stop until they have all been banished from the dream dimension. I couldn't live with myself if people died while I did nothing.

I reread the passage shocked. My dad was a Knight like Shawn? Is that why they came to my home town? He was trying to find a way to get rid of the goblins for good, but he failed. I wondered if Shawn ever thought about it.

January 31, 1998

It feels like all is lost. A mare killed Jon's father last night. The council chose Jon to be the new head of our territory. He hasn't spoken to me about it yet, but I think he will try to force me to abandon my research. He is my best friend, but I will not stop looking for a way to save everyone from the goblins no matter what he says.

I was given a rune today. I was told it has been passed down to the strongest Knight in our clan for as long as anyone can remember. I asked Sven what it did, but he didn't have an answer. All he told me was I should keep it close to me and when the time was right to hand it over to the next Knight I thought was worthy.

I have worn it since he gave it to me and have noticed nothing. Everything is the same as it was before I received it. I will do as tradition demands, but I see no point in it.

I got out of bed and pulled the tin out from under it. I pulled the rune out and held the leather thong in my hand while I looked at the rune. Was this what my dad had been talking about? Should I give it to Shawn? It probably belonged with his family since it should have been handed off to the next strongest Knight. I sat it on my nightstand thinking I would give it to Shawn the next day when he came over to study.

I picked the journal back up and reread the passage. What kind of research was my dad doing? Wasn't Shawn's dad name Jon? Jon was a pretty common name, but there were too many common factors for them not to be the same. I pulled out the picture of the boys from the day at the lake. I turned the photo over to see if there was anything written on the back but there was nothing. I looked at each of the boys trying to see if one of them looked like Shawn, but they were too far way and I couldn't see any resemblance. I went back to the journal.

April 9, 1998

> *I do not know how much more of Jon's demands I can take. I have not had a night off in weeks, but I think I know how the mares are entering the dream dimension. A door or a gate is open in their realm allowing them to enter.*

> *We have moved three times since Jon took over. As soon as I zero in on the location of the gate he makes us move. I think he is following me or spying on me. How else could he know how close I am to coming up with a solution to the problem before making us move?*

There was a gate? The goblin said he had to come back after Shawn killed him. If we found a way to close the gate maybe we could get rid of the mares for good, but if my dad couldn't do it why would I?

July 4, 1998

> *I am leaving. I have not told anyone yet, but I can't continue this way. I confronted Jon about why we were leaving each area before all the mares were neutralized. He said job security. I was speechless and walked away. He is happy with his life and the money we make.*

> *We are nothing more than mercenaries. Pay us and we will save you from dying in your sleep. We are Knights! How can we worry about job security when people's lives are at stake?*

I took a deep breath. Jon was greedy, I hoped it didn't carry over to Shawn. When I thought about Shawn, greed was the last thing I thought. He had a job, and it sounded like he did it well. He had a higher calling and wasn't drawn to the money. I hoped I wouldn't meet Jon any time soon though, I didn't know if I could keep what I was learning to myself.

September 9, 1998

I am leaving this place tomorrow. I am going to California, there are always a lot of Mares there and the terrain should make it easy to find a gate. I will save all the people I can. I am going to steal one of the nets. I created them, I see no reason why I can't take one with me. If I can find a gateway, maybe I can figure out how to close it and I won't have to spend my life fighting off nightmares.

From what he wrote, killing them did not stop them from returning or new mares coming. Based on what I read a gate needed to be closed. They needed to be locked out. I looked at my watch, I wanted to find Shawn and tell him about my father, but it was late, and he was probably already working. We could talk about it the next day.

January 1, 1999

It has been hard. I have been distracted I admit it. I met a woman, and she is amazing. We are destined to be together I can feel it. I am still working, but I fear it is fruitless. While there are Mares all over I have not been able to find the gate they are coming through. California might not have been the best place to start my search.

March 3, 1999

I was married to the love of my life today. It was a small ceremony with just her friends and family present. I had to lie to her about where my people were. I could not jeopardize my plan. If Jon found me he would try to stop me. I will not let him interfere with closing the gate. After I close a gate, I will take my findings to the council, and they will agree with closing the gates. I don't care if I spend the rest of my life as a janitor if it means souls will no longer be stolen by the goblins.

We don't want to raise our children in California. Sandy has convinced me to move to a small mountain town in Colorado. I have looked it up, there have been bouts of the sleeping death there in the past. I will continue my research there and hope I will have more to show for it than I have had in California.

I always wondered why they moved here, it didn't seem like a logical thing to do. It had been what my father needed though, a concentrated area with mares. I wondered if my mom knew about him.

April 26, 2000

I found it! Now I need to figure out how to close it. My daughter will be here in a few months and I pray she will not have to live the life I have.

I wiped a tear away from my face. The last entry was the day before he died. He failed in his attempt to save Twisted Pine from the mares. I didn't understand everything he was talking about, but I bet Shawn would.

I was buzzing from the information in the journal, but it was late, and I needed to sleep even if it meant I would be tormented by the mare.

CHAPTER 16

I woke up in a cold sweat, clutching at my covers, and looking for the mare who had terrorized me most of the night. I had been having the nicest dream. Shawn and I were on the lake fishing. It wasn't the real Shawn, but the Shawn my dreamscape had created. I was reeling in a huge lake trout. When Shawn got ready to net it, the trout turned into the mare. He gabbed Shawn, pulled him overboard, then dragged him down into the dark cold water. I tried to jump in the water to go after him, but the damn force field wouldn't let me. Every time I jumped toward it, I would hit the barrier and bounce back into the boat.

I woke up wanting to jump out of bed and make sure Shawn was alright, but I stayed where I was. I had to believe it wasn't the real Shawn. I finally got up and went into the bathroom to brush my teeth and get cleaned up for the day, remembering Shawn was coming over to study. *Crap,* I thought. I forgot to tell my parents about it.

I went downstairs and found them decked out in their ski gear. "You guys are going skiing?" I asked, getting a cup of coffee.

"Yeah, sorry we didn't invite you, but you shouldn't be skiing with your head still healing," Dad said, taking a spoonful of his oatmeal.

"Is it okay with you if Shawn and I get together to study for our history test?" I took a sip of my coffee.

They both froze and looked at each other like they had no idea how to respond. "Where are you planning on studying?" Mom finally asked.

"It's Sunday so the library's closed. I was just going to have him come here. I didn't know you guys were going skiing. You wouldn't have cared if it was Billy."

"Give us a minute," Mom said, pointing toward the living room.

I turned, went into the living room, and sat on the couch with my coffee. I clicked on the television to my favorite morning show and settled in. I was a little worried, they had never acted like this before. They had always trusted me. What had I done other than go on a date to earn their distrust? I told them almost everything going on in my life. If they weren't going to trust me maybe I would stop telling them what was going on.

A few minutes later, Mom called me into the kitchen. I got up with my now empty coffee cup went back to the kitchen and straight to the coffee pot. I refilled my coffee and turned to them trying not to look as mad as I felt.

"Shawn can come over and study," Dad said, folding his arms in front of his chest.

I was ready to argue, but then his words registered. They were being reasonable. I couldn't believe it.

"Understand, sweetheart, you haven't done anything to make us not trust you, so we are going let you do this, but please be smart and study," Mom continued for Dad, who didn't look happy about the situation.

I rolled my eyes. "If we were going to do something else, I would have told you what we were planning." I was beginning to understand where teenage angst came from, parents not trusting their kids to the point of insanity.

"Don't be a smart-ass." Dad brought his arms down and took a step toward me. "No hanky-panky. Do you understand?"

"Yes, Dad. We will be good little high school students and study. I promise." I took a sip of my coffee. I really wanted to let them know how I felt about their trust issues, but I got what I wanted, there was no need to make him mad and have it taken away.

"With that settled, we are off. Be good." Mom kissed me on my cheek before going out the garage door.

"I'm sorry, sweetie, this is just really new for me," Dad said, giving me a hug before following Mom out.

I slumped where I stood. They were acting so weird, they wouldn't have batted an eye if Billy had been coming over. What was wrong with Shawn and what made Billy so great in their eyes?

I went up to my room, opened my laptop, and clicked on my Facebook page. I clicked on the messenger button and sent Shawn a message.

Hey, my parents went skiing today. Let me know when you want to come over to study.

He must have been on his computer because he responded almost instantly.

Did you sleep well?

Part of me didn't want to tell him about the nightmare, but he was someone who could protect me.

No, my stalker wouldn't leave me alone. I found something I need to talk to you about.

I closed the lid on the computer and swung my backpack over my shoulder before going down to the dining room. When I opened the lid again I had another message from Shawn.

I will be there around eleven if it works for you. I can't wait to hear what

you want to talk about.

I looked at the clock. It was ten, so I had an hour. I typed back, **Sounds Good.**

I closed my computer and started reviewing what our test would be covering. I looked at the clock when I finished, it was almost eleven. I moved to get something to drink when someone put their hands over my eyes.

"Nice Jeep."

"Billy." I jumped and turned around to see him standing in the doorway. "What are you doing here? How are you already back from your trip?" I loved Billy like a brother, but I didn't want him there when Shawn arrived.

"We made it halfway before Tommy's machine died. We spent the rest of the day fixing it. We ended up camping where we were and decided to just come home, no need to tempt fate." He walked to the head of the table and put his hands in his pockets

"I'm glad you guys are safe," I said, only paying attention to half what he said. I need to come up with a way to get him out of the house before Shawn showed up.

"Yeah, we were never in trouble or anything. Hey, I kind of missed you." He was up to something, and I didn't think I was going to like it.

"Why? Need me to fix Tommy's machine?" I folded my arms over my chest.

"And make fun of him for not knowing how to fix it himself." He pulled out a chair and sat. "We have a history test on Wednesday, right?" he asked, looking at my book on the table.

"Yeah, actually Shawn is on his way over to study for it." Honesty was the best policy, right?

"He is, huh? I bet I'm cramping your style." He leaned back

in the chair, he had no intention of leaving. "Heard you guys had quite the date on Friday."

"We had a great time, but I don't know why it's any of your business." I moved to stand by the doorway.

"I don't think he is right for you, Liz." He brought the chair back down.

"Why?" He was not going to have an answer to make me stop seeing Shawn, but I would listen.

"Who knows how long they will be here. They move all the time. I just don't want you to get your heart broken."

"Is there anyone who you would be okay with me dating?" He was starting to sound like my dad.

"I can think of someone." He stood and took a few steps toward me.

"Who?" I asked, taking a step back when he got too close.

"Me," he almost whispered but then found his courage. "Me," he said firmly.

My mouth opened and closed, but nothing came out. Mom had warned me about Billy, but I ignored her. How could Billy want to date me? "Billy, I—" I didn't know how to tell him. He put his finger on my lips to quiet me.

"Think about it." He started walking toward the front door and I followed behind him.

I should tell him I would never date him, I thought to myself, but I was a chicken. I didn't want to hurt his feelings.

"Billy," I said, finding my courage while he opened the front door.

He turned to face me, pulled me into his arms, and kissed me. I was too surprised to do anything at first. Once I realized what he was doing I pushed myself away from him and slapped him as hard as I could across the face.

It was too late though. I heard the tires squeal and looked up in time to see Shawn fishtailing out of the driveway. "Crap," I ran my hands through my loose hair. "What the hell, Billy? Did you do that on purpose?"

"I did it because I've wanted to for years and now seemed to be the right time. If Shawn was here to see it, all the better." He ran his hands over a welt in the shape of my hand on his cheek. "I want you to go out with me, I want to be your boyfriend."

"Billy, you're like a brother to me. I could never think of you like that." I folded my arms across my chest. I was killing him, but he just screwed everything up for me and Shawn. I needed to get rid of Billy and call Shawn. "I'm sorry if it hurts to hear. You are my best friend and I don't know what I would do without you, but you need to leave right now. I need to call Shawn and explain what happened."

"Why are you suddenly so interested in guys? You never gave anyone the time of day before Shawn. I thought you were waiting for me to make a move." Billy wasn't going anywhere, and I rolled my eyes at him.

"Because I have never been attracted to anyone before. If I liked you in that way, I would have made a move. Now, please go."

"Fine, but this isn't over, Liz." Billy stomped to his truck and I ran inside slamming the door behind me.

I ran for the phone, dialed Shawn's number. It rang and rang before going to voicemail. "Shawn, its Liz. I'm guessing you saw Billy kiss me, what you didn't see was me slapping him. He just showed up and I was trying to make him leave. Please call me, I want to explain what happened." I hung up the phone and carefully put it back on the charger instead of throwing it across the room. My eyes were starting to burn. I didn't know what to do. I went to my computer and sent a message on Facebook to him, then lay down on the couch and waited for him to respond. When an hour passed without a word, I sent him another one. After another hour passed with no response I could not help the tears that started to fall. I let them come and I cried until I fell asleep.

I was running through the forest looking for Shawn, he was hurt, and he needed me, but I couldn't find him. I ran, calling his name. If I could find him I could save him.

"Liz," I heard him yell from behind me. I turned around but there was no one there.

"Where are you?" I called, turning in a circle. I was surrounded by twisted pine trees and I could not see beyond them. I pushed through the branches running toward Shawn's voice. When I broke free from the trees, I found myself at the opening to the mineshaft from my dream.

"Liz, help me." The voice I thought was Shawn's turned scratchy and cracked.

I froze, my stalker was back, and I remembered where I fell asleep, on the couch without my dreamcatcher. The mare wouldn't know the barrier between us wasn't there. I just need to wake myself up and I could escape.

"Wake up," I yelled at myself. Nothing happened, I was still standing outside the mineshaft and the wind started to pick up, instead of coming from the mineshaft this time, it came from behind me. It was trying to push me toward the opening. I looked at opening of the shaft, and I saw the mare waiting there for me, ready to welcome me into his home, where he would feast on my soul.

Not today, I thought to myself, digging my heels into the ground, and bending my knees, trying to stand my ground.

"Come now, Liz, it will only hurt for a second. Then you won't have to worry about your Knight or your other boyfriend," his voice swept across the wind almost stinging me when the words reached my ears.

"Billy's not my boyfriend," I yelled back at him. It was not the time to debate my relationship with Billy with a goblin, but I was so mad at Billy.

The goblin laughed grabbing his stomach. "Whatever, you think I care? The only thing I care about is eating your soul for dinner." He moved his hands in a complicated pattern, and the wind gusted.

I dropped to my knees and grasped at the sparse vegetation, trying to keep myself from being blown into the shaft. Another wind gust hit, and I lost my grip on the ground. I was lifted off my feet and flew straight toward the opening. *Is this how I die?* I thought, trying to think of anything to save me. A weapon, I was able to manifest a gun the other night. I thought frantically, while flying through the air, of a weapon I could use to kill the goblin. My hunting knife finally came to mind, I looked down at my hand to see the shining metal in my hand. The wind died, and I started to fall from the sky, the goblin was directly below me waiting to catch me with his arms out.

I felt his arms take my weight right before I hit the ground. He pulled me towards his mouth and I flung my knife into his back. He screamed and dropped me on the ground. I tried to jump to my feet, but he was on top of me in less than a second.

"You think your puny knife is going to stop me?"

I tried to punch him, but he caught my right wrist in his hand and started to lean over me. His grip on my wrist burned so badly, tears formed in my eyes. I squirmed and jerked trying to think of anything that would save me from him. I had one hand free, I brought it up to the side of his head as I thought of an icepick and slammed it into this ear. He screamed in pain and grabbed the side of his head.

I pushed him off me and got to my feet. He fell on his back and looked up at the sky. I didn't think he was dead for a second, but I was mad. I ran over to him ready to give him a kick to the head when his arm shot out stopping me.

"You think you beat me, little girl? The joke is on you. I marked you, no matter where you go I will find you, and eventually I will take your soul." He laughed dryly before melting into the ground like rain on a parched desert floor.

"Liz, wake up." I opened my eyes to my mom shaking me.

"I'm awake." I took a deep breath trying to slow my racing heart. I was covered in sweat and my hands were shaking. My wrist still hurt from where he had gripped me. I wanted to look at it but not with my mom there. It took me a second to remember where I was. I looked around remembering everything from earlier in the day.

"You know you shouldn't fall asleep out here. Where's Shawn?" Mom sat on the couch next to me.

"Billy ruined everything." I didn't want to cry in front of her, but I couldn't stop the tears from falling.

"What did Billy do?" Dad asked, walking into the room.

"He came over before Shawn got here. We talked and when I walked him out he kissed me. Shawn saw the whole thing and peeled out of the driveway. He didn't even wait to see me slap the crap out of Billy." I sobbed into Mom's shoulder.

"Did you try to call him?" Mom asked, patting my back trying to sooth me.

"Yes, and I sent him a message on Facebook. He hasn't responded. Damn Billy, he ruined everything," I yelled, letting go of Mom and reaching for a tissue. I blew my nose loudly.

"I'm sorry, sweetie. I'm sure you'll be able to talk to him tomorrow and work it out," Dad said, sitting down in the recliner. "If not, he isn't worth it."

"Your father's right. If Shawn's worth it, you two will work it out. If not, then you will find someone else."

"I'm going to kill Billy. How dare he kiss me?" I got up and started pacing.

"I'm surprised he waited so long," Dad mumbled, kicking the recliner back and folding his hands together to rest on his lap.

"You knew he had a crush on me?" I asked, stopping in front of him and putting my hands on my hips.

"Billy has been in love with you since you were ten." Mom leaned back on the couch and put her feet on the coffee table. "I tried to tell you," Mom said.

"I know I just didn't want to believe it?" I threw my hands in the air. "I wish I could have taken care of this years ago. I love Billy like a brother. The thought of him kissing me is disgusting." I wiped my mouth with the back of my hand.

"We kept waiting for him to make a move. I didn't think it would happen like this, but it's not a huge surprise," Dad said.

"Why isn't it a huge surprise?" I asked, stopping in front of him again.

"Sometimes, boys won't make a move until they are threatened, and Shawn threatened him," Dad said, trying not to laugh.

"Guys suck." I looked at the clock, it was already four o'clock. "I have to study," I said, going into the dining room, and sitting down in front of my history book. I wanted to drive over to Shawn's house and force him to talk to me, but I didn't want to fail my history test. So, I stayed home and studied.

After studying for a few hours, my parents forced me to eat dinner then I went up to my room. I sat on my bed and thought about the dream. I was lucky. I looked down at the burn I woke up with on my wrist. It was almost a brand, there were two interlocking lines of angry red welts wrapping all the way around my wrist.

I needed to talk to Shawn more than ever now. The goblin said I was marked, that I would never escape him. Then there was everything I had learned about my bio-dad in his journal. I didn't know if Shawn would ever talk to me again, but I needed his help if I was going to survive.

CHAPTER 17

I tossed and turned all night, never making it to REM, which was a relief in some ways. If I had, I would have to deal with my goblin stalker, but when my alarm went off in the morning I felt like I had just gone to bed. I took a quick shower, braided my hair while it was still wet, threw on a pair of jeans and a T-shirt without looking at it. I pulled a hoodie off a hanger and decided I had to face the day.

I should have been excited to drive my new Jeep, but I was freaking out about seeing Shawn and Billy. I wanted to corner Shawn and explain to him what happened, and I wanted to slap Billy again for the kiss. Even thinking about his lips on mine made me want to throw up.

I stopped at the top of the stairs and looked at my wrist. It looked the same as it had the night before. My mom would freak if she saw it, thinking I did it on purpose. I shoved my arms through the hoody and pulled it over my head. I didn't like hiding things from my mom, but there was no way she would believe the truth.

I went downstairs and got a cup of coffee before sitting at the bar. I had no appetite, I just wanted to get the day over with.

"Good morning, sweetheart," Mom said in a singsong voice when she came into the kitchen already dressed for work.

I grunted and took a sip of my coffee.

"Liz, it will be alright. Talk to Shawn and explain what happened."

"Mom, I tried to talk to him yesterday after he left, and he wouldn't return my calls." I rested my forehead on the counter.

"If he's worth it then he'll listen to you." She patted my head then went to the refrigerator.

"You're right, but it wasn't my fault. It was Billy's, and he did it on purpose."

"You are going to have to deal with them both, dear. It's part of growing up."

"Then I don't want to grow up." I got up and took my lunch sack off the counter and put it in my backpack.

"You'll be alright. Don't let a boy ruin your mood." She came up to me and gave me a hug. "They aren't worth it."

"Thanks, Mom, I have to go." I pulled out of her embrace. "I'll see you after work." I put my coat on, grabbed my bag, and went out to my Jeep.

The sun was out and warm on my face, but I didn't enjoy it. I wanted thunder and lightning to match my mood. I got into my Jeep and started it up. The last thing I wanted to do was go to school, but my parents would be really mad if I ditched because of a boy. Instead, I took the long way to school enjoying my new Jeep and listening to Hair Band Radio to take my mind off my problems.

When I got to school, I parked my Jeep and forced myself to face the day. I stared at Shawn's empty Jeep in the parking lot as I walked. I wanted to find him and force him to talk to me. I looked at my watch, unfortunately I didn't have time to find him unless I wanted to be late to class. I picked up my pace and made it to class with seconds to spare.

I tried to pay attention in math, but my eyes seemed to stray to the clock waiting for class to be over. I wanted to find Shawn and make him talk to me. It was the longest class of my life, the seconds slowed down to minutes and the minutes turned into hours. When the bell finally rang, I jumped out of my seat and ran for the door. I was going to camp out by Shawn's locker and not leave until he would talk to me. Unfortunately, Billy was waiting outside the door of my classroom, and I knew I wouldn't get away from him.

"Liz, wait. Would you talk to me?" He grabbed my elbow, stopping me.

I tugged my elbow free of his grasp. "No, Billy. You messed everything up for me and Shawn. I'm not ready to talk to you. Leave me alone." I turned and stormed down the hall to my locker, I didn't have time to go by Shawn's, thanks to Billy, and got my books for my next class. I looked everywhere for Shawn while I walked, but he was nowhere to be seen.

"Jo," I called, seeing her turn down the hallway in front of me. I ran after her hoping she would stop so I could talk to her about Shawn. She was waiting for me when I turned the corner.

"What do you want?" she asked, leveling her eyes on me.

"Where's Shawn? I need to talk to him. I need to explain." I felt the back of my eyes start to burn and I blinked hoping I wouldn't cry in front of her.

"He saw everything he needed to on Sunday. I never took you for a slut, but I guess it's my fault for trusting someone I just met."

"Billy kissed me," I almost yelled. "Shawn left before I slapped the crap out of Billy for doing it."

"You don't have to explain yourself to me." Jo turned and walked away.

"I just want to talk to Shawn," I called to her. "I need his help," I said, rubbing the burn on my wrist. I wanted to tell her more, but she didn't know I knew about her.

"Not my problem." She continued walking to class.

I went to my class, depressed that not only had I lost Shawn, but Jo too. I was scared I was going to be on my own in my dreams and I didn't know if I was strong enough to beat the mare. My dad had failed and from what I had read he was one of the best Knights they ever had. I had zero training and no help, how would I survive when he had failed?

Lunch time came, and the cafeteria was the last place I wanted to go. I took my lunch and went out to my Jeep. I turned the radio on and ate my sandwich by myself. The last thing I wanted to do was sit at my table with Billy. The next two classes I had were with Shawn, and I wondered if I could get him alone to talk to him.

I got to auto-shop early and waited by my station for Shawn to come in. He walked in right before the bell and Mr. Pearson started talking. When he was done explaining what we needed to do Shawn went to his station on the other side of the garage without even looking my way.

I let out a frustrated breath and got to work, trying to think of an excuse to go talk to Shawn, but came up with nothing. When I finished with the assignment I went over to his station.

"Can I talk to you for a second?" I asked, in a small voice.

"I'm really busy right now," he said, polishing his carburetor with a rag.

"Look, Billy came over, I was making him leave when he turned around and kissed me. You left before you could see me slap him." I put my hands in my pockets and shuffled my feet back and forth.

"Who you kiss isn't my problem anymore." He didn't look up as he talked, only concentrated harder on the already gleaming carburetor.

"I did not kiss him," I said a little louder. "He kissed me, then

I slapped him."

"I need to get to work. Please leave me alone." He turned his back on me and I struggled to keep from crying as I walked back to my auto-shop locker.

I took my coveralls off and left. I didn't care that class wasn't over. I needed to leave before I made a fool of myself by crying in front of the guys.

I walked numbly to my school locker to get my history book. I opened it and stood there staring at the contents like it was the first time I had seen any of it. I didn't know what to do. This whole situation was Billy's fault. I should have stayed at the dining room table and not walked him out, but then Shawn would have seen him leaving. Would he have still thought something was going on between Billy and me if he saw Billy leave the house right before he got there?

Maybe Shawn was too jealous to be with me. I did hang out with the guys a lot. Maybe my mom was right. If Shawn didn't want to listen to me and believe me when I said Billy kissed me without permission, then he wasn't worth my time. The bell rang, and I noticed the people all around me.

I was done feeling sorry for myself. This was not my fault. Shawn could suck it. Switching gears, I walked to class wondering how I was going to figure out how to get rid of the burn on my wrist and the goblin on my own.

Billy was in his usual seat when I arrived, and I took a seat in the front row as far away from Billy as I could get. He gave me a hurt look when I accidently made eye contact with him, but I ignored him and opened my book. I forced myself to keep my eyes on my book while the seats around me were taken. I only looked up when class started.

I told myself I didn't care where Shawn was sitting. I didn't need him to mess up my future. I didn't need Shawn or anyone.

When class was over I went to my locker without making eye contact with anyone I passed. I threw my books in my backpack and headed for the parking lot, excited to go to work. At least I wouldn't have to think about the mess my life was for a few hours.

Working after being gone for a week was exactly what I needed. Bob had a ton of stuff for me to do to keep my mind off the problems ruling my life. I was only interrupted by Billy, who came in to buy some milk. He tried to talk to me, but I ignored him, and only said what I had to—what his total was. I was still so mad at him for messing up what Shawn and I had. For the first time in my life, Billy had no idea what was going on with me. Even if we weren't fighting and I told him what was going on in my dreams I doubted he would believe me.

Mom was pulling dinner out of the oven when I got home, so I ran up to my room and dropped my backpack off then came back downstairs ready for dinner.

"How was your day?" Mom asked tentatively as she put a piece of roasted chicken on my plate.

"It sucked." I saw no reason to lie to my parents about it.

"What happened?" Dad asked, looking a little too eager.

"I'm not talking to Billy and Shawn wants nothing to do with me. One date and my entire life has been flipped upside down." I took a bite of my chicken.

"Why aren't you talking to Billy?" Dad asked.

"Because this whole thing is his fault. If he hadn't kissed me everything would be fine." I couldn't believe my Dad didn't understand what was going on.

"Things were going to get complicated one way or another." Mom took a bite of her salad. "Billy thought he was losing his chance with you. He was bound to do something drastic."

"Well, neither of them are worth my time. I am just going to hang out on my own and focus on my future."

"Good. Boys can wait till you are done with school," Dad said, after wiping his lips with a napkin.

My mom rolled her eyes but kept quiet. She wanted me to have a social life and not spend my time under cars or in books. Well, until I found someone worth spending time with, I would keep myself busy.

After dinner I went to my room and studied for a while then pulled up my favorite search engine and looked for information about gateways to other dimensions and how to close them. Unfortunately, all I found were websites about video games and volcanos. I had no idea where the gateway was, but my bio-dad thought there was one near Twisted Pines and the closest volcano was the super volcano under Yellowstone. There had to be another way to find it. I took a picture of the rune on my nightstand and did an image search for it, but nothing came up. Frustrated, I gave up for the night and tried to get some sleep, hoping my stalker would give me some peace.

I dreamed restlessly that night. Billy and Shawn were fighting over an ice-cream cone. I tried to break them up, but it was like I wasn't there. When I tried to get between them they would move away from me. All I could do was watch them punch and kick each other, neither of them winning, just beating the crap out of each other. All the while my stalker goblin tried to get in on the action, but the boys were intent on killing each other and ignoring the goblin.

CHAPTER 18

I went through the motions of getting ready for school the next day, but I was still miserable. I was exhausted and mad. I needed to find a way to get rid of the goblin, or I would never get another good night's sleep, but I had no idea where to start looking without being able to talk to Shawn. I ate breakfast and said goodbye to Mom then went to school.

The day started better than the previous day. I was determined to put on a brave face and not let Billy or Shawn get me down. Everything was going smoothly until lunch. Tommy and Sam were my friends too, and there was no reason why I should freeze to death eating in my car when there was a perfectly good table I could sit at and ignore Billy.

I arrived late on purpose. I wanted to sit as far away from Billy as I could. The cafeteria was full of students when I got there, and I went to my normal table figuring Shawn and Jo would be sitting somewhere else. Not only was I wrong, but Tiffany was sitting between them. Shawn saw me and quickly looked away. I couldn't leave now unless I wanted to look weak. I pulled my shoulders back and walked to the only free seat at the table, luckily it was on the end furthest away from Billy and Shawn.

"Hey, guys," I said, sitting down with a smile on my face. "How's your sled, Tommy? Did you get it fixed yet?"

"Oh, no I haven't had time to look at it yet," he answered me like he was surprised I was talking to him.

"If you need help let me know." I opened my bag and took out my sandwich and bottled water.

"Yeah, I will." Tommy's eye rolled from me, to Billy, to Shawn, then back to me.

"Hey, Tracy, how was prom dress shopping?" I think it was the first time I had ever started a conversation with her.

"Drama. Kelly and Laura wanted the same dress and I had to figure out who it looked better on. To tell the truth, it didn't look good on either of them. I tried to talk them both out of it, but Laura bought the dress and Kelly blames me. Be happy you didn't come."

"Yeah, doesn't sound fun. Did you find a dress?"

"Yes, it is going to look amazing on me." Her whole face lit up when she talked about it. "It's long and fitted, bright green with a ton of sequins."

"Yuck, green? Really?" Tiffany said, flipping her hair, and hitting Shawn in the face with it.

It took everything I had not to start laughing as Shawn pulled a few loose hairs out of his mouth. Jo rolled her eyes after making eye contact with me.

"What is wrong with green?" I asked, a little harsher than I intended.

"Everyone wore green last year, but I guess you wouldn't have known since you were sophomores." She rolled her eyes, like being a year younger was the worst.

"Crap," Tracy mumbled, looking down at her hands.

"Don't worry I'm sure you'll look great, and since its *green* you will stand out more than if you wore whatever this year's color is."

She gave me a sideways look then smiled. "Thanks," she whispered before eating the rest of her lunch.

"Are you even going?" Tiffany asked, putting her arm around Shawn like she owned him. He shook her arm off and gave her a dirty look.

"I haven't decided yet, but maybe you could tell me what this year's color is, so I can make sure to buy a contrasting color."

"You don't have a date yet? Are you going by yourself?" She let out a ridiculous laugh.

"Last time I checked I didn't have to report who I was dating to you. Now if you will excuse me, someone's perfume is making me sick to my stomach." I picked up my empty bag and left.

It took everything I had to hold myself together, but I managed. I had twenty minutes before my next class started so I went to the library.

I found the only book on runes the library had and started to skim through it. There were diagrams of them and I studied them looking for the rune on my bio-dad's stone but I didn't see anything like it.

I wanted to start reading the book from the beginning, but the warning bell rang, so I took it to the counter and checked it out. I put the book in my locker then ran to shop class, making it just before the bell rang.

I stood at my station while my teacher went over what we needed to accomplish and didn't look over at Shawn once. When he released us to get started, I put my head down and got to work.

I finished just as the bell rang. I ran to my locker to get out of my coveralls and get back to my regular locker to get my history book. I didn't want to be late or have to talk to anyone.

I took the same seat as I had the day before, away from both Billy and Shawn and successfully ignored them during class. When the final bell rang, I left the room and walked quickly to my locker. I was looking at the floor to keep myself from staring at Shawn when I found shoes blocking my path.

I looked up, finding Billy blocking my path. "Move."

"Liz, can we talk?" He shuffled his books from one hand to the other.

"I am not ready to talk to you yet. You ruined everything, Billy." I pushed past him and walked away as quickly as I could without running.

I threw everything I needed for the night into my pack and instead of leaving by the front entrance like I normally did, I went out the gym exit and walked around the school to the parking lot. Tears I could no longer hold back started streaming down my face. I kept my eyes down and hoped I wouldn't run into anyone.

Once I was safely in my Jeep I wiped my eyes and looked around. Shawn was standing in front of his Jeep talking to Tiffany, who was flipping her hair and laughing. I saw him roll his eyes and look around the lot. His eyes met mine for a second before I looked away. I started my Jeep and left, making sure not to drive too fast, I didn't want him to know how much he was hurting me.

When I got home, I sat at my desk in my room and pulled out the book on runes. They originated in northern Europe and were used until they adapted the Latin alphabet. They were not only an alphabet but many had special meanings. I picked up the stone by the leather thong and looked at it for a long moment. I had a feeling the symbol on the stone was more than a letter, it had to mean something. Maybe it could help me lose the goblin. I held it up to the light and was about to put the thong around my neck when I heard a car pull into the driveway. I dropped the necklace and went into my parents' room to see who it was.

Billy was getting out of his truck and walking to the front door. He was the last person I wanted to see, but, knowing him, he wouldn't leave until he said his piece, plus he had a key.

I went downstairs and opened the front door part way.

"What do you want?"

"I'm sorry, Liz. I should have talked to you about how I was feeling. I had no right to mess up what you and Shawn had. I told him what happened after school today."

"Too little, too late, Billy. You saw Tiffany hanging all over him at lunch." Tears threatened again, but this time I held them back.

"He doesn't like her, Liz, he couldn't take his eyes off you during History." He shoved his hands in his pockets and rocked back on his heels.

"Look, Billy, you need to go. Maybe I'll be ready to talk later this week."

"Yeah, I just wanted to let you know I'm trying to make it right." He spun around and went back to his truck.

I shut the door and ran back to my room. I flopped face down on the bed and cried. I was tired of crying; this dating thing was not as fun as I thought it would be.

Once I cried myself out, I read more about the runes and looked at all the diagrams, hoping to find some similarities between them and the stone. After an hour of finding nothing, I ate dinner with my parents, then went back to my room, and pulled out my homework. I studied until I couldn't keep my eyes open any longer then I went to bed, praying I would get a good night's sleep.

I was sitting on the couch in the living room watching a Bronco game with my parents. They were winning by one touchdown and the clock had just hit the two-minute warning. I was staring at the screen willing the defense to hold the Patriots back. We needed to win for some reason. The Patriots quarterback had just received the ball from the center, he threw the ball far down field with a Hail Mary pass when the screen when blank.

"What the hell?" I called, getting up from the couch and walking over to the television. I didn't know what I was going to do, but it didn't matter, the goblin's face filled the screen and I took a step back.

"Why are you putting off the inevitable? You will never escape me. Why not give in and save yourself from the pain?" he asked, with hungry eyes.

"Go away," I yelled, at the monster as it crawled out of the screen. "Why won't you leave me alone?"

"Because," he paused, finding his feet, and looking at my parents who were still staring at the now black TV screen. "I need you or my plan will fail. Now what is it going to take to convince you to give in."

"I will never give in." I closed my eyes and imagined my dad's .45 revolver. It was heavy and difficult to shoot, but it could take down most large animals if you got close enough. I aimed the barrel at the mare and pulled the trigger. The gun went off and my arm came up with the recoil. It hurt, and I thought I hit him, but I wasn't sure. The goblin was on the ground screaming in agony.

My mom got up from the couch and went to the monster. "How could you shoot this man, Liz? He is a friend of ours." She looked at me with disappointment in her eyes.

"Mom. No don't. He's a goblin, he'll eat your soul and you will die like Victor. Please get away from him." As soon as the words left my mouth the goblin's cries of pain turned into maniacal laughter. Shawn's plan of shooting the goblin didn't work, dang it. He grabbed my mom by the neck and twisted her head off in one smooth motion. Blood spurted from her neck and he threw her severed head at me.

I caught it as tears began to roll down my cheeks. "See, Liz, I told you there was no reason to shoot the man," Mom's head said, smiling up at me. I screamed, dropped it, and jumped away.

Dad was on his feet running towards mom's body. "Dad, no, stay away from him," I yelled, trying to get to him before he reached the goblin, but it was too late. The goblin grabbed Dad by the shoulders and brought his mouth down on Dad's and I froze with fear as the goblin sucked the soul from him. I ran toward them. I wanted to rip the goblin's head off, just like he did to my mom, but when I was a foot away I ran face first into the barrier that separated us.

The goblin lifted his head and laughed. "You can't touch me while you have your protection. I'm going to enjoy killing everyone you care about until you face me without it."

"No," I screamed, falling to my knees while he bent back to my dad and continued sucking the soul from his frozen body. The smoke alarm started to go off and I looked around expecting the house to be engulfed with flames, but there wasn't any smoke in the air. I closed my eyes and told myself to wake up. I needed to check on my parents.

CHAPTER 19

I opened my eyes and looked around my bedroom. *It was just a dream*, but was it? My heart was racing, and I was covered in a cold sweat. I jumped up out of bed and went to my parents' room. I had my hand on the doorknob ready to run in to try to save them when I heard first one voice talking softly then the other. I let out a shaky breath and went back to my room to get ready for school. The goblin had been messing with me, my parents were fine.

I got in the shower and cried. I was so relieved my parents were alive. My hands shook so badly I dropped my loofa twice. I closed my eyes and counted to ten. Everything was alright. There was nothing to freak out about. It was only a dream. Except it wasn't, if I didn't find a way to get rid of the goblin I would never be safe, and if anyone I knew ever slept without their dreamcatcher, I was sure that goblin would find a way to make me watch while he killed them.

I turned off the shower and got dressed. I didn't know what I was going to do, but I had to figure something out to keep everyone I cared about safe.

I made it through the day trying not to think about my dreams and the goblin, but it was hard. I would think about how tired I was, and I knew it was because of him. When lunch came around, I was in a daze. I was the first one to show up at our table, forgetting I wanted to be the last one. I turned to look at the doors; if anyone saw me leave they would know something was wrong with me. I made myself sit down at the far end and pulled my lunch out. I tried to act as normal as possible, but I had never felt so vulnerable in my life.

Billy was the next one to join the table and he sat in the middle and opened his lunch. "Hey."

"Hey," I said, hoping he would not move down to my side of the table.

Tommy and Tracy sat next to Billy before he could move or say anything else. "What's going on, kids?" Tommy asked, before taking a bite of his pizza.

"Same old, same old." I mumbled.

"I hope Tiffany doesn't sit with us today," Tracy said, stabbing some lettuce with her fork. "She's such a bitch."

"No joke," I said around a mouthful of food.

"Looks like we have the gang back together," Sam said, sitting down next to me.

"I guess." I went back to eating my lunch until Jo and Shawn showed up. I looked at them for a second then went back to my lunch.

"Hi, how's it going?" Jo asked the table while sitting down.

"Just another day?" Billy asked, sounding different than he usually did. I shot him a confused look, but then remembered I was mad at him and looked back down at my food.

"Are you ready for the history test?" Shawn asked, and this time I kept myself from looking up.

"I hope so, what about you?" Billy asked, he almost sounded nice while talking to Shawn. That was a first.

"I should be alright," Shawn said, sounding like he always did, amazing.

"Hey, Shawn," Tiffany's squeaky voice penetrated my ears. "Is there room for me?"

"Um," Shawn said.

I looked up in time to look around the table, it was full thank God, unless he let her sit on his lap.

"Sorry, looks like we are full up," Shawn said, looking at me before I could look away.

"Where am I supposed to eat?" she whined.

"There's a table right over there." Billy pointed to an empty table in the back of the room.

"I don't want to sit all by myself." She huffed and crossed her arms under her boobs to try to make them look bigger.

"Sorry, we are talking about our history test. I'm sure you can find somewhere else to sit."

"Fine." Tiffany huffed and stalked away.

"Sorry about that," Shawn said to the table. "I said hi to her once and she thinks we're soulmates. I don't think I will ever understand women."

"I completely understand," Sam said, finishing his pizza.

Done with my food, I got up to leave. "See you guys later." I picked up my trash and left the cafeteria. I was starting to think about finding a new table to sit at. Sitting so close to Shawn but not being able to touch him was killing me.

I walked down the hall to my locker, thinking about what happened. Why was Billy acting so weird with Jo? Shawn had actually smiled at me. I thought he hated me. Billy said he would make it right, but how could he? If Shawn didn't believe me, why would he believe Billy?

I stopped in the middle of the hall. What did any of it matter? I was done with Shawn, and I still wasn't ready to talk to Billy, but then I thought about my dreams and how badly I needed help. Maybe there was a way Shawn and I could just be friends. I didn't need a boyfriend to be happy, but I didn't know how long I could go on with the goblin terrorizing my dreams. I put a smile on my face and went about the rest of my day pretending everything was fine. I would just fake it till I made it.

I let out a breath as I set my test on Mr. Anderson's desk. I knew I could have done better but I was so tired, and even though I studied for it, I should have put in a few more hours instead of trying to find the meaning behind the rune. It was too late though.

After school, I went to work and spent my time stocking shelves and helping customers. When I was done stocking and fronting all the merchandise I worked on the weekly orders to keep busy.

The house smelled amazing when I got home. I left my backpack at the base of the stairs and followed my nose into the kitchen. "Mom, did you make stew?" I asked, coming around the corner.

"Yes, it sounded good." She turned from the stove with a spoon in her hand. "How did your test go?" Mom always had a reason for making stew.

"What's the occasion?" I asked, leaning against the bar.

"Nothing dear, just sounded good." She didn't look up as she spoke.

"Mom, you always have a reason, give it up." I crossed my arms over my chest.

"I know you and Shawn aren't together anymore, but do you still want to go shopping this weekend?" She went to the cabinet and pulled out three bowls.

I let out a breath. Prom and Shawn were two things I didn't want to think about, and I had been planning on spending Saturday at the library researching the gates and the rune, but Mom was looking at me like I would break her heart if I did not go. "We can still go, Mom. If I find a dress and don't go to prom I can always wear it next year." I gave her a smile, hoping it did not look as fake as it felt.

CHAPTER 20

I opened my eyes and found myself in Shawn's padded room. I got up and looked around. How had I ended up here? The last thing I wanted to do was talk to Shawn. I walked around the room running my hand over the wall, looking for a door but found none. I wanted to get out of there before he showed up. I closed my eyes and thought of my room, but it was too late.

"What are you doing here?" Shawn asked from behind me. "How did you get here? This is my dream."

"I have no idea. I went to bed, hoping not to have another nightmare, and I ended up here." I crossed my arms over my chest and thought about how mad at him I was, not sad. If I was sad, I would start crying, and I didn't want him to see me cry.

"Well leave." He turned his back on me and took a few steps away.

"You know what? No." He needed to know what was going through my head. "I need to tell you a few things."

"I don't want to hear it." He crossed his arms and disappeared.

I looked around the empty room. "Shawn," I yelled, closing my eyes. He was going to listen to what I had to say. *I needed his help damn it*, I thought to myself.

When I opened my eyes, I was looking directly into Shawn's. It took him a minute to recognize me, but as soon as he did, he backed up a step. "How did you? Never mind, leave me alone." He was gone again.

I sighed, I was not going to give up. I had nowhere else to turn. I closed my eyes and thought of him. When I opened them again he was standing on a beach looking out at the ocean. "Shawn, I have to talk to you." I tried to use my calm voice, but it came out a little harsher than I wanted.

"Are you going to follow me around until you've said your piece?" he asked, not looking back at me.

"Yes." I crossed my arms over my chest.

"Then let's go back to the padded room." He closed his eyes and we were back in his safe space. "You want to talk, then talk." He crossed his arms over his chest and leaned against the wall.

"What you saw was bad, believe me it wasn't enjoyable for me either, but instead of talking to me about it you just left. You didn't find out what was going on. You assumed. We could've had something special if you would have gotten out of your Jeep and talked to me or punched Billy." I put my hands on my hips.

"I didn't have anything to say." He turned his head to avoid meeting my eyes.

"Look, I've said my piece and I would walk away and let you live your life, but I need help and I don't know where else to go." The thought of the goblin showing up at any second made tears prick my eyes.

"What are you talking about?" He looked up to meet my eyes.

"The goblin, the one you killed. He won't leave me alone. He has been in every dream I have had since Sunday. I tried to kill him, but my protection goes both ways. He can't hurt me, and I can't hurt him. He said he would kill everyone I loved until I gave myself to him." A tear leaked out and I quickly wiped it away. I wasn't sad, I was just so tired I couldn't control my emotions any longer.

"I killed that goblin, it must be a different one." His voice was gentle, but his eyes were hard.

"He told me it was him, that he came back, he always comes back."

"Why is he obsessed with you?"

"He said I have enough power to bring him over to our dimension. Shawn, last night I had a nightmare where he ripped my mom's head off and sucked out my dad's soul. I don't know what to do." I crumpled to the floor, cradled my head in my arms, and let the tears come, no longer caring if he thought I was tough or not.

"What's on your wrist?" he asked, coming over to where I lay and picking up my hand.

"I fell asleep on the couch on Sunday, I didn't have my dreamcatcher and he said he marked me. I woke up with it."

Shawn dropped my hand and took a step back like I had the plague. "You've been marked. This is not good." He ran his hands through his hair.

"Do you know how to get rid of it?" I asked, rubbing the burn.

"I don't. I've read about it, but I have never seen anything about removing it." He turned to the wall.

"Okay, well thanks anyway." I got to my feet and closed my eyes, thinking of my room.

"Don't go," he all but whispered.

I opened my eyes and met his. They looked soft for the first time since our date. "Why?"

"Because I like you. This week has been so messed up. I'm pretty sure I failed the history test because I couldn't take my eyes off you." He looked away and put his hands in his pockets. "Billy talked to me yesterday. He told me how he has had a crush on you for years and I forced him to make a move. He also told me you rejected him and if I didn't make things right with you he was going to kick my ass."

I laughed, Billy said he was going to make it right, but still. "So, you believe Billy, but you don't believe me? This is a small town, Shawn, no one can get away with seeing two people at the same time without getting caught."

"Hey, I just moved here. I've heard people talk. You and Billy are always together. I understand being friends, but it's hard to believe something else isn't going on."

"What about Tiffany? Are you two dating now? Your interest in me didn't last long."

"Tiffany? When she heard about our fight she started following me around. I only let her sit with us at lunch because I felt sorry for her, but she isn't a nice person."

"No kidding." I laughed again.

"Who do you really want?"

"You." I backed away from him. "If you can handle me being friends with Billy and being marked by the goblin."

"I can handle it, if you promise not to kiss him again. Don't worry we'll figure out how to get rid of the mark." A small smile played on his lips.

"Him kissing me was the grossest thing that has happened in my life so far. It would be like you kissing your sister." I looked at my wrist and ran my finger over the mark. "Do you think there is a way to get rid of it?"

"Kissing my sister? Gross," he took a step closer to me. "I don't know if we can get rid of it, but I won't let the mare get you."

"Really?" My eyes widened.

His lips were on mine, just like I remembered them, soft and plump. Goosebumps broke out on my arms as I wrapped them around his neck. My lips missed him, it was almost like they were meant to always be together. Shawn's arms came around my back and squeezed me tight. I hoped he was right, and we would find a way to get rid of the mark.

I pulled away when my lungs started screaming for air. "I'm so scared, Shawn."

"Don't worry, we'll find a way to get rid of it." He smiled and came back in for another kiss, but he stopped before he met my lips. "Crap, I'm on duty I have to go. My dad is looking for me."

"Okay, I'm glad we talked." I took a step back from him.

"Me too. I'll see you tomorrow okay?" His eyes were bright and the smile on his lips reminded me why I liked him so much.

"Okay." I closed my eyes and thought of my room. This time when I opened my eyes, I was where I thought I would be. I got into bed and pulled the covers over my head, praying the mare would leave me alone for a change.

CHAPTER 21

I woke feeling centered and happy, Shawn and I had made up but what if it had been a dream? I hoped it wasn't, but at least I had been able to sleep without having to deal with the goblin.

Then there was Billy. I was getting tired of being mad at him. He said he would make it right and he did. Part of me wanted to thank him for talking to Shawn but the other half of me was still mad. The fight with Shawn was because of him in the first place.

"What about dress shopping Saturday?" Mom asked later, while I ate a piece of toast covered in peanut butter.

I shrugged. "Sure, Mom, if I don't go to prom I'm sure I'll find some reason to wear it."

She knew I hated shopping. That I agreed to go at all, was enough for her. "Okay we will leave early, so we can get to Denver right when the stores open."

"Sounds good. I'll see you tonight," I said, grabbing my backpack and leaving for school.

I checked the parking lot out of habit for Shawn's Jeep when I arrived. It was there, as always. Butterflies filled my stomach as I walked into school and down the hallway to my locker. I needed to calm down, I never saw Shawn before lunch and it was hours away. I needed to get control of myself, or I wouldn't make it to lunch. I was looking at my feet as I walked to my locker, and when I got there I looked up to see Shawn leaning against it.

"Hi," I said with a small smile while I nervously adjusted the straps of my backpack.

"Hi," he said, returning the smile, and pushing off my locker to stand a few feet away.

"So, last night wasn't just a dream?" I moved to my locker and dialed in the combination before opening it.

"Not just a dream." He sounded nervous too.

I hung my backpack on the hook, then my coat. I pulled my books out and put them on the shelf. "I'm glad." I looked over to him and smiled as the butterflies in my stomach disappeared.

"Yeah, me too." The bell rang indicating we only had a few minutes to get to class. "Will you have lunch with me? I want to talk to you."

"Yeah, where do you want to meet?" I pulled what I needed for class down from the shelf then closed the door.

"I'll meet you here," he said, putting his hands in his pockets.

"I'll see you then," I said as he walked away. It was still awkward, but it was worth it.

I was walking to math class when I saw Billy shut his locker. "We need to talk," I said to him before he could walk away.

"Okay at lunch?" he asked, giving me a hesitant smile.

"No, I'm having lunch with Shawn, after school alright?" I met his eyes for a second before looking away.

"Sure," he said, looking down the hallway with a frown. I turned and went to class. This was going to be hard on Billy, but he was going to have to move on if we were going to continue to be friends.

I spent the rest of the morning watching the clock tick slowly by. I couldn't wait for my lunch with Shawn. I was excited we had made up and wondered what he had planned for lunch. I almost ran to my locker when the bell rang and found Shawn waiting for me when I arrived.

"Hey, how's it going?" I asked, opening my locker, putting my book in, and pulling my lunch out before closing it.

"Not too bad for a day at school." He bounced off the locker he was leaning against and took my hand before walking down the hallway away from the cafeteria.

"Where are we going? We aren't allowed to eat anywhere except the cafeteria." I let him pull me for a moment before I quickened my pace.

"It's a surprise," he said, squeezing my hand.

I had forgotten how good it felt to hold his hand, I squeezed it back and felt my face turn red in the process. He led me to the doors of the gym and pulled one open. "Shawn, we will get in trouble if anyone catches us in here."

He pulled me inside and I expected it to be completely dark, but there was a battery-operated lantern sitting on a card table with two chairs around it. "It's alright I got permission to do this." He led me to the table and pulled my chair out for me, then went around to the other side and sat.

"This is romantic," I said, putting my paper bag on the table, and pulling my lunch out. I looked up at him with a grin.

"Well, I wanted to talk to you where we wouldn't be overheard, and this seemed like the best spot after last night." He let out a breath. "I'm sorry I was a dick to you this week. When I saw Billy kissing you I blew a gasket. I thought you were pranking me, the new kid initiation or something. I've watched you be miserable all week, so I set this up yesterday."

"Wait, you set this up yesterday? Before we talked last night?" I asked dumbfounded.

"Yeah, well last night just reinforced the truth." He ran his hand through his hair nervously. "I was wondering if you would..." he trailed off and the lights in the gym came on.

I blinked a few times while my eyes adjusted to the light. When I could see again there was a huge banner hanging off the bleachers. "Go to PROM with me?" I laughed putting my hand over my mouth. I couldn't believe he did this.

"Yes." I got up, moved around the table, bent over, put my arms around his neck, and kissed him lightly. His arm went around me, and he pulled me into him, deepening the kiss.

My stomach growled, and he released me. "Sounds like we need to feed the beast."

"Hey, I'm not a beast." I went back to my side of the table and sat.

"I don't know. You can be kind of scary when you want to be."

"Thanks, you can be a dickhead when you want to be." I narrowed my eyes at him.

"Prom is going to be amazing." He changed the subject before taking a bite of his food, smart boy.

"I'm just glad I agreed to go shopping with my mom on Saturday. I told her if I didn't go this year I could always wear the dress next year and she almost lost it." I ate a bite of my sandwich.

"What are you doing after school?"

"I have to talk to Billy after school. I need to make this right." I took another bite of my sandwich. "Then I was going to go to the library and see if I could find anything about the mark. Do you want to come?"

"Yes, but what are you going to tell Billy?" He pulled his eyebrows together looking concerned.

"That he is still my best friend and I can't not have him in my life." I opened my bag of chips and dug in.

"Are you going to tell him I'm your boyfriend?" he asked, munching on a chip.

I felt my cheeks beginning to burn again. "Why would I tell him that?"

"What am I to you then?" He put his sandwich down and crossed his arms over his chest.

"I don't know, we have only been on one date. I don't know if that means we can be boyfriend/girlfriend yet. Plus, with this mark I'm not sure how long I will be around. Are you sure you want to get more involved with me and my drama?"

"You aren't counting our dreams though. If you count those, we have been on a bunch of dates and yes, I want to be very involved with you. We will find a way to get rid of the mark." He pulled his eyebrows together.

"Are you asking me to be your girlfriend?" I dropped my sandwich on the table.

"As long as your answer is yes then I am. If your answer is no, then let's just pretend this conversation never happened." He ran his hand through his hair and looked around the empty gym.

I thought about It for a second. "Yes, I want you to be my first boyfriend."

"Good I want you to be my girlfriend." He gave me one of his dazzling smiles.

"Alright." We finished eating, and I could not keep the smile off my face. We would find a way to get the mark off my wrist, then we could be together without all the drama.

"I've been thinking about last night and how you came to me," he said, stuffing his trash into his bag.

"What about it?" I took the last bite out of my apple before putting the core in my bag.

"The only way you could have done it is if you were a Knight Flyer, like me." He put his elbows on the table and laced his fingers together.

"You said I had to be born with it, right? Which means one of my parents must be one too?"

"Yeah, they must be. I never heard of one who didn't have ties to Iceland though, and neither of your parents look like they came from there." He was trying to be gentle.

"Burt's not my real dad. My real dad died before I was born. It was right after he and my mom moved here." I needed to tell Shawn what my dad was trying to do before he died. "I'm pretty sure he was a Knight Flyer."

"How do you know?" Shawn asked, cocking an eyebrow.

"I found his journal in the garage. He talked about fighting mares and trying to find the gate where they came from. He wanted to figure out how to close the gates and get rid of the mares for good."

"Can I see it?" Shawn leaned forward, and I could almost see his gears starting to turn.

"Yeah, I can show it to you whenever."

"What was your dad's name?" He relaxed his hands and put them on the table.

"Victor Robinson, I think he knew your dad, at least he talks about a Jon a lot in his journal." I looked down at the table. I didn't want Shawn to know that if it was his dad referenced in the journal they didn't get along.

"What's wrong?" Shawn took my hand, causing me to look up at him. "I don't recognize his name, but I'll ask my dad when I get home."

"I don't think they got along very well, and if it is your dad he talks about, I don't want it to mess everything with us up."

"Don't worry, we won't let it. My dad is the leader of our clan, but that doesn't mean he's perfect." He gave me a half smile.

"Whatever happens between you and me, let's not let other people influence our relationship, okay?"

"Okay." I smiled back at him then looked down at the table and saw the time. "Do we need to get this cleaned up before lunch is over?"

"Just part of it. I'm going to take the banner down after school." He stood and folded his chair and I copied him.

He put our trash on the floor and flipped the table over to release the legs to fold it up. "I just have to get this table put away before the end of lunch."

I picked up our trash bags and took them to the trashcan while he took the table and chairs over to the equipment closet. I waited from him to come back over to me. "Do you have to give everyone a ride home after school?" I asked.

"Yeah, but after I drop them off, I can meet you at the library."

"That will work perfectly since I am going to talk to Billy after school."

When we got to class, we reluctantly went our separate ways although we stared at each other almost the entire time. After shop was over, we went to my locker, then his, to get our books for history.

Billy was sitting in his normal spot, so I sat next to him and Shawn sat on the other side of me. "What, you two back together?" Billy asked, before the teacher started.

"Yes, but let's talk about it after class," I said, opening my book.

"Fine." He was trying to sound mad, but I could tell he was happy I was talking to him again.

When class was over, I walked with Billy to his locker. "So, what did you want to talk about?" he asked, walking with his head down, and his arm hanging like limp noodles at his side.

"Look, I can't stay mad at you. I don't want us not to be friends, but I need you to promise me something."

He looked up at me with a half-smile. "Yeah?"

"It's actually two things. One: Don't be a dick to Shawn because he's my boyfriend and you're not." I waited for him to agree as we arrived at his locker.

"What? Boyfriend? When did this happen?" He turned and opened his locker.

"At lunch," I said as he grabbed his backpack and slammed his locker shut.

"Who else knows?" he asked as I turned and started walking to my locker, hoping Billy would follow. He caught up to me and matched my pace.

"You're the first person I've told, because you're my best friend. I want to be able to talk to you about things, and for you and Shawn to be friends too."

"Fine, I'll try and be nice to him, but I'm not promising it."

"Okay, moving on. Number two: Don't ever try and kiss me again or I won't slap you, I'll punch you." I pushed his arm hard, making him stumble.

"Fine, I promise I won't try and kiss you ever again." We got to my locker and I spun the lock before entering the combination.

"I have a condition too, though." He leaned against the locker next to mine.

"What?" I opened my backpack and loaded it with the books I would need for the night.

"I know we're BFFs and all, but I don't want to hear about any of the kissing and making out crap girls like to talk about with each other."

"Billy, when have you ever known me to talk like a normal girl?" I asked, zipping up my bag.

"Well, you did get a boyfriend. Who knows how else you are going to change."

"Alright, I promise not to talk about making out or kissing him with you." I pulled my pack out and slung it over my shoulders.

"So, we're good?" Billy asked as we walked toward the front doors.

"I guess." I felt myself relax for first time since Sunday. All was right with the world for a change.

"What are you doing this weekend?" Billy asked before we split up to go to our vehicles.

"Hanging out with Shawn tomorrow night probably, prom dress shopping with Mom Saturday. Working half a day on Sunday and studying the rest of the time."

"No Billy time?" he asked, looking bummed.

"Come hang at work with me on Sunday morning, you know how dead it will be."

"Alright, I'll see you then. If you get lonely in the meantime, you know how to find me."

I rolled my eyes and started walking to my Jeep. "Bye, Billy."

"Bye, Liz."

I found an empty study room at the library and checked it out for two hours. I left my backpack inside then went to the computers to look for books about northern European mythology, nightmares and how to get rid of them. I knew it was a long shot, but I had to try something. Twisted Pines did not have a big library, but I did find a few books that might point me in the right direction. After I pulled them, I went back to the room and stacked them in front of my chair.

I had just opened one when my cell phone started to vibrate. I pulled it out of the front pocket of my bag and smiled before answering it. "Hi, are you still coming?" I asked Shawn, feeling all warm and fuzzy at the thought of spending time with him outside of school.

"I'm here, where are you?" he asked in a low voice.

"Oh, sorry, I'm in study room two." I stood and went to the doorway and looked out. He was walking around with his phone to his ear looking completely lost.

"Over here," I said, waving my hand in the air. He looked around and nodded his head.

I hit the end button on my phone and went back into the room. I sat and moved my bag off the table to give us more room to work.

"I feel like a complete idiot," he said, coming in and closing the door behind him.

"Why? I'm guessing you have never been here and I never told you where I would be."

"Still, everyone was staring at me like I didn't belong." He sat in the chair across from me and put his bag on the floor. "What are you looking for?" he asked, looking over the books between us.

"I wish I knew. I need to get this mark off, but I am also looking for the meaning of the rune I found in my bio-dad's stuff."

"What does it look like?" He pulled his eyebrows together in a frown.

"Here," I said, pulling my phone back out and scrolling through the pictures. "I took a picture of it, so I could see if I could find something like it here." I handed him the phone.

"It looks almost like something we use before we can protect ourselves from the mares but it's different." He put the phone on the table and pulled a notebook out of his bag. "I'm going to try to draw it, then I can look in our library at home. I would have you send me the picture, but I don't want my dad to see it if he checks my phone."

"You have a library?" I asked, wishing I could take a peek at it. I bet that is where my bio-dad had found out about the gate, not at the local public library with books full of myths and legends.

"Yeah, most of the books are super old, and, unless you read ancient Icelandic, you won't be able to read any of it, but there are a bunch of books with pictures of runes in them. Maybe I can cross reference them." Done drawing the rune he gave me my phone back.

I looked at the books I pulled and blew out a breath. "Do you think I am going to find any answers here?"

"Maybe, but I doubt it." He pulled one of the books in front of him and thumbed through it.

"What am I going to do?" I had no idea even where to start looking for the information I needed. "I know you kill monsters in people's dreams but why? How did this all start?"

"We will find something. I'll ask my dad if we don't figure it out soon. To answer your second question, we were cursed to protect people from the mares, or goblins.

"Our clan came from Iceland, we are not sure when they settled there, but it was around two hundred AD. The legend says a man named Sindri was hunting after a brutal winter and found a cave. There are many caves on the island and they were known to our people, but this one was new. He ventured into the cave and found a door covered in runes he had never seen before. When he touched the door, It flew open pushing him to the ground. He saw nothing but felt pure evil escaping out of the doorway. He had no idea he had allowed the goblins to cross into the dream dimension.

"The evil he felt terrified him, and he ran back to the village, with a terrible feeling that something bad was about to happen to his people. He was relieved when he returned and found no trace of the evil he felt come out of the cave. He relaxed, thinking he had hallucinated the entire thing. He told his wife what had happened, and she laughed at him. The next morning, he awoke to find half the clan dead, never waking up from their dreams. He went to our leader and told him what happened in the cave. The leader was beyond himself. Their numbers were too few as it was, the leader told everyone they needed to move as far away from the cave as they could. Sindri had cursed them, the only way for them to survive was to move away.

"For nine days they packed up their lives with no idea where they would go and for eight nights people went to sleep and many never woke up. On the ninth night, the night before they were set to leave, Sindri entered his wife's dream and killed the goblin who was trying to kill her. The next morning, she remembered what he did, and they went to the leader and told him what happened.

"They stayed another night and the leader told each man what had happened in the dream and each man of the village went to sleep ready for battle. They ended up staying where they were and killing all the mares or dream goblins.

"Word came many years later of another village having the same problem with the sleeping death. A band of men from the village went to fight the mares. They tried to teach the others how to fight the goblins, but they were unable to."

"So how did we end up with this gift?" I asked.

"It's been passed down through the generations. Like I said it is a curse."

"Or a gift," I said thinking about the ability to save people.

"That is a constant debate among the knights. What I don't get is how anyone lives here. There is a huge concentration of mares here, yet everyone is alive and well. Then there is this protection you have."

"The answer is simple. There's an old legend, if you don't sleep under a dreamcatcher you will die in your sleep. Everyone in town has them over their beds. Even the hotels and the rentals have them."

"Wait, seriously? A dreamcatcher? It's that easy?"

"Don't you sleep with one?" I asked, giving him a confused look.

"No, but I don't spend much time in my own dreams."

"I can't believe you and your family are still alive. There are always a lot of deaths from campers and tourists who don't stop by the visitor's center and pick one up. So, can everyone fight them? What about the babies and kids?"

"We all wear a special rune to keep the nightmares away until we can defend ourselves. It is similar to your dreamcatchers, but it requires the magic of a holy person to bless them. They are very rare and expensive. When you come of age, and can fight your own mares, you have to give it back. It is kind of a coming of age thing. Will you show me your dreamcatcher?"

"Sure, but what am I going to do in the meantime?" I asked as my phone started to vibrate again. I looked at the screen. "It's my mom, I didn't tell her I was coming here." I hit the answer button.

"Hi, Mom." I rolled my eyes at Shawn.

"Liz, where are you? Did you get called in to work?"

"No, I went to the library after school. I'm sorry I forgot to tell you."

"Okay, well dinner is going to be ready in thirty minutes."

"I'll pack up and be home soon then." I wanted to talk to Shawn more about Knight Flyers, but it was going to have to wait.

"Drive safe."

"I will, love you, Mom."

"Love you too." I ended the call and looked at Shawn. "I have to go."

"It's alright, I'll find you later." Shawn got up as I picked up my pack. I looked at the books, he was right, I doubted I was going to find anything in the books to solve my problems.

"Are you on duty tonight?" I asked as we left the room and walked toward the exit.

"No, I actually have the night off." He took my hand as we went through the door and emerged into the parking lot.

"Good, I might need you to save me from the goblin."

"I would love to be your knight in shining armor," he said as we stopped by my Jeep. "I missed you, Liz."

"I missed you too." He came in and pressed his lips to mine for a quick second. "I'll see you later."

When I opened the mudroom door, the smell of my favorite food surrounded me, and I couldn't help the smile on my face. "Mom, I'm home," I called, taking my shoes off, and hanging my jacket up. I took my backpack to the base of the stairs then went into the dining room. "Sorry I'm late."

"What were you working on for so long?" Mom asked, coming in with a plate full of steak, green beans, and salad.

"Just a history project," I said, skirting the truth. I was looking up ancient history.

"I'm glad to see you back to your old self," Dad said, cutting into his steak.

"Yeah, well Shawn and I made up. I talked to Billy too, and I think everything is going to be better now." I cut a piece of my steak and looked up when Dad started coughing.

"Are you alright?" I asked, ready to jump up and pound on his back.

"Yes, what do you mean, you and Shawn made up?" he asked, taking a sip of water.

"Shawn and I made up. He asked me to go to prom with him at lunch." I looked down, trying to hide my blush.

"Well, that's wonderful," Mom said, getting up and kissing me on the cheek. "See, I told you everything would work out."

"I don't know about this, Sandy, look at how upset she has been for the past week." Dad put his fork and knife down and folded his hands together.

"Sweetheart, we've talked about this." Mom narrowed her eyes at him and I wondered what they had talked about. "We are so happy for you, Liz."

"Thanks, actually, I know you guys don't know him very well and I thought maybe he could come over for dinner tomorrow night, so you could get to know him better." I hadn't really thought about it, but it might be a good way for them to trust him.

"That is a wonderful idea," Mom said, looking at my dad and almost daring him to object.

"I haven't asked him yet, so I will let you know tomorrow."

After dinner I went up to my room and did my real homework. No matter what was happening to me I wasn't going to let my grades slip and ruin my chances to get into the Air Force Academy. When I was done, I crawled into bed, excited to see Shawn in my dreams. When he was there the goblin wasn't, and I needed a break.

When I opened my eyes, I was in Shawn's padded room and he was sitting on a white leather sofa waiting for me. "Hi," I said, walking over to him.

"Hi, how was the rest of your night?" he asked.

"Good, I think. I told my parents we were back together, and we were going to prom." I sat next to him on the couch and he draped an arm over my shoulder.

"What did your dad say?"

"Dad wasn't thrilled I took you back, but Mom was happy and kept giving him the evil eye."

"Maybe someday I will win him over." Shawn laughed and kissed the top of my head.

"Yeah, I was thinking the same thing. Do you want to come over for dinner tomorrow? It might help smooth things over." I looked up.

"Yeah, maybe it will help."

We spent the rest of the night talking about anything but the mares. It was so nice just to hang out and not worry about the nightmares trying to ruin my life.

CHAPTER 22

The next day at school everything had gone back to normal and I was relaxed for the first time all week. Shawn met me when he could and would walk me to my class. Billy sat on one side of me at lunch and Shawn sat on the other. We laughed and talked about the upcoming weekend. Billy kept staring at Jo and I could not figure out what was going on there. When the last bell of the day rang I was glad the week was over.

I drove home with the music from the satellite radio blaring and singing along with all the songs I knew. I parked in the driveway, went inside, and took my backpack up to my room. I threw it toward my desk then fell backwards onto my bed. *What do I do now?* I thought to myself. It was Friday, normally I hung out with Billy, Tommy, and Sam. We had all spent so much time together growing up and I thought we always would be together, but things were changing, and I was going to have to get used to it.

I sat up and bent over to pull the tin with my biological father's things in it from under the bed. I wanted to show everything to Shawn, maybe if he looked at everything we could understand a little more of where I came from. I pulled everything and out and organized the contents. I put the pictures in one pile, the letters in another, and put the journal on my desk. I picked up the stone by the leather thong. It had to be important, all the journal had said was that it was passed down to my father because he was a powerful knight. I rested it in the palm of my hand and felt something creeping up my arm, through my skin, and weaving itself around my body. It didn't hurt, it was almost soothing, or protective. I wanted to put the necklace on and never take it off. I held it up ready to put it on but paused. With all the crazy things going on in my life, I had better figure out what it was before I put it on. I put it on top of the journal and felt its presence leave me.

I looked at the time, then around my room. Shawn would not be in my room, but it was kind of dirty, and I needed to keep busy, so I started cleaning. When I was done with my room, I went downstairs picked up, dusted, and vacuumed. I thought about what movie we could tell my parents we were going to watch. It needed to be something we had both seen in case they quizzed us about it later. I went back upstairs and sat at my computer.

I had a message from Shawn on my messenger. I clicked it open.

Hey, are we still on for dinner? What time?

I clicked the reply box.

We are good to go for dinner; we usually eat around seven.

I finished cleaning and had just finished setting the table when Dad walked in.

"Hi, Dad," I called, going to meet him in the kitchen.

"Hi, Liz," he said, sounding like he had a rough day. "Is Shawn still coming over for dinner, or did you break up again?" he asked, taking his shoes off, and hanging up his coat.

"Yes, he is still coming over. Why would we break up again?"

"I don't want you to get hurt again." He leaned against the counter and folded his arms over his chest.

"He's a good guy. He thought I was messing with him when

he saw Billy kissing me. He needed to cool down, then we talked, and we are all good now."

"I'm going into the man cave. Have your mom come see me when she gets home." He stalked off.

I shook my head, I was going to have to figure out a way for Shawn to win him over. With the table set, I went into the kitchen to do the few dishes in the sink. Mom walked in while I was starting the dishwasher.

"Hi, sweetie, where's Dad?" She pushed off her boots and put her slippers on.

"He went into the man cave. He's butt-hurt that Shawn and I didn't break up today and is still coming to dinner. He asked me to tell you to go see him when you got home."

"Overprotective, was he ever a teenager?" Mom mumbled under her breath as she went down the hall to the man cave.

With nothing left to do I went into the living room and switched on the television. I started a Modern Marvels episode I had recorded a few months before but hadn't watched yet.

Mom came in a little while later. "What time is Shawn coming?"

"I told him seven," I said, turning the television down. "Is Dad okay?"

"Yes, he's having a hard time with you growing up is all." She patted my head and turned toward the kitchen.

"Mom?"

"Yes, sweetheart?"

"Let me know if you need help with dinner."

"I think I've got it, but you could set the table."

"I already did and vacuumed and dusted."

"Thanks."

"No problem." I went back to my program and tried to pay attention to it and not the clock. I finally heard Shawn's Jeep pull into the driveway and turn off. A minute later the doorbell rang, and I jumped up to answer the door.

Shawn stood there with an arm full of flowers. "Hi, what are those?" I asked.

"What do they look like smarty?" he said, coming in while I shut the door behind him.

He stomped his feet on the mat. "Should I take my shoes off?"

"Please, I just vacuumed." I took the pile of flowers from him while he pulled his boots off then his coat. I gave the flowers back to him, took his coat and hung it in the closet.

I turned back to him and he gave me one of the bouquets. "These are for you." I took them and buried my nose in them. They smelled of everything spring.

"Thank you. Are those for my mom?" I asked, leading him into the kitchen.

"Yeah, hostess gift, you know," he said shyly.

"Shawn's here, Mom," I said, going to the cabinet where we kept vases. I pulled two down while Shawn waited for Mom to look up from making a salad.

"Thanks for having me," he said, offering her the flowers when she looked up.

"Thank you, Shawn, they're beautiful. Liz, will you get me a vase?" she asked, then turned and saw me at the sink with two vases. "Oh, perfect, you put these in water while I finish up dinner. Shawn have a seat at the bar and tell me what you think of Twisted Pines so far."

"Well, Mrs. Lawson," he said while taking a seat. "It's colder than I am used to, but it's beautiful. I can't wait to see it in the summer. Everyone has been friendly. It seems like a close-knit community."

I finished cutting the ends of the flowers and stuck them in vases. "Those are beautiful. Liz, why don't you put one on the dining room table and the other one in your room? Shawn, where were you before you moved here?"

I rolled my eyes and picked up the flowers. "I'll be back." I put one of the vases on the dining room table then took the other up to my room and put them on my desk, so I could see them from my bed.

I went back downstairs and opened the door to the man cave. "Shawn's here. Are you going to come out?" I asked Dad.

"I can hear him, and I'll be out in a few. Please close the door."

I closed the door and went back into the kitchen where Mom and Shawn were chatting. "Liz, did you tell your father Shawn was here?" Mom asked, spooning some green beans into a serving bowl.

"Yes, he said he would be out shortly." I sat at the bar next to Shawn. Our eyes met, and I gave him the, *is everything okay*, look and he nodded his head. "How did you do on the history test?" I asked.

He groaned. "C- I should have gotten an A but my mind was elsewhere. How did you do?"

"A, I should've gotten an A+, but my mind was elsewhere," I said, mimicking his excuse. We were probably both thinking about each other.

"Liz, Shawn, do you want to take the food into the dining room. I'm going to go get your dad, so we can eat."

We took the food to the table and sat across from each other. "Is your dad okay with me being here?" Shawn whispered to me.

I wanted to say yes, but Shawn deserved to know the truth. "No, but it's not your fault. He doesn't want me to grow up."

"I get it, my dad did the same thing when my sister started dating." He chuckled.

"What's so funny?" Dad asked, taking his seat at the head of the table.

"Oh, I was just telling Liz about how my dad acted when my older sister started dating." Shawn sat up straighter in his chair.

"How did he act?" Dad was not in the mood for jokes and I hoped Shawn picked up on it.

"He loved her, and he didn't want anything bad to happen to her. He did background checks on every guy who came to pick her up." Shawn took the napkin from under his plate and laid it on his lap.

"Good idea, I may need some information from you. Why was it funny?" Dad took his napkin and did the same.

"I'm four years younger than her. I didn't understand why my dad was making such a big deal about it, my sister could take care of herself. It was just a kid thing." Shawn was backtracking and the expression on my dad's face was not getting any better.

"How was work today, Dad?" I asked, trying to change the subject.

"One of the girls you go to school with is pregnant," he answered, not taking his eyes off Shawn.

"Sweetheart, isn't it against the law for you talk about your patients?" Mom asked, putting the roasted chicken on the table.

"I just can't say their names. She's younger than you." Dad stood and started carving the bird.

"What do you want me to say, Dad? I'm sorry she made poor life choices she will have to deal with for the rest of her life. I won't be making the same choices. I have goals."

"Good, I just wanted to hear you say it in front of Shawn," he said, without looking up.

"So, Shawn where were you living before New York?" Mom asked, changing the subject.

"We were in Quebec for a year, before that we were in Beaver, Wisconsin for a few years," Shawn said, giving my mom a quick smile.

"Wow, it sounds like you have moved around a lot," Mom

continued as Dad finished carving the chicken and took my plate from me, put a thigh on it and gave it back to me, then served Shawn.

"Yeah, I've never spent more than a few years anywhere, my dad's work keeps us moving. I think we are going to stay here for a while though. My mom is adamant we spend my senior year in one place."

"What are your plans after high school?" Dad asked, sitting down, and taking one of the chicken breasts for his plate.

"My dad wants me to work for the family business, but I want to go to college. I'm not sure where yet."

"What do you want to study?" Mom asked.

"I'm thinking psychology, but I've thought about chemistry as well."

"Liz wants to go to the Air Force Academy, and she is well on her way there," Dad said, making me blush.

"Impressive, it's a tough school to get into." Shawn raised his eyebrows at me. "I know you'll get in."

"Thanks, I need to keep my grades where they are and do well on the ACTs, then I might have a chance," I said, loading up my plate.

We all dug into our food and were quiet while we ate. When we were done eating, Shawn and I cleared the table and started doing the dishes.

"That was so good. I wish my mom was that good of a cook," Shawn said, as he rinsed the plates then handed them to me to load into the dishwasher.

"I'm sure she isn't as bad as you are implying." I laughed.

"She tries, but she doesn't understand seasoning. One night it will be perfect, the next it has too much salt or pepper. We ate out a lot before we moved here." Done with the dishes Shawn rinsed the sink out.

"I was going to try and find a movie for us to watch but I have no clue what you are into," I said, leading him into the living room.

"I'm a guy so anything with action and adventure. I love all the superhero movies."

"What are you kids up to?" Mom asked, coming into the living room smelling of her favorite perfume.

"We were going to watch a movie if that's okay," I said, looking at her from my position on the couch.

"As long as you're good it's fine. Your dad and I are going to the Andersons' for cards. We won't be home too late."

"Just remember what I told you about the patient I saw today," Dad said, coming down the stairs, going to the closet and pulling out Mom's coat then his own.

"Don't worry, we'll be good," I said, looking at Shawn who was sitting on the other end of the couch.

"I would never disrespect your daughter, or you, sir."

"Then have fun and we'll see you later."

"You too," I said, looking over to Shawn and trying to tell him with my eyes I wish they would leave already. When I heard the garage door open I relaxed. "Thank God, I have never seen him be such a jerk before."

"It was definitely a little intense for a while there. He just wants to make sure you're safe."

I moved over to sit next to him. "Yeah but it was bad. If you want to leave and never speak to me again I will understand."

"He's not going to scare me off." Shawn put his arm around my shoulder. "Are we really going to watch a movie?"

"No, I want to show you my bio-dad's stuff." I got up and went to the stairs. "I'll bring it down."

"Not going to let me see your room?"

"Not when I have no idea when my parents are going to be home. I'll be right back." I ran up the stairs to my room. I put everything in the tin and brought it back down to the living room.

Shawn was sitting on the couch when I came down channel

surfing. He looked up when he heard me. "I thought we better turn something on in case they came home."

"Good idea." I sat and put the box between us. "Here is everything I found. Some of it isn't related, but a lot of it is. I pulled out the photos and gave them to him. He flipped through them quickly until he stopped at one.

"That's my dad, and there's Jo's dad, so that must be your dad." Shawn pointed at the photo of the boys at the lake.

"I wondered if you knew any of them." I let out a breath I didn't realize I was holding.

"I haven't had a chance to ask my dad about Victor yet, but I will as soon as I can." He flipped through the rest of the pictures then set them aside. "Can I read his journal?" he asked, eyeing it.

"Sure, there isn't anything too personal in it." I gave it to him and sat back while he read the few passages it contained. When he was done he gave it back to me then turned and took my hand.

"You are a Knight Flyer Liz. We need to ask my dad if you can train with us." He smiled but it never reached his eyes, instead they showed concern.

"I would love to, but what aren't you telling me?" I took his hand and gave it a squeeze.

"I'm just worried, if you don't get the training then you won't know how to defend yourself. Plus, with the mark, it makes you much easier to find."

"Here is the rune my dad had," I said, holding up the leather thong with the carved stone on it.

"I'm sorry, I haven't had chance to research it yet. Hopefully I will have time tomorrow."

"It's okay, it's been a crazy couple of days. I didn't realize I had never touched the stone until this afternoon, it makes me feel weird." I watched, and he let the stone sit in his hand then dropped it like it burned him.

"Did it hurt you?" he asked, rubbing the spot on his hand where it touched him.

"No, it was almost like it was covering my body in something. It didn't hurt though, I guess it felt soothing. Like I had a protective layer all around me. Did it burn you?"

"Yeah." He looked down at it then back up to me.

"I wouldn't touch it until we can find out more about it. You don't want to end up like Gollum." He half laughed.

"I was thinking the same thing." I put everything back in the box and looked at the time. Shawn followed my gaze to the clock.

"I should get home," Shawn said, pulling me into a half hug before getting to his feet.

"Are you on duty tonight?" I asked, getting up and going to the closet to get his coat while he put his boots on.

"No, I was hoping I could talk to you more about all this later." He stood and came to me.

"I don't think my father would approve of that." I went to hand him his coat, but he pushed my hand away, took me in his arms, and kissed me. Warmth erupted in my belly as his tongue flicked across my lips asking for admittance.

I opened them, not really sure what to do, but when our tongues met it was instinctual. "Wow," I said when we came up for air.

He took a step away from me, I stumbled and almost fell to the floor. "Whoa, are you alright?" he asked, grabbing my arm to steady me.

"Yeah, it was just, wow." I smiled shyly.

"I'll see you later." He let go and went to the door.

"Yeah, see you later." I followed him as he opened the door and stepped out.

"Thank you for a nice night," he said before turning and walking to his Jeep.

"Thank you. It was nice. Drive home safe," I called before closing the door and watching him back out of the driveway. With a little more bounce in my step I locked the door. I turned off the lights and grabbed the tin before going upstairs to my room. My room smelled amazing from the flowers Shawn gave me. I walked over to them and stuck my nose into the blooms, then got ready for bed. Right before I turned out the light there was a knock at my door.

"Come in."

"Hey, we're home. We are going to leave pretty early in the morning, so you might want to set your alarm," Mom said, peeking her head in.

"Okay, did you have a good time at the Andersons?" I snuggled deeper into my bed.

"Yes, but your dad was nervous about leaving you here with Shawn." She laughed. "Did you two have a good time?"

"Yeah, we watched Deadpool, then he left." I felt bad, lying to them, but they would never believe me if I told them the truth.

"Good, sleep tight."

"You too." She shut the door.

I set my alarm, turned off the light, and willed myself to sleep so I could meet up with Shawn in dreamland.

CHAPTER 23

I was at work, and nothing was going right. People kept coming and paying with cash and I didn't have enough change. They were starting to yell at me and pound their fists on the counter demanding their money. The chime over the door went off and I looked over to see my goblin walk in, pick up a bag of chips, open them, and start to eat them. When did I start calling him mine?

"This is a pretty boring dream," he said around a mouthful." Why don't you come and play with me, Liz, my girl?"

"Why would I want to do that? Why won't you leave me alone?" I yelled, putting my hands over my ears, and closing my eyes.

Because you are mine, I marked you. You are going to be my ticket out of the dream realm and into the waking one. His voice was in my head, I turned and ran for the garage, slamming and locking the door behind me.

"When are you going to figure out you can't outrun me? No matter where you go, or what you do, I will be waiting for my chance to eat your soul and become the most powerful goblin in all the realms."

I knew he couldn't hurt me, I had my dreamcatcher over my bed like I always did, but I was so tired of trying to outrun him in my dreams. I opened my eyes and ran at the mare, ready to tackle him to the ground and beat him until there was nothing but mush left. He looked startled at first, then a smile crossed his face. He dropped the bag of chips and held his arms out to me. I jumped when I was two feet away, ready to tackle him, but instead of tackling him, I bounced off an invisible barrier and landed on the hard, concrete floor of the garage.

"Your protection goes both ways. I can't touch you, and you can't touch me." He laughed long, grabbing his belly, and squeezing his eyes shut. "Why are you even trying? It's going to be you and me for the rest of your life," he said, then looked around and shook his head. "I'll see you later, lamb chop."

"Hey, princess," Shawn said, wrapping his arms around me from behind. I jumped and turned around, relieved it was Shawn and not the goblin. "Are you okay? You're shaking."

"Don't call me princess." I leaned back into him, enjoying the feel of my back resting on his chest. "You just missed the goblin."

"Did he hurt you?" Shawn asked, wrapping his arms around me, and pulling me tight against him.

"No, I tried to hurt him, but my protection goes both ways. He can't touch me, and I can't touch him."

"Let's go to the padded room," he said, pulling away from me.

"Good idea." I gave him a smile. I always felt safe in his padded room.

I closed my eyes and thought of Shawn's safe place. Moments later we were there. "What am I going to do? I can't take much more of him tormenting my dreams. When you aren't with me he is always there, and I wake up more tired than when I went to bed."

"We'll figure something out. My dad will be back tomorrow, and I will talk to him about it. I just hope he will help."

"Why do you say that?"

"He can be weird about Knight Flyer stuff. We are a secret

organization, but if you can do what we do, he should be excited." He took my hand. "Hey, you never showed me your dreamcatcher. Will you show it to me now?"

"Sure." I closed my eyes and pictured my room. I opened them and walked to the head of my bed. "It's right there."

"Was it blessed by a Shaman?"

"No, I bought this one from the gas station, I liked the colors and the feather. We buy them in bulk, I think there was a 'Made in China' sticker on it."

"This is the only place I've been where something so simple works to keep the mares out."

"Yeah, no one knows why they work, or even who found out they work, but they do." I sat on the bed, not really sure what to do. I didn't have any of the answers I needed, and neither did Shawn. I didn't know what to do besides be relieved that when I was with him the goblin would leave me alone.

"What are you doing the rest of the weekend?" Shawn sat next to me.

"I'm going dress shopping in Denver with my mom tomorrow, we are getting up at the butt-crack of dawn to get to the stores before they get busy. I have to work on Sunday morning, then I will spend the rest of the day studying. What about you?"

"I'm on duty tomorrow night, then training and studying I guess. I want to see you again this weekend though."

"We might be able to study together on Sunday as long as Billy doesn't show up and kiss me again. The jerk."

"Okay, maybe we can go to my house this time? There will be less of a chance of Billy showing up."

I laughed. "Good plan, as long as it's alright with my overbearing father it should be fine."

"He really cares about you." He wrapped his arm around my shoulder and pulled me into his chest. "I do too."

"I care about you too." I wrapped my arms around his midsection. My alarm started to sound through the room and I groaned. "See you later," I said before waking up in my room alone.

CHAPTER 24

I hated shopping, I was never comfortable stripping in a tiny cubicle and putting on clothes with tags and anti-theft devices poking me. Mom made me try on twenty different dresses before we finally settled on one. It was black, with a strapless, fitted top covered in sequins, and a long chiffon skirt. Mom liked the cut, I liked the color. She wanted me to get a pastel color, but I had to put my foot down, I was not a pastel kind of girl and we found a pair of black kitten heels since no one would see my feet.

We got manicures and pedicures, the lady who did my nails was able to get all the grease and oil off my hands and gave me some special soap to use to keep them clean. After, we had lunch at our favorite café then we started back to Twisted Pines.

"Have you kissed Shawn yet?" Mom asked, as she swerved around the traffic on I-70.

"Mom," I groaned, looking out the window and feeling my face turn red. "Didn't you and Dad see him kiss me goodnight last week?"

"I did, but I wanted to hear it from you."

"Yes, we have kissed a few times." I kept my eyes on my window. It was not a conversation I wanted to have with my mother.

"Is he a good kisser?" she asked, giggling.

"I don't know, Mom. I haven't really kissed anyone before. How do you know?" I looked at her for a second then turned back to the window.

"He's a good kisser if he gives you goosebumps and you never want it to stop." Her voice sounded far away as she spoke.

I felt my face burn even hotter than before. "Then, yes. He's a really good kisser."

"Then I am glad your first kiss was from a good kisser."

"Um… Thanks?" I wasn't really sure how to respond. "Hey, Mom, you know when Billy and I were cleaning out the stuff from my old Jeep in the garage?" I needed to tell her I found the tin with my bio-dad's stuff. Being trapped in the car with her was probably the best time to bring it up.

"Yes, dear, I meant to thank you and Billy for putting the Christmas decorations away." She looked at me for a second then back at the road.

"No problem, but while we were putting the boxes on the shelf I found this really old tin…" I trailed off.

"You did? What was in it?" she asked, not taking her eyes from the road.

"A bunch of Victor's stuff." I let the sentence hang as I watched her face change from relaxed to tight with anger. "I'm sorry I looked, I just wanted to know a little about him."

"It's fine, sweetie, really." She gave me a tight smile. "I was going to wait until you graduated to give it to you. Your father was into some pretty strange stuff."

"Did you read his journal?" I asked, wondering if she would understand half of what he was talking about.

"Journal? Oh, you mean the novel he was writing? Yes, I read it. I loved him so much, but he was not a fiction writer."

I gaped at her. She thought his journal was a novel? I loved my mother and I thought she was pretty smart, but how could she think his journal was a novel. I wanted to talk to her about it, but before I opened my mouth I thought about it. Maybe it was best she didn't know what Victor, or I, was. She tended to worry too much as it was.

"Yeah, not a very good book," I finally said, and looked out the window. "You don't mind if I keep it?"

"No, of course not, like I said, I was going to give it to you next year."

"Thanks, Mom, you looked beautiful in your wedding dress," I said in a quiet voice right before my phone started playing *Come Out to Play*, by the Offspring. I clicked the answer button. "Hey, Billy, what's going on?"

"Just hanging out, where are you? You sound like you are in the car."

"Mom and I went shopping in Denver. We are on our way back."

"Nice, hey are you hanging out with Shawn tonight?"

"No, he has to work why?"

"Do you want to come over and play Call of Duty?"

I thought about it for a second. Billy and I needed to get back to normal, but I was afraid Shawn would be mad if I hung out with him. Then again, I could not let a guy dictate who I hung out with. "Sure, I'll call you on my way over."

"Okay, later," he said before hanging up.

"You and Billy made up?" Mom asked as she got off on our exit.

"I think so, but we have a ways to go. He needs to get used to me having a boyfriend."

"So, it's official?"

"Yes." I was embarrassed but proud that Shawn was mine. I loved my mom but talking about boys with her was not something I thought I would ever be comfortable with. I picked up my phone and sent a text to Shawn. **I'm going to play Call of Duty at Billy's tonight. Just an FYI.**

"Are you asking Shawn if it's okay?" Mom asked.

"No. I'm letting him know I'll be with Billy. I don't want to have any more misunderstandings with him about my friendship with Billy." My phone buzzed, and I clicked it on.

Great, have a good time!

"Good, don't ever have a man who tells you who you can, and cannot, hang out with."

"I don't plan to. They both need to deal with me having them in my life. If they can't, then one of them will have to go."

"I'm proud of you, sweetie, and don't worry about your dad, he just wants you to be happy and perfect. He sees a lot of bad stuff at the clinic, he doesn't want anything bad to happen to you."

"I know, but I'm not going to do anything to mess up my future."

We lapsed into silence for the rest of the way home, but it felt good talking to my mom about Billy and Shawn. She listened and understood better than Dad did.

"Why did you knock?" Billy asked, when he opened the door a few hours later. "I thought you were one of the church ladies for a second."

"I don't know. I thought I should is all." I looked down at my feet. I wasn't mad at him anymore, but it was still weird being around him.

"It doesn't matter. Come on I have the game ready to go." He moved back from the doorway and he let me go in before him. I took my coat off, then my shoes, and hung my coat on the hook I had claimed when I was six.

"How was shopping?" he asked, as I followed him down to the basement where the game room was.

"I hate shopping, but I found a dress for prom, so it wasn't a complete loss."

"I thought you didn't want to go. If I recall you said, 'prom wasn't your thing.'"

"Things change. It sounds like fun now." I sat on the couch and picked up a controller and headset. "Come on, let's play. Did you order pizza yet?"

"Yeah, we have at least thirty minutes before it gets here."

We stopped talking about life and got into the game until the pizza showed up. Billy got us plates and napkins while I opened the pizza box on the coffee table.

"Do you know if Jo has a date for prom?" he asked, sitting down across from me, and putting a slice of pizza on his plate.

"Jo? I have no idea. You want to ask her?" I took a bite of my pizza. I felt a little hurt he was already over me. How could he be so quick to change his affections?

"I was thinking about it. She seems really cool, and you like her, which says a lot."

"How so?" Why did what I think matter?

"You don't like most girls, and you like her, so I figured she would be more my type." He picked up his slice and took a bite.

"Then go for it. I don't know her well, but she's nice. I don't think she will put up with any of your bullshit."

"Good, finish your pizza, let's go kill those guys from California."

"Do you want to spend the night?" Billy asked, as I stood to stretch, we had been playing for hours and it was already past eleven. "We could make a night of it?"

I let out a groan as my joints popped. "No, I don't think it would be appropriate anymore, Billy." I turned and started up the stairs.

"I wasn't trying to put the moves on you or anything." He followed me up the stairs.

"I know, but we are growing up. I have a boyfriend and you are going to ask Jo to prom. How would it look to them?" We reached the top of the stairs and I bent to put my shoes on.

"Yeah, I get it. If we were both guys, or girls, it wouldn't matter."

"But we're not. It'll be okay, we just have to find a new normal." I put my coat on and went to the door.

"It's going to be hard."

"I know, but we will make it through. You are my BFF." I opened the door and turned to look at him.

"You're mine too. Drive safe, alright?"

"I will, see you Monday." I left, thinking about how quickly things changed between Billy and me. It made me sad, but it was bound to happen eventually.

It was late, and I was tired as I drove home. The sky was clear but there was no moon which made it so dark it felt like my headlights were on dim even though I had the high beams on. I was turning around the corner where I had met the moose when a deer picked its head up from the middle of the road.

My mind jumped back to the moose. I tried to remember everything I was supposed to do, but I couldn't get the image of the moose landing on my hood out of my head. I shook my head, slammed on the brakes, and blared the horn. She tried to run but the road was too slick. She fell, regained her footing only to fall again. She was not going to get out of the way in time.

I pushed my foot harder into the brake pedal, and squeezed my eyes shut, waiting for impact, but none came. I opened my eyes; the Jeep had stopped less than a foot from the deer. She blinked at me then walked to the other side of the road. I blew out a breath and forced my fingers to release the steering wheel. After I regained the feeling in them, I put the Jeep in gear and drove the rest of the way home, relieved I hadn't killed the deer or wrecked my Jeep.

Mom and Dad were already in bed, so I made sure the lights were off and went up to my room to sleep.

I was back at the mineshaft. The wind was blowing me away from it this time. The voices called out for me to save them, but the wind was keeping me from getting to them. I tried to call Shawn with my mind. I wanted him to see what was going on in my dream, but he was either busy or he couldn't hear me.

I wanted to help them but there was nothing I could do. "Aren't you going to help them, Elizabeth? Isn't that what your kind do?" The cracked voice of the goblin said from behind me.

"What are you doing to them?" I asked, turning to face him. He looked different than he did the last time I had seen him. He was trying to look like Shawn, but his voice and lack of a nose gave him away.

"They are the souls I'm saving for dessert, yours will be the main course. You can try to save them if you want." He laced his hands together behind his back and started to walk in a circle around me. "All you have to do is go down the shaft and let them out of their cages. They aren't even locked."

The voices seemed to get louder as he spoke. I turned my head toward the shaft, *it wouldn't be too hard to go down the shaft*, I thought.

"Yes, go down the shaft and save the lost souls," he whispered in my ear.

I jumped and turned to face him and met the holes where his eyes should have been. He was smiling, his pointed teeth gleaming at me. "You must think I'm dumber than I look. Leave me alone." I closed my eyes and thought of my room, a safe room where he could not follow me.

When I opened my eyes, I was in my bedroom, alone. I ran to my bed and jumped in. I pulled the blankets over my head and waited for the alarm to go off, praying the mare would not follow me.

CHAPTER 25

Work the next day was quiet as usual for a Sunday before Memorial Day weekend, when tourist season officially started. I worked on homework between waiting on customers. Billy sent me a text, saying he wasn't going to make it by before I got off work. His mom was making him go to church. My shift was almost over when I saw a black suburban pull up to the curb.

It looked like the one Shawn was in the first time I saw him. I put my book away and watched a man get out and come inside. As soon as I saw his face I knew he was Shawn's dad. He stared at me for a moment before walking down the aisle to the dreamcatchers hanging on the wall. He stared at them as if it was the craziest thing he had ever seen.

"Hi, can I help you" I asked, watching him.

"No, just looking," he called back not taking his eyes off the display. I pulled my phone out of my pocket and sent Shawn a text.

Did you tell your dad about the dreamcatchers?

Yes, why?

I'm pretty sure he's here looking at them.

Don't worry, he knows who you are.

"Does your boss approve of you texting while you are working?"

199

Shawn's dad asked from the other side of the counter. I jumped, startled he was able to get so close without me hearing him.

"I'm sorry, no, he doesn't normally mind. Did you find everything you needed?" I asked, trying not to make eye contact with him. I scanned the carton of eggs he put on the counter.

"Yes, you're Liz, the girl my son is dating right?" I looked up and met his eyes. He took a step back like he recognized me.

"Yes, it's nice to meet you, Mr. Ericson." I tried give him a genuine smile, but it was hard after reading what my bio-dad had written about him.

"You as well, please call me Jon." He looked at the register.

"Okay, that will be $2.57" I said, looking at the total on the screen.

"You're coming over to the house later to study with Shawn?" He gave me three dollars.

"That's the plan." I made change and gave it to him. "Would you like a bag?"

He looked down at the eggs as if he forgot what he was buying. "Yes, please, my wife will kill me if I break them."

I put the eggs in a plastic bag and handed it to him. "Have a good day." This time I gave him a genuine smile.

"You too. We'll talk when you come up to the house." He took the bag and left without another word.

I sent a text to Shawn. **He just busted me for texting at work. ☹ I'm off in a half hour then I will be over.**

See you soon, he replied.

I tried to go back to my math homework, but I kept thinking about Shawn's dad and how weird he looked at me. It was almost like he recognized me from somewhere and I wondered if I looked that much like my bio-dad. Before long, Bob came to take over the store, and he took my mind off Shawn's dad as I gave him a run down on what had happened that morning.

Before I left, I went into the bathroom to make sure I looked my best before I went to Shawn's. I looked in the mirror, the bruises from my run-in with the moose were almost gone. I smiled to myself to make sure I didn't have anything stuck in my teeth and they were clean. I took the braid out of my hair, ran my fingers through it and let the waves cascade down my back. With my hair down, I couldn't see the stubby hair where my stitches were all but gone. I came out of the bathroom and pulled the straps of my backpack over my shoulders. I yelled to Bob I was leaving and headed to my Jeep.

The mansion was about ten minutes from the Gas N'Go. It was on a mountain next to the mountain where my house sat but it still had a great view. It was built by Thomas Freeman, the first miner to find gold nearby. He lived there with his wife and two children until they died tragically. He was so overcome with grief it was believed he died of a broken heart, but now I wondered if the mares had something to do with it.

I had been inside once many years before when there was talk of turning it into a museum. My parents dragged me through it as part of an open house to raise the money needed to refurbish it. The town had been unable to raise the money and it sat vacant until Knight Inc. bought it and started to renovate it.

I pulled into the lot and parked next to Shawn's Rubicon. I took a nervous breath. I wasn't looking forward to meeting his mom and talking to his dad. I wondered if he felt the same way before he met my parents. My longing to see Shawn won out, and I grabbed my bag before getting out of the Jeep.

I started walking toward the front door, dragging my feet with every step. "Liz," a voice called, and I turned to see Shawn making his way toward me. I stopped and watched him half-jog, half-walk over to me. The butterflies in my stomach evaporated and I smiled.

"The main entrance was set up for the company, the side door is the entrance for the residence," he said, pulling me to him and giving me a quick kiss before taking my hand. "How was work?"

"Quiet except for your dad. It was weird." I shivered even though the spring sun was warm on my face.

"He has been known to create strange situations. Come on, my mom is dying to meet you." He held the door open for me and we went inside.

He took my hand once we were in and led me down a hall to a staircase. The mansion had changed a lot since I had been there. It felt like a home now, instead of the vacant ominous place filled with dust and cobwebs. When we got to the second story, Shawn led us down a hallway and into a commercial kitchen that smelled like heaven. Meat of some kind was roasting in the oven and it made my mouth water.

"Mom? Are you in there?" Shawn called out.

"Back here," a voice answered from behind a narrow door.

Shawn let go of my hand and went to open the door. A woman in her mid-forties came out with an arm full of vegetables. "Hi," she said, nodding her head toward me. "Give me just a second." She went to the sink and dropped everything in her arms into it. She dusted her hands off on her apron and walked over to me with her arms out like she was going to hug me. "Shawn has told me so much about you." She took my hands instead of hugging me, to my relief, and looked me up and down.

"It's nice to meet you, Mrs. Ericson." I wasn't sure what to do, so I just stood there and let her look at me.

"You have your father's eyes and mouth." She nodded her head as if she was trying to convince herself.

"You knew my father?" I asked in awe as she let go of my hands and went back to the sink.

"Of course, he was Jon's best friend for many years. I would recognize him anywhere." She turned on the sink and started washing the vegetables. "Shawn, your father is waiting for you two in his office, you had better get up there. Liz are you staying for dinner?"

I looked at Shawn, he nodded his head and pushed his palms together in a prayer gesture. "Umm, as long as it's okay with my parents I will."

"If they say no, let me talk to them. I'll convince them to let you stay," Mrs. Ericson said, without looking up from the sink.

"We'll see you in a while, Mom, after we talk to Dad we're going to study."

Shawn took my hand and led me out of the kitchen and down another hall to a closed set of double doors. He knocked lightly on the door. "Come," his dad called. Shawn opened the door and we walked into his dad's office.

"Liz, good to see you again," he said from behind his desk not taking his eyes off his computer. "Please, take a seat." He pointed at the chairs in front of his desk.

"You too," I said, giving Shawn a sideways glance, and sitting.

"So, your father was Victor Robinson?" Jon said finally closing the lid on his laptop.

"From what I understand, yes. I never met him." I looked down at my hands and laced them together to sit in my lap.

"Do you know what happened to him?" Jon asked, putting his elbows on the desk, and lacing his fingers together.

"Only what my parents told me. He died in his sleep shortly after moving here. Is that why you moved here?"

"No, Victor left our clan before he met your mother. He cut all ties with us. I had no idea he had died until Shawn told me. He was a good man. I miss him every day."

"I'm sorry, he left my mom with no information about his friends or family, otherwise I'm sure she would've contacted you."

"Yes, well there is nothing to be done about it now. Shawn tells me you have inherited your father's gift for dream shifting." He changed the subject effortlessly, but there was something in his eyes, relief maybe, that he would never see Victor again.

"I guess so, I had no idea I was doing it until Shawn told me about what you do." I looked down at my hands again, feeling uncomfortable. I remembered everything Victor had written about Jon in his journal and wondered how much of it was true.

"Well, what do we do with you now?" Mr. Ericson asked no one in particular. He leaned back in his chair and looked at the ceiling.

"Can't we train her to be a Knight?" Shawn asked, surprising me. The thought had never crossed my mind.

"How old are you, Liz?" He glanced at me before turning his attention back to Shawn.

"I'll be seventeen at the end of May." I had no idea why he needed to know.

"Shawn, you know the rules. She's too old. I won't lose another apprentice because they started too late."

"But she can already do almost everything I can," Shawn protested. "If we don't give her the weapons she needs, how long will she last out there on her own?"

I pulled the sleeve of my hoodie up. "What about this? The mare who is stalking my dreams said he marked me." I showed him the angry red scar on my wrist. "How do I get rid of it?"

Jon's eyes went wide, and he pushed away from his desk like the mark was contagious. "You were marked? There is no way to get rid of it, it is truly too late for you. There is no escaping once you have been marked. It is only a matter of time before he will get you. Now, if you will excuse me, I need to get back to work, and I believe you two need to study." He looked at Shawn as we stood and shook his head.

"Shawn, you know what happens when someone is marked. Are you sure you want to spend any more time with this girl? It will only hurt more when her time comes."

"Dad, we need to help her, not write her off." Shawn began pacing around.

"No one who has been marked has survived over a year and you know it. Think of your aunt," Jon's voice dropped, and he almost sounded sorry. "There is nothing we can do for you, Liz, I'm sorry your life will be cut short. Now, if you will excuse me." He turned back to his computer.

I looked at Shawn, I didn't know what to do. This man just told us no one had ever been able to remove a mark or survive it for more than a year. "There has to be a way to fix it. Remove the mark, something." I glared at him, angry instead of depressed. If I was angry I wouldn't cry.

"You can sleep under your dreamcatcher, since it seems to work, but someday you won't have it and the mare will find you and take you. I'm sorry, I know it would not have been what Victor wanted for you." Jon looked up from his computer and shook his head.

"This is bullshit. Come on, Liz, let's go." Shawn offered me his hand and I took it. I wasn't going to get anywhere with Jon.

We slunk out of the room giving each other wary looks. Once we were outside the office with the door closed Shawn let out a breath. "Well, it could've gone worse."

"It could've gone a heck of a lot better too." I stood waiting for Shawn. My body started to shake, I was going to die and there was nothing I could do about it.

"Come on, we can talk in my room." He led the way back down the hall to the stairs. We walked up two more flights before he turned left down a hallway until we reached the first door on the right and he stopped.

"Before we go inside, just keep in mind I tried to clean up, but Dad had me training all morning." Shawn opened the door, walked in, and held the door for me.

It looked like a boy's room. The walls were covered in posters of half-naked women and vintage rock band posters. A desk, piled high with old leather-bound books, sat against the window overlooking town. There was a full-size bed in the middle of the room with a forest-green comforter sitting on top of it. The hardwood floor was covered with area rugs that matched the bedding. There was a bookshelf along the wall across from the bed filled with paperback books.

After he closed the door he took me in his arms. "Don't worry we will find a way to get rid of the mark." He released me then walked over to his desk and took a book off the top of the pile.

"How?" I asked as tears filled my eyes.

"We will start with this. There has to be a way to get rid of it." He dropped the book on the bed and wrapped his arms around me. "I'm not going to let you go without a fight." He squeezed me tighter then let go.

"Can you teach me how to fight them?" I asked, slipping my shoes off, and pulling my legs onto the bed to sit cross-legged. "At least then I will have a chance until we find an answer."

He looked at me with a smile on his face. "Yeah, I can, and maybe my sister will help. I'll be right back." He got up and left the room.

I picked the book up off the bed and started to page through it. At least it was in English. I had just found a section on goblin marks when the door opened and a beautiful woman with long, light-blonde hair came in. She had high cheekbones and a high forehead. She was slender with barely any curves. She looked like she could be walking the runway in Paris not in Twisted Pines. She looked familiar, and I figured out where I knew her from quickly.

"I'm Heather, I don't think we were introduced last time we met. Nice to meet you in person," she said, standing next to the bed.

"You too." She was the woman who helped save me from the mare the night I hit the moose.

Instead of offering me her hand she pulled me into a hug. "I'm Shawn's big sister in case you hadn't already figure it out."

"Yeah, well he said he was going to get his sister." I gave her a nervous smile. I didn't think I had ever met anyone who acted so casual right after meeting a stranger before.

"He's told me all about you. I'm glad you're here. Are you staying for dinner?"

"Crap, I need to call and ask my parents." I looked at Shawn.

"I'll fill her in while you call them. You can go in the hallway if you want."

I dug my phone out of my pocket and pushed the button for the house phone. Mom picked up on the second ring. "Hey, Mom."

"Liz? Is everything alright?" She sounded concerned, I rarely called her unless something important was going on.

"Shawn's mom asked me to stay for dinner. Is it alright if I eat here?"

"I don't see why not, but I want you home by nine. You have school tomorrow."

"No problem, thanks, Mom. I love you."

"Love you too, sweetheart, have fun."

I disconnected the call and went back into Shawn's bedroom where he was explaining what their dad said about training me and the mark. They looked up when I walked in. "Close the door," Heather said in a low voice. I did as she asked then went back to the bed and sat.

"If we do this, we must be careful, if he finds out, there will be hell to pay, but I agree with you. We need to find a way to remove the mark but teaching her to fight them will extend her life until we do."

"When do we start?" I asked, looking back and forth between the two of them.

"We will have to work around our work schedules, but we will start tonight, since we are both off." Heather got up. "So, your dad was Victor?"

"Yeah, do you know anything about him?"

"I know he was one of us. He was Dad's best friend from childhood. I know they got into a fight, but I have no idea what it was about. Victor took off and left everything behind one night and he was never heard from again." Heather got up from her spot on the bed. "Are you staying for dinner?"

"Yeah, I just have to be home by nine since it's a school night."

"Perfect, I'll tell Mom. You guys have fun and keep it clean. We'll talk more later." She winked at us, got up, and left the room closing the door behind her.

"I see you started without me," Shawn said, looking at the open book on his bed.

"Yeah, I know we should be studying for history, but..." I looked down at the book.

"You're right, that's why I snuck these books out of the library." Shawn went to the desk and picked up another book. "We can read our history books whenever we want."

We got to work, and I tried to leave thoughts of our dads' fight behind. I read the section on marks and found nothing useful. I had just closed my book when Shawn shut his book with more force than he needed to.

"What?" I asked.

"It said to put the marked person out of their misery to save their soul."

"Mine described what the marks looked like and how to spot them. There was nothing about removing it or saving the person marked. I'm not giving up." I got up from the bed and got another book from the pile.

"I'm not either," Shawn said, following me to the desk.

We spent the rest of the afternoon looking for anything that would help me but found nothing.

Heather stopped by later to tell us dinner was ready. I packed up my stuff, since I was planning to leave after dinner and we went to the dining room. Shawn's mom made pot roast with roasted potatoes and vegetables.

Jon said grace before we dug in. Mrs. Ericson insisted I call her Jenny. We talked about what it was like growing up in such a small town and what they could expect once tourist season started. Jon didn't say much, but he kept looking at me with pity in his eyes.

After dinner Shawn walked to me to my Jeep. "Your dad kept staring at me, like I had a terminal disease and I was going to keel over any second," I mumbled, watching my shoes as we walked across the parking lot hand in hand.

"I noticed, I wish he would stop feeling sorry for you and help us find a way to save you." We stopped at the driver's side of my Jeep.

"Me too, are you going to keep looking?" I asked, opening the door, and throwing my pack into the passenger seat then turning back to face Shawn.

"Yeah, but I have to get some homework done since I didn't get much done today." He moved in closer to me.

"Me too, thanks, Shawn," I managed to say before his lips met mine and I was jelly in his arms. When he pulled back I sucked in a breath. "I have to drive now?" I laughed and got in the Jeep.

"Are you going to be alright?" He watched while I put my seatbelt on and put my keys in the ignition.

"Yes, I'll be fine." I smirked. "I'll see you and Heather later?"

"Yeah, we'll come to you."

"See you then." Shawn shut the door and I started the engine.

It was dark once I got to my road, but the weather was clear, and I could see better with the new Jeep's headlights than my old one. I drove slow though, looking for anything out of the ordinary. When I pulled into my driveway, my heart was racing, and my breathing was shallow. I needed to get over the fear of hitting another animal soon. I couldn't take the panic attacks anymore.

Mom and Dad were watching television when I finally got myself under control and went inside. I set my backpack down by the stairs and went into the living room to tell them I was home.

"How was dinner?" Mom asked, looking away from the television.

"It was good. Shawn made it sound like his mom wasn't a good cook, but we had pot roast and it was really good." I sat on the arm of the couch.

"Did you have a good time?" Mom asked.

"Yeah, I met his parents and his sister. Heather is really cool, and his mom is nice."

"What about his dad?" Dad asked.

"Well, I'm not sure. It turns out he knew Victor." I did not want to elaborate in front of my dad.

"You mean your biological father?" Dad asked, sitting up in the recliner.

"Yeah, they grew up together."

"Small world." Dad ran a hand through his hair. "How did he figure it out?"

Crap, I thought to myself. I was not going to tell my parents about the Knight Flyers. "He said I looked familiar and asked about my parents."

"You must really look like him." Dad kicked back in the recliner as his show came back on.

"Shawn's mom said I had his eyes and mouth." I wasn't really sure what to say. Dad had been the only father I had ever known, it was weird to talk about Victor with him. "Well I'm going to head upstairs. It's been a long day." I got to my feet.

"Goodnight, Liz," they both said as I picked up my bag and climbed the stairs.

I sat at my desk a few minutes later and pulled out what was left of my homework. I tried to concentrate, but my mind kept going back to the mark and what Jon had said: I would be lucky if I made it a year, and there was no way to get rid of it. I pulled the sleeve of my hoodie over the mark. We would find a way to get rid of it. There was no other choice.

CHAPTER 26

"You stayed up late," Shawn said when I opened my eyes and found myself in the padded room with him and Heather. "Did you make it home alright?"

"Yeah, I needed to finish my homework." I rubbed the mark on my wrist.

"Don't worry, Liz, we are going to find a way to get rid of that mark. In the meantime, I want to see what you can already do," Heather said, taking a step forward. "Shawn said you showed up in one of his dreams. Do you know how you did it?"

"I think so. I just thought about him and I was here." I was glad Heather was going to help us. The more help I had the better my chances were of living a full life.

"Good, why don't we try it with someone else?" Heather looked at Shawn then back at me.

"Alright who?" I asked, looking between them.

"Billy?" Shawn suggested.

I shrugged my shoulders and thought of Billy. When I opened my eyes, we were in Billy's bedroom, the lights were low, and he was moving around on the bed. I blinked and realized there was someone on top of him. I wanted to run to him and pull the mare off, but Shawn put his arm in front of me to stop me. He pointed to his ears. He wanted me to listen. I strained my ears and the moaning became apparent. Billy was having a sex dream, gross.

Heather giggled, and Shawn cleared his throat. I closed my eyes and thought of the padded room. "I think I'm scarred for life," I said when I opened my eyes and put a hand to my stomach.

Heather and Shawn were laughing. "We forgot to warn you. When you enter someone's dream you never know what you are going to find," Heather said, wiping a finger under her eye.

"When the mares are after them it's a little better. Normally there isn't any sex, but you never know," Shawn said, putting his hands on my shoulders and rubbing them.

"How do you know where the mares are going to be?" I asked, leaning into him.

"We have a *Mare Sensor,* it casts a net over an area then feeds information into a computer and plots the activity on a map. Victor actually designed the first one. Then all a Knight has to do is think about the location and they are there." Heather walked a few steps away from me then back again. "There is a lot more technical stuff to it, but we will go over it later."

My bio-dad's journal had talked about taking a net, but I still didn't understand how it worked. "If you're dreaming, how do you know where to go?"

Shawn pulled something out of his ear and put it in my hand. It looked like a hearing aid. "It's a very high-tech radio. A technician, normally someone who is in training or who wasn't born with the gift, mans the computers and tells us where we need to go. We sleep with them. They broadcast at a frequency we can understand and hear while we sleep. It takes some getting used to, but they're great."

I gave the radio back to him. "So, how do you kill them?" I put my hands in the pockets of my jeans. "Wait, do you really kill them?"

"To answer your first question, it depends on the mare. Different weapons work better on different mares. It's a guessing game but typically a knife or a gun works well," Shawn said.

"Do we really kill them?" Heather repeated my question. "Why would you ask that?"

"My stalker said he was the same one Shawn killed the night I hit the moose and who killed my bio-dad."

Heather looked at Shawn. "We were taught they died, but if what you say is true, then we've been lied to." Her face fell, and she stared at the ground.

"Liz found Victor's journal and we both read it. He believed the mares come through a gate, or a door between their dimension and our dream dimension. He believed when we killed them they go back to their dimension, like when you die in a video game, you start back at the beginning of the level. All they have to do is find the door and they can come back through." Shawn looked at me for agreement.

"My bio-dad was trying to figure out how to close the gate when he died. His journal said he had a plan, but first he needed to find a gate."

"That's perfect," Heather said, grabbing my hands, and jumping up and down.

"What?" Shawn and I asked at the same time.

"Don't you see? If we close the gate and kill the mare, you'll be safe."

"But we don't know how to close it, or where it is," I said, pointing out the obvious.

"Then we will find it and figure out how to close it. In the meantime, we will teach you how to fight." Heather let go of my hands and took a few steps away. "That way if he ever catches you without your dreamcatcher you'll have a chance."

"I have already manifested a gun and some other things. I stabbed the mare with my knife and an icepick. Do you think it killed him?" I asked thinking of stabbing my stalker in the back when I fell asleep without my dream catcher.

Heather looked at me like she didn't believe me. I thought of the .22 rifle my dad gave me for Christmas when I was twelve and it appeared in my hands. I opened the bolt to check the chamber. It was loaded and ready to go.

"I can't believe you did it. It took me three years before I could manifest a weapon that complicated," Shawn said, taking it from me. He unlocked the bolt, pulled it back, checked the chamber, then pushed the bolt back into it and locked it down. "It's loaded too."

"Nicely done," Heather said, smiling. "Most rookies can manifest a gun, but they forget about the ammunition."

"How is she able to do this? It took us both years to get this far." Shawn gave me back the rifle.

Since I didn't need it, I told the gun to go away and it was gone. I reached out and took Shawn's hand, this was starting to freak me out.

"Natural talent or Victor? Tomorrow, I'm going to see if I can find any information on him and the research he was doing. I'm on duty tomorrow night so Shawn will relay anything I find out to you." She took a step back. "I think we've done enough for tonight, so I will leave you two. Sweet dreams."

"You too," I called as she disintegrated before my eyes.

Shawn turned to me. "You have an amazing talent. I might be a little jealous."

"Why? I have no idea what I'm doing. I'm the one who deserves to be jealous. You get to go out there and kill these guys." He pulled me closer to him.

"Not tonight, tonight I am with you." He bent his head and touched his lips to mine.

CHAPTER 27

The next day at school everything went back to normal if there was a normal the week before prom. The sun was out, and the temperature was on the rise. I was still grossed out when I saw Billy and remembered the dream I intruded on. Billy and I were talking again, Shawn and I were together as much as possible, and prom proposals were going on left and right.

Monday at lunch we were all sitting at our table, eating, and talking about what we wanted to do over the summer. Billy was sitting to one side of me and Shawn was on the other.

"Billy, please stop shaking your leg, my butt is falling asleep." I bumped him with my shoulder.

"What?" He looked at me with bulging eyes. "Oh sorry." His leg stopped shaking and he looked down at his untouched food.

"What is going on? Are you alright?" I whispered to him, starting to get worried.

"Yeah I'm fine." He pushed his chair back and stood. "Jo?"

"Yeah?" Jo looked over from where she had been talking to Tracy.

"Will you go to prom with me? I know its last minute and all, and if you already have a date or just don't want to go with me I'll understand." Billy rushed on, looking at his feet.

"Billy?" Jo almost giggled. "Yes, I'll go to prom with you." She smiled.

"Really?" His red face glowed with excitement.

"Yes, I already have a dress and everything." Her face turned red to match Billy's.

Tracy and Shawn started clapping and I fist-bumped Billy. "Sweet, now sit down and eat your lunch."

"Yeah, lunch." He sat back down and pulled his chair back to the table while I tried not to laugh at his anxiety.

After school, Shawn walked me to my car, holding my hand. "Are you working tonight?" I asked, hoping he wasn't.

"I don't think so, but you can never tell with my dad."

"How will I know if we are going to be training or not?" We got to my Jeep and I hit the unlock button then leaned against the door.

"I'll let you know on Messenger." He stepped closer to me and ran his finger over the strap of my backpack.

"I think we need a code system. With the way my dad has been acting he's probably cyberstalking me." I couldn't help my smile as he stepped closer, our bodies were all but touching.

"Not a bad idea, I don't trust my parents to stay out of my accounts either," he said in a low voice.

"Shawn," Jo yelled from across the lot. "I have stuff to do."

"Hold on," he shouted back. "If I say, 'sweet dreams' we are on for training."

"If you can't meet me say 'see you tomorrow'," I offered. Making up a code was fun.

"If my sister is going to meet you I'll send you, 'my sister says hi'."

I laughed. "That was easy." I looked at my watch. "I'm going to be late if I don't leave now."

"Have a good time at work and I will talk to you later." He pulled me in for a kiss that had me steadying myself against the Jeep to keep me from falling over when he released me.

"Later," I called as he walked to his Jeep while the kids he gave a ride to yelled catcalls to him.

I got in my Jeep and headed to work a little faster than I normally did and made it on time. After work, I went home, and studied at the dining room table. I tried to keep my mind on homework, but I couldn't help but wonder if Heather had found out anything about how to remove the mark or my bio-dad and the gates.

"How was your day, Liz?" Dad asked as he cut into the steak sitting in front of him.

"Just school. Billy asked Jo to prom, he was so scared I thought he was going to have an aneurysm." I laughed and took a sip of my milk.

"Billy asked someone to prom?" Mom asked, looking skeptical.

"Yes, he was sweating bullets, his leg would not stop shaking. It was too funny."

"Who is Jo?" Dad asked.

"She started after spring break. Her dad works with Shawn's dad." I took a bite of food.

"What did she say?" Mom asked, looking hopeful.

"She said yes. We are all going to go together." I took a sip of milk.

"Billy got over you pretty fast." Dad took a sip of his water.

"Thank God. The last thing I needed was him trying to derail me and Shawn again."

"I'm glad you're going to prom together. I'm sure you will have a good time," Mom said, looking over at my dad.

"I'm sure Billy will make sure you stay safe," Dad said, looking back down at his plate.

"Why do you think I would be in trouble to start with?" Dad was becoming harder and harder to deal with.

"It's prom," he said not looking up.

I stared at him for a minute. Why would prom be such a bad thing? I was so tired of him not trusting me. "I'm so glad you trust me." I stood, stomped to the kitchen, and put my plate in the sink.

"Liz don't run off," Mom called.

"I am not going to sit there and let him act like I am going to get pregnant on prom. I'm going to bed." I grabbed my backpack and stomped up the stairs to my room, slamming the door behind me. I was throwing a fit, but it was hard not to when I didn't understand where his distrust came from.

I threw my bag on the bed then fell onto it to stare at the ceiling. I was in no mood to study, but I didn't want to go back downstairs and deal with them. I sat at my desk and was just about to open the journal to look for anything I might have missed when my computer pinged. I went to my desk, shook the mouse to wake the screen up and clicked on my Facebook. There was a message from Shawn: **Sweet Dreams**

Smiling, I closed my computer and got ready for bed. I hoped Shawn would have some good news about removing the mark.

"Took you long enough." Shawn took me in his arms and kissed me before I knew where I was.

"Sorry, I was so excited it took me forever to fall asleep." I pulled back from him and looked around, we were back in the padded room. "Did Heather find anything out about the mark or the gate?"

"She pored over the archives, and finally found a file about Victor. It was almost like it was buried on purpose. I'll sneak it to you at school tomorrow. There isn't anything personal in it, only his work and training history." Shawn paced around the room. "He worked with the Knights until he turned twenty, but she can't find any paperwork or log of why he left."

"The way his journal made it sound, he picked up in the middle of the night and didn't tell anyone he was leaving. I wish I knew what happened to the rest of his things. I'm sure what I found in the box wasn't even close to all the notes he would have made on the gates."

"Did you ask your mom?"

"No, but I think I will, it's more important than just learning about him. He might have information that could save not only me, but everyone in Twisted Pines." I shivered and looked around. It was time to get started. "So, what are we doing tonight?"

"You are going to fight fake mares. I want to see how you fight, get a baseline of what we're working with. I want you to use whatever you can think of to fight them. Use any weapon you think will work."

"Will you protect me if I fail?" The idea of fighting a mare made my head spin. I didn't think I was ready.

"Yes, I will control them. I promise you won't get hurt. Are you ready?"

"Do I have a choice?" I thought of my dad's Colt 1911 .45 as a monster that looked similar to a yeti came running at me. He, it was definitely a he, was tall, at least eight feet, covered with white shaggy fur, standing on two feet, with long arms dangling at his side. His eyes were small and black, matching his bearlike snout. He opened his mouth and roared at me. His mouth was covered in fangs made to rip flesh from bone.

I pulled my weapon up, aimed at his head, and pulled the trigger. I hit him in the head, but the bullet didn't stop him. *Too bad he wasn't a zombie*, I thought to myself and started shooting at his knees. Hoping to slow him down. After three shots his right leg gave way beneath him, but he still hobbled toward me. I took aim at his left knee and pulled the trigger until it clicked empty. He was almost on me, I froze. He was going to kill me, and I was out of bullets. There was no way I would have time to conjure up another fully loaded clip, drop the empty one, and load the fresh one before he was on me.

I started to panic, I wasn't going to make it. I needed to think of something, but my brain could not move past my paralyzing fear. I finally broke out of my paralysis and thought of a sword that would take his head off. A sword was in my hand replacing the Colt in the next instant, but it was a flimsy fencing sword. I threw it at the beast and tried again to come up with a better weapon, but it was too late. A massive arm swung out toward my face and I screamed before everything went black.

"Liz, you're fine. Remember, it wasn't a real monster." I cracked my eyes open to look up at Shawn. My head was resting on his lap, he was looking down at me and pushed my hair out of my face.

"What happened?" I sat up and crossed my legs, so I was facing Shawn.

"I made him leave before he could touch you. You only passed out for a second." He laced his hands together in his lap.

"I'm sorry. I panicked." I looked down at my legs.

"You did great, but tell me what you were thinking when you ran out of bullets?"

"That I didn't have time to think of a full clip and reload before he got to me, then I froze in terror. My mind wouldn't let me think of anything besides the fact he was going to kill me."

"But you were able to work through it, why did you think of a fencing sword?"

I thought back. "I was scrambling for anything at that point."

"Do you understand what you did wrong now?"

"I didn't think of something specific, or when I did, it wasn't what I needed to get the job done."

"Yep, all you had to do was imagine the clip full again and it would have been. Thinking generally of a weapon will never get you what you want. You need to think of the weapon with as much detail as possible. I think you are good with the guns because you know a lot about them. You've handled them and shot them. You need to look at pictures of other weapons, learn about them. If you can, try one out. We have a bunch at the house, but I'm not allowed to show you our training rooms."

"Okay, I'll work on it. What do we do now?" I asked, not sure if I was ready to face another monster.

"We can go again, or we can be done for the night. It was a lot."

"Let's go again, I need to get this figured out." I huffed out a breath and stretched my arms over my head.

"OK, let's start by thinking of a weapon that would have killed the monster."

I closed my eyes and thought about what might kill it. The mock-mare reminded me of a monster in an old *Star Wars* movie and I chuckled as I opened my eyes and looked down at the lightsaber in my hand. I pushed the button and brought the handle up to the middle of my chest.

"Well, you do have an imagination," Shawn laughed. "Should we see if it works?"

"Let's do it." I wrapped my hands around the hilt and held it like a baseball bat.

A moment later the mock-mare was back and running straight toward me. His mouth hung open showing me his razor-sharp teeth, he held his arms out like he was going to tackle me, and the claws on the end of his fingers sparkled in the light. I held my ground until he was in range then brought the lightsaber around and connected with his neck. His head went flying away from his body, but not before his claw dug into the skin on my arm and I screamed in pain.

The mock-mare was gone in the next instant and Shawn's arms were around me. "Are you alright? Why did you scream?"

I brought my arm up for him to see "I wasn't quick enough." I laughed around the throbbing pain radiating up and down my arm.

"Shit." Shawn pulled away from me and pulled his shirt over his head. I felt myself blush despite the pain at seeing his pale skin stretched taut over his pectoral muscles and the eight pack on his stomach. "I'm sorry, Liz, I should have been quicker." He tore his shirt in half then wrapped half of it around my arm as I grunted in pain.

"How am I going to explain this to my parents?" I asked, fighting through the pain that changed from throbbing to burning.

"This is a dream, it won't be there when you wake up." Shawn took me over to the wall and made me sit down.

"It won't?" It felt like it was going to be there when I woke up. "If this is just a dream then why does it hurt so bad?"

"You've never gotten hurt in your dreams before?"

I thought about it. "No, I guess I haven't."

"Knight Flyers feel the pain, most people don't, but we do." He pulled me against his chest. "You did well against him, but we need to work on your fighting skills." He kissed the top of my head and I relaxed into his chest, content to let him hold me.

"I agree, if I can't kill them with a gun, I need to learn to fight with weapons and hand-to-hand." I let out a calming breath as the pain turned into a dull ache.

"That's why we are here." He wrapped his arms around my waist.

"When did you start training for this?" I asked, wondering how long it was going to take me to be as good as he was.

"When I was ten, it was very different than what we are doing with you."

"Why?"

"You already have the basics down. I started from scratch. The first thing I learned to do was control my dreamscape. I thought it would be easy when my dad told me what I needed to do. I had a good imagination as most ten-year-old's do, but it took me a long time to figure out how to gain control over my dreams."

"Ten? Great, it's going to take me years to be as good as you."

He kissed the top of my head. "No, it won't. You already have the basics down, we just need to teach you how to fight, and manifest weapons. I wouldn't be surprised if you were better than me before the summer is over. The best part is, my dad still doesn't know about half the stuff I do."

"Are you talking about the padded room?"

"Yes, it's one of the things he never figured out. I have others, I'll show you sometime, but not tonight, I'm too comfortable." He yawned and squeezed me tighter.

"Me too." I closed my eyes and drifted.

CHAPTER 28

Shawn was right about the gash from the mock-mare. When I woke up in the morning there wasn't even a scratch on my arm, thank God.

Shawn brought the file on my bio-dad to me the next day and it felt like I was getting to know the man who donated part of his DNA to me.

The file gave me his parents' names, Iva, and Stephon Robinson, they were both Knights too. It didn't say if they were still alive or where they were though. It listed his training scores, which I didn't understand and that he was the youngest to ever complete the training program. It listed his mare kills over time. It didn't give me an in-depth look at the man, but it made me proud. My bio-dad was badass. I made a copy of the file, so I could look at it whenever I wanted to and gave it back to Shawn. He needed to sneak it back into the file room before anyone knew it was missing.

As the week passed I found a rhythm. I got up and went to school, then I would either go to work or go home and study. Before I went to bed each night, I would look at Google images of weapons and do my best to memorize them. I looked at their specifications, and what they were used for. By the end of the week I could manifest three or four different swords. When I went to sleep, I spent my dreams training with either Shawn or Heather.

Heather was still searching for a way to remove my mark and for any information on what the rune meant. I hid the fact I was terrified that each night I went to sleep, I didn't know if I would wake up the next day. My goblin stalker had disappeared since I had been spending every night training with Heather and Shawn. I felt rested for the first time since I hit the moose and by Friday, I felt like I knew what I was doing.

School dragged, everyone was excited for prom and no one wanted to be in class. Our history class would not be quiet, so our teacher gave up and let us talk about our plans for the upcoming weekend.

"What are you doing tonight?" Shawn asked me.

"My parents are making me stay home. They don't want me getting too tired," I moaned. "I think they don't want me to have too much fun."

"Bummer, I was hoping we could hang out," Billy said.

"I could ask them if we could have a movie night. The new Avengers movie is out on pay-per-view."

"Could Jo come?" Billy asked, turning red.

"If it's okay with my parents, yeah."

"Well, let me know as soon as you can. I will run it by Jo as a maybe."

When the bell finally rang we gathered up our books and walked down the hallway together. "I'll shoot my mom a text before I leave and let you know."

"Sounds good see you later." Billy stopped at his locker while Shawn and I kept going to mine.

"I hope your parents say it's okay. I want to hang out with you in real time," Shawn said.

"Me too, they have been acting so weird since we started dating. I don't get it." I came to a stop in front of my locker and spun the dial before turning it to enter my combination.

"You're their only child, they are being overprotective from the new kid in town." He deepened his voice and tried to sound like a bad boy.

"I know, I just wish they would get over it already." I opened my locker and put my history book in my pack. I grabbed my jacket and my pack then closed the locker.

"My parents aren't thrilled about us either."

"Because of my mark or because of Victor?" We walked down the hall toward his locker. "Because they think you are a distraction, which you are." He turned and winked at me. "But I wouldn't want it any other way."

"They should be happy though, we are only encouraged to date other Knight Flyers, there is less to explain, and it continues the bloodline." He shrugged.

"Isn't it a little narrow-minded?" I asked, raising an eyebrow as he turned to his locker.

"Yes, but I understand where they are coming from." He spun the dial and shrugged. "If two Knights have a child there is a ninety percent chance it will be a Knight."

"Is that why you are dating me?" I was confused, his words did not sound like him.

"No, I'm dating you because I like you. It doesn't hurt you are one of us though." He opened the locker and started moving things around.

"Do you have to marry another Knight?"

"If I want to stay part of the clan." He pulled his backpack out and slung it over his shoulder. "One of my sister's friends was kicked out because he eloped with a girl who was not part of the Flyers.

"Is your dad in charge of the whole thing?" We started walking toward the main entrance.

"No, he is only in charge of our clan. There are a bunch of other clans scattered across the globe who are fighting mares."

"Wow, so it's a pretty big dating pool then." He took my hand and squeezed.

"I don't need them when I have you."

"Since I'm not technically a Knight, you're breaking the rules, I've got myself a bad boy." I laughed to myself.

"No, because your dad was one. You are safe even though my dad won't let you join. He is being such a pain in the ass about it."

"It's alright I have other plans anyway." We reached my car and I turned to him. "I'll send my mom a text as soon as I get in the Jeep and I'll let you know about tonight."

"Okay." He leaned in and brushed his lips across mine. I closed my eyes and moaned at his touch. I didn't think I would ever get tired of him kissing me.

Shawn's phone started to ring, interrupting our kiss, so he pulled away and took his phone out of his pocket. "It's Heather, I wonder why she's calling."

I shrugged my shoulders as he pushed the answer button on the phone. "Hey, what's going on?" he asked.

I hit the unlock button on my jeep, opened the door, and put my backpack on the passenger seat while listening in on his side of the conversation.

"You did? That's great. What does it say?"

I turned to look at him with my eyebrows high in question.

"What? Okay, I'll see what she can do. I have to drop off the guys and I'll let you know." He hit the end button and looked up at me.

"What?" I asked, barely containing my excitement.

"Heather found something on the rune."

I blinked, letting his words sink in. Were we actually going to figure something out? "What?"

"She wants to tell us in person. Can we come over after I drop everyone off?"

"Yeah, of course. Did she give you a clue?"

"No, but she sounded excited. Go home, we will meet you there as soon as we can." He pulled me to him and gave me a quick kiss before turning and running over to his Jeep where everyone was waiting for him.

I got into my Jeep, pulled my phone out and sent a text to my mom. It would take her a while to respond to me, so I drove home thinking about Shawn's kisses and how many more there would be over the coming weekend.

When I got home I put my backpack in my room and grabbed the tin with my bio-dad's stuff and set it on the dining room table. I didn't know when my parents were going to be home and I hoped they wouldn't mind if Shawn and his sister came over. I knew they wouldn't mind if it had been Billy, so I didn't bother calling them. They were going to have to get over this double standard, or I would force them to.

I heard cars pulling into the driveway and I ran to the door. I couldn't wait to find out what Heather had. Shawn got out of his Jeep just as a Subaru parked behind him and Heather got out. I threw up a bit in my mouth at the sight of Heather driving a Subaru but pasted a smile on my face. I would talk to her later about her choice in cars.

Shawn waited for Heather before they came to the door at a fast walk. "Hi, come on in," I said, holding the door for them. After they took their shoes off and we went to the dining room and sat, Heather opened the book.

"Okay, let me start by saying I am not the best at translating but I'm pretty sure the rune you have is an ancient weapon." She pointed to a hand-drawn diagram on the page. There was text I didn't understand around it.

I picked up the stone by the thong and set it on the book, so we could compare the symbol. They matched, I could not believe she had found something that matched it so completely. "What do you mean an ancient weapon?" Shawn asked.

"Well, if I'm reading this correctly. It says if the person who wears this is of pure heart and wants nothing but the best for humanity it will not only protect them from darkness, but it will aid them in their fight against it." She looked up at me. "You said when you touched it, it felt like something was covering you in a protective bubble, right?"

"Yeah, but when Shawn did, it burned him." I looked from Shawn to Heather and my gut tightened. "If what you say is true then I am of pure heart and Shawn isn't?" I didn't want to think about what that meant.

"No, I don't think so." Heather turned the page. "It also says once it has chosen its bearer, no one else will be able to use it until the said bearer has died or is given to another freely."

Shawn let out a relieved breath. "Thank God, I didn't think I had any latent homicidal tendencies," he said with a half-laugh.

"I think we're all relieved to hear that," Heather said.

"So, what do I do? Wear it when I go to sleep at night?" I asked.

"It doesn't say how it works, or what it will do, only it will help whoever wears it." Heather touched the leather next to the rune.

"Start wearing it. We will experiment on it next week with the goblin. See if we can figure out a way to make him back off," Shawn said.

I picked up the stone and looked at it for a second. As soon as my skin touched it I felt the soothing feeling wash over me again. I put the necklace over my head and under my shirt. "This is going to take some getting used to." I closed my eyes and let out a sigh as all the stress and fear that had been plaguing me for the past few weeks evaporated.

"Good, I have to go. See you guys tomorrow." Heather got

up and almost ran out of the house.

"What now?" I asked, opening my eyes, and looking at Shawn. His expression made me melt.

"You look so happy right now, I don't know if I have ever seen you like this."

"Well you never saw me before all this crap started."

"I hope I will get to see more of it then." He looked at his watch. "I have to get home but let me know if we are on for movie night."

"I will," I said, walking him to the door.

"Don't worry, Liz, we are going to figure this out." He leaned into me and kissed me quickly before leaving.

CHAPTER 29

I let out a deep breath and looked around the living room. There was an empty pizza box on the coffee table and empty cans of soda surrounding it. Billy and Jo were sitting next to each other on the couch, doing everything they could to keep from touching, while I was lying with my head in Shawn's lap with my legs hanging over the arm of the love seat.

"That was a good movie." I rolled onto the floor, landing gracefully on my knees before getting up and starting to pick up the mess we made.

"I agree." Jo jumped to her feet and started to help me clean up while the boys stared at the credits.

With our arms loaded we went into the kitchen and threw everything away. "Are you having fun with Billy?" I asked, pulling the now full trash bag out of the can.

"Yeah, he's really nice. I just don't know if will be worth it to get too invested in him."

"Why do you say that?" I asked, then remembered my conversation with Shawn earlier in the day. "Never mind Shawn told me about the rules." I went into the laundry room to get a new trash bag. When I came back Jo was staring at me with her mouth ajar. *Oops, forgot Jo didn't know I knew about them*, I thought to myself.

"What did Shawn tell you?" she asked, taking a step closer to me. I thought she was going to hit me for a second.

"I know everything. My dad was one of you." I saw no point lying to her.

"He was? Wait, you mean Dr. Lawson was a Knight Flyer?"

"No, he's my stepdad. My biological dad was Victor Robinson, he died in his sleep before I was born."

"Victor?" She looked at me sideways like she was trying to believe me.

"Yeah." I cocked an eyebrow. "You knew him?"

"No, he was friends with my dad. He used to talk about Victor all the time, and I have seen pictures of him. You look like him, but then do you have the gift?" She put her hands on her hips.

"What is taking you guys so long?" Billy asked, walking into the room, and standing next to Jo.

"Just girl talk." I smiled brightly and fluttered my eyelashes at him. "You know the stuff you didn't want me to talk about in front of you."

"Gross, well come on let's start the next movie before your parents come down and kick us out."

"Actually, I better get home, Billy, tomorrow is going to be a big day." Jo left the kitchen with Billy following her like a lost puppy. *Crap, she wasn't taking the news very well*, I thought to myself.

"What's going on?" Shawn asked, standing up from the couch when Jo went to the closet to get her coat.

"I need to get home, tomorrow is going to be a long day." With her coat on she went to her shoes and started shoving her feet into them.

"Yeah, we will all get to hang out tomorrow night." Billy put his shoes on and went to the door with Jo.

"Yeah, see you guys tomorrow." I shot a look to Shawn trying to say, *shit is about to hit the fan*, but I didn't think he got what I was trying to say.

When the door closed I let out a breath. "We might have a problem," I said, locking eyes with Shawn.

"What would that be?" Dad asked, coming out of the man cave. "You didn't get in another fight with Billy did you"?

"No, Dad," I rolled my eyes, perfect timing as always. "I don't think Jo is as into Billy as he is into her. I have a feeling there could be some drama tomorrow night."

"There is always drama on prom night." Dad smiled at me then looked at his watch. "Would you look at the time? Don't you think you should let Shawn get home, so you can get your beauty rest for tomorrow?"

"I was just leaving," Shawn said, putting his shoes on, and going to the closet to get his coat.

"Good." Dad turned and stalked back to the man cave.

"I accidently told Jo I knew about you all," I whispered.

He straightened and looked straight into my eyes. "Did you tell her about your training?"

"No, but I told her who my biological father was." I shrugged.

Shawn ran a hand through his hair. "I'll handle her. I'm on duty tonight with Heather so you are going to be on your own, but you have your rune, so you will be good. Right?" He put his hand on the doorknob.

"It should be a good test if my stalker shows up," I whispered.

"If you need me, you know how to find me." He planted his lips on mine for too brief a moment before pulling away and opening the door. "See you tomorrow night."

I shut the door after him, called a goodnight to my parents, and went to my room, wanting to be alone and avoid their incessant questions. Knowing I would be on my own in my dreams, I didn't want to go to sleep. I had my rune, and it was supposed to protect me, but I didn't know how to use it.

I read until I couldn't keep my eyes open any longer, then I turned out the light, and snuggled into my comforter. My fingers found their way to the stone around my neck. I rubbed it, praying the goblin would leave me alone, before tucking it under my shirt and falling asleep.

I was in the auto shop working on my engine. I was trying to pull the carburetor out and the nuts refused to loosen. I stood and stretched my back out. Shawn would be there soon, maybe he would get them started for me. I started to check the hoses on the radiator when I heard the door open and close. I stood, expecting to see Shawn, but it was only my stalker. I shrugged, I was dreaming, and since Shawn and Heather were busy it wasn't a surprise the goblin showed up.

"You are kind of a chicken," I said, preparing myself for the struggle the rest of the night was going to be.

"No, I'm not." He looked down at his nails then polished them on the outside of the coveralls he was wearing.

"Yes, you are. You only show up when I am alone in my dreams. You know I can't touch you and you can't touch me. If you weren't scared, you would show up when my friends were here." I wiped my hands off on a rag then stuck them in my pockets. I wondered if I could get to him now that I was wearing the stone.

"I just don't want to lose any more power than I already have. When your boyfriend killed me the night we met, it was the first time in almost two decades since someone had killed me. Do you understand how much power I lost?" He walked around me, poking at the invisible barrier that kept us from killing each other.

"Not enough if you are still here bothering me." I pulled my hand out of my pocket and rubbed the rune under my shirt. How was it supposed to work? If it was a weapon did I need to activate it?

"Silly girl, nothing on this plane will kill me. It may weaken me, but all I have to do is find a soul and eat it. You will never be rid of me." His head jerked up as the door to the shop opened. "Oh good, now we can play."

"Hey, Liz, what are you doing in here? The party is in the gym," dream Billy said, stopping dead in his tracks when he saw the goblin.

"Billy, run," I yelled. I wanted to jump and tackle the goblin, but I knew I would just bounce off the barrier. I knew it wasn't the real Billy, but I didn't want to watch the goblin torture him. I thought of the grenade launcher I had been looking at the day before and it materialized in my hands. I checked to make sure it was loaded then rested it on my shoulder. Billy's eyes grew huge and he turned to run for the door, but he wasn't quick enough. The goblin jumped, landing on Billy's back as he screamed in pain.

"Hey, you piece of crap." I sighted down the barrel and waited until the goblin looked up from where he was chewing on Billy's neck before I pulled the trigger. The grenade launched toward him and the black holes where his eyes should have been seemed to grow as the grenade flew at him.

I dropped the launcher ready to celebrate when the grenade hit the barrier between me and the goblin and exploded. The shock wave pulled me off my feet and I flew a couple of feet through the air before I fell hard on the concrete floor. I groaned as every part of my body exploded in pain.

I rolled to my side and looked up when a pair of feet entered my field of vision. I looked up to see the goblin grabbing his sides as he laughed, or I was guessing he was laughing, I couldn't hear anything after the explosion. The rune didn't do squat.

CHAPTER 30

I sat up in my bed and checked myself for injuries, it felt like I broke every bone in my body when I hit the concrete floor. After searching my body and not noticing any shooting pain I let out a breath. I took a shower and tried not to this of my dream from the night before. It was going to take hours for my hair to dry and mom wanted to put it in curlers to set.

When I was cleaned up and dressed in a button-up shirt and capris-leggings, I pulled the rune out from under my shirt and looked at it. Whatever book Heather had found the information about it in was lying, it didn't help me at all with the mare. Part of me wanted to put it back in the tin with my dad's stuff, but the other part of me wanted to keep it close by. It was one of the only reminders of him I had. I ended up leaving it on and I went downstairs in search of breakfast.

Dad was cooking bacon and eggs when I went into the kitchen. "Morning, Dad," I said as I went to the coffee pot and poured myself a cup.

"Morning, sweetheart. It's going to be a big day." He started moving the bacon to a plate covered in paper towels.

"It's just prom, what's the big deal?" I asked, taking a sip of coffee.

"Has your mom told you what you are in for yet? She has the entire day planned."

"You're kidding? Where is she anyway?" I looked around the room realizing for the first time she wasn't there.

"Getting supplies, and Shawn's boutonniere." Dad put some scrambled eggs and bacon on a plate then handed it to me. "I was chosen to make you breakfast. Your mom doesn't want any accidents today. She doesn't want you to get nervous and back out." He filled his plate then joined me at the bar.

"I would only back out if Shawn did, and I think he is more excited than most of the girls at school." I took a bite of my eggs. "Thanks, this is really good."

"You're welcome. I was also deemed fit to give you the 'prom talk.'" He made air quotes as he said, 'prom talk.'

"I will not be having sex with Shawn tonight if you mean the sex talk when you say, 'prom talk.' I've only been dating him for what, two weeks? It's way too soon." I bit off a piece of bacon and chewed noisily.

"But what if he wants it and won't take no for an answer?" Dad pushed his eggs around on his plate refusing to meet my eyes.

"He won't, but if he does I'll kick him in the balls. You taught me how to defend myself, I take that stuff seriously." I finished my eggs and took my plate to the sink. I turned around to find Dad with his head in his hands. "Dad, what's wrong?" I ran around the bar to his side and put my hand on his shoulder.

He looked up with red eyes brimming with tears. "When did you grow up? Yesterday you were playing Tonka trucks with Billy in the driveway now you're dating and going to prom with a boy we barely know."

"Dad, Billy and I haven't played with Tonkas since last summer at least." He laughed and wrapped me in a hug. "I'll always be your little girl. Just because I'm going to prom doesn't mean I'm not the same girl you raised."

He hugged me back and we stood there until we heard the front door open and Mom yelled for help. I let go of Dad and ran down the hallway to help Mom with the dozen or so bags she was bringing in.

"Mom, what is all this?" I asked, taking half the bags from her.

"Makeup, hair products, perfume. We are going to make you even more beautiful than you already are." I followed her into the living room where she deposited the bags.

"Dad made breakfast if you're hungry," I said, no longer looking forward to this prom thing.

"I already ate, come on let's start working on your hair, getting it in rollers is going to take forever."

I stopped by my room before the fun began, grabbing my phone and found a new message from Shawn.

I talked to Jo, she understands now.

I let out a breath and text back. **Did you explain everything?**

Yes, she wants to help us.

Sweet, glad she is good with it.

Me too. I can't wait for tonight.

I smiled. If I survive the torture my mother is putting me through, it will be fun.

I have to go help my dad. Pick you up at six.

Bummed I didn't have anyone to text with while my mom blew dry my hair I looked through my contacts. I was going to whine to Billy about it, but then I found Jo's number. I wondered if she was going through hell too.

Is your mother torturing you like mine is me?

"Relax, Liz, this should feel good," Mom yelled over the blow dryer.

I tried but she was yanking the hair out of my head with her brush. My phone buzzed, it was a picture from Jo. She was sitting in a beauty chair with her hair wrapped in tinfoil and what looked like marshmallow spread all over her face. Maybe I didn't have it so bad after all. I took a photo of my mom blow drying my hair and a pained expression on my face. I sent back to her. **My mom says it should feel good.**

My mom said it's the price of beauty. See you later! Jo sent back to me.

When my hair was almost dry, Mom put the rollers in, then she doused it with enough hair spray that I needed a warning label that said, 'Caution Flammable.'

I spent the rest of the day getting fluffed and buffed. I was surprised she let me eat anything when lunchtime came around. I finally found the courage to ask my mom about my bio-dad's stuff while she was applying foundation to my face.

"Mom, what did you do with the rest of Victor's stuff when he died?"

She froze and looked down at me before catching me watching her face and resuming. "Why does that matter?" she asked.

"Because he is part of me and I would like to learn more about him." I needed to learn more about him because of the mares, but I couldn't tell her that.

"You know Burt is your dad in every way it matters." She put the beauty sponge down and picked up the blusher.

"I know, Mom, and believe me I love him as my father, but what is so wrong about wanting to learn about the first man you fell in love with and married?"

She huffed out a breath while spreading the blush on my cheeks with a brush. "I don't have any of it anymore. The tin you found is all that is left." She was getting irritated at my questions and I didn't believe her answers.

"What did you do with it? Just throw it away?" I grabbed her wrist and forced her to look at me.

"You don't understand what I was going through, Liz. We had just moved here, I didn't know anyone in town. I was pregnant and on my own, I didn't even have a job. I got evicted from the house Victor and I rented. They locked me out. All I had was the stuff he had left in the car and a few of my things." She pulled away from me and grabbed a tissue from the counter to blot her eyes. "I didn't even have enough gas to go to my friends in Denver."

I had no idea my mom had such a hard time after Victor died. I didn't know what to say so I put my hand on her shoulder. "Mom, I had no idea. I'm so sorry."

"All he cared about was his stupid dreams and finding a way to save the people in Twisted Pines from dying in their sleep. It was so stupid, I don't know why I agreed to help him. If I hadn't fallen asleep that night, he would probably be here now."

My jaw went slack, no wonder Mom hated to talk about him. "Mom, it wasn't your fault. He should have been better prepared for who he was fighting." I cursed myself as soon as the words left my mouth.

"How do you know?" she asked, turning to face me.

"The same goblin that killed him is stalking me," I whispered. I didn't know if she would believe me or not, but I was tired of hiding it.

She burst into tears again and threw her arms around me. "We'll leave then. As soon as school is over we are going to move far away from here."

"Mom, we can't, and besides it's too late." I pulled the sleeve of my shirt up and showed her the mark.

She grabbed my hand and turned it around looking at the brand marking my skin. "Jon said I'm marked and it was too late. No matter where I go the goblin will follow me. That is why I need Victor's stuff. He was trying to close the gate, and we think if we close the gate, and kill the goblin, he won't come back, and the mark won't matter anymore."

"Jon, Shawn's dad? Is that why they moved here? To close the gate?" She turned back to me looking hopeful.

"No, they came to kill the goblins, but Shawn, Heather, and I want to find a way to close the gate."

"No, absolutely not. You're just a kid and I will not risk losing you." She turned her back on me.

"Mom, I am telling you this because you have a right to know. I'm not asking for permission." I didn't like fighting with my mom, but she needed to understand she wasn't going to stop me from doing this. "If I don't try then I probably will die within the year. You know how tired I was when Shawn and I were fighting?"

"Yes."

"That wasn't all because I was heartbroken. The goblin who marked me is tormenting my dreams. If I don't find a way to get rid of him, I don't know how long I will be able to go on."

"I don't want to lose you like I lost Victor," she said, turning back to me, and cupping the sides of my face with her hands.

"You won't, I'm not alone."

She blinked back tears then looked at her watch then changed the subject. "Well, we had better finish getting you ready if you don't want to keep Shawn waiting."

"I love you, Mom," I said as she started applying my eyeshadow.

"I love you too, please be careful."

"I will."

She finished doing my makeup and hair in silence. She was scared for me, heck I was scared for me, but I wasn't going to let it stop me from living my life on my terms.

Once she was done, and I was dressed, I looked in the full-length mirror and didn't recognize myself. I looked five years older, with perfect skin and hair. I turned to my mom and gave her a hug. "Thank you so much." She hugged me back.

"You're welcome but stop before you wrinkle the dress or mess up your makeup. I haven't gotten a photo yet." She pulled away and went in search of the camera. She was acting like everything was normal, but her bloodshot eyes betrayed the truth.

I took my overnight bag off the bed. It had a change of clothes for the after-prom party and other necessities I might need.

She came back in with the camera in hand. "Put the bag down and stand up straight," she said, and started snapping pictures from every angle. "No one is going to believe you are my tomboy daughter."

The doorbell rang, and I bent down to pick up my bag. "Mom, Shawn's here. I have to go."

"He can wait for a second." She snapped another picture. "Give me your bag, I'll carry it downstairs for you." She reached for the bag and I gave it to her. "Stay here for a minute. I want to get pictures of you walking down the stairs."

"Fine," I fumed, but did as she asked. It had been a hard day for her, at least I could do this for her. I waited until I heard her greet Shawn, then I opened the door and walked to the top of the stairs. With a death grip on the railing, I made my way down, trying not to trip and fall on my face.

When I met Shawn's eyes, I realized all the torture I endured getting ready was worth it. His eyes were bright, his mouth hung open, and I wasn't sure if he was breathing. He was wearing a black tuxedo with white shirt and a black vest with silver lines swirling around the fabric. When I got to the bottom of the stairs he took a step toward me. "Hi," I said in a low voice, looking at the floor.

"Hi, you look gorgeous," he said, taking my hand causing me to look up and spun me in a circle. "Wow. Oh, this is for you." He gave me a clear box with a white rose corsage.

"It's perfect." I opened the box and pulled it out. It had a wrist band thankfully. I was about to slide it on my wrist when my mom spoke up.

"Wait, Shawn, you put it on for her." She was still taking pictures. I had forgotten she was there. I rolled my eyes and gave Shawn the corsage. He put it on my wrist, covering my mark, while my mom oohed and awed, still snapping pictures.

"Mom, where is Shawn's boutonniere?" I asked, looking around the room.

"Burt, will you get it? It's on top of the freezer in the garage," Mom asked, still taking pictures. "I want to get some posed shots with them."

"On my way." Dad sounded relieved to get out of the situation.

"Okay, stand against the wall," Mom dictated. "Put one arm around her and hold her other hand, perfect."

"Here it is," Dad said, handing it to me and giving me a wink.

"Thanks, Dad." I opened it and took out the white rose with a spray of green behind it. "I'll try not to poke you." I pulled his lapel away from his chest and attached the boutonniere with some difficulty, while my mom never stopped taking pictures.

"Honey, I think you can stop taking pictures now," Dad said, standing next to Mom. "Enjoy the moment."

She brought the camera down and smiled. "I am, I just never thought she would go to prom." She wiped the tears away and hugged me. "Have fun and be safe."

"I will, I love you, Mom." I pulled back and went to my dad.

"You look beautiful, sweetheart." He took me in his arms giving me a bear hug. "Be careful tonight."

I pulled back from him. "Thanks, Dad, we will. I'll see you tomorrow."

Dad went over to where Shawn was standing. "You will respect my daughter and make sure nothing bad happens to her. Do you understand?"

"Yes, sir," Shawn said, extending his hand to shake my dad's. He took it, shook once then let go and put his arm around Mom again.

"Have fun kids," Dad said, holding my mom's hands down to stop her from taking more pictures as we walked out of the house and toward Shawn's Jeep.

"I'm sorry Mom was freaking out," I said, once we were seated in the car. "I kind of told her about the goblin and my mark when I was trying to find out where the rest of my bio-dad's stuff was."

"What? She knows about the Knights now?"

"She already did, Shawn. She didn't know it was Knight Inc, but I had to tell her. She has a right to know what is going on in case something happens, and I don't make it."

"I know, I just hoped it wouldn't come to that. I wanted to have the mark gone and everything back to normal, so you would never have to tell her. Does she still have Victor's stuff?"

"Me too, but it's too late now. No, she doesn't have his stuff." I told him about everything my mom told me. I finished just as we pulled into the parking lot at the mansion.

"I feel so bad for her," Shawn said, putting the Jeep in park, and turning to look at me.

"Me too, it's hard to imagine. Listen, I don't want this to ruin our prom. Can we just forget about it until tomorrow?" I looked out the window and saw Billy's mom's car pull into the parking lot.

"Deal, I don't want it hanging over our heads all night either."

We got out of the car and I prepared myself for another round of photos. Billy and Jo looked perfect together. Jo's dress was long and bright blue, and Billy's vest was the same color. They both looked nervous but excited.

Pictures at Shawn's were not as bad as they had been at my house, but only because it wasn't my mom taking eight million of them, it was Mrs.

Ericson, Billy's mom, and Jo's mom. Shawn's dad made a quick stop to say hello and tell us to stay out of trouble before he disappeared again. Heather smiled from behind her mom laughing at how many pictures everyone wanted.

"You look amazing," Heather said, while Billy and Jo were taking their turn in front of the camera.

"Thanks, I feel like I have ten pounds of makeup on." I wanted to scratch my nose, but I didn't want to mess up my makeup.

"You look perfect. I'm surprised Shawn can take his eyes off you. Have fun tonight," she said before walking away.

"Thanks, we will."

After we all piled into Shawn's Jeep and were on our way to dinner we all let out a relieved breath. "No more parents," Billy said.

"Thank God," I said, laughing. "Now we can be ourselves and have a good time."

"I'm starving. Where are we going to dinner?" Jo asked, from the backseat. "My mom wouldn't let me eat all day, she was afraid I wouldn't fit into my dress."

"The Diner, you can pig out all you want," Shawn said, laughing.

"Perfect I want the biggest cheeseburger they have," Jo said.

"Me too," Billy chimed in.

Shawn parked the car, came around to my side and opened the door for me. I stepped down, glad there wasn't any ice on the road for a change. "You are the most beautiful woman I have ever seen," he whispered in my ear and offered me his arm.

"Thank you. You look like a stud," I said, taking his arm, and walking toward the diner's door.

We sat at one of the few tables in the middle of the room. There were a few other couples and groups from school and everyone looked nervous eating in their formal clothes.

"Liz, I almost didn't recognize you," Mrs. Baneberry said, as she handed me a menu. "You look beautiful."

"Thank you," I said, ducking my head down. I didn't think I would ever be used to people telling me I was beautiful.

"Billy, you clean up well too," she said, giving him a good once-over.

"Thanks, Mrs. Baneberry." Billy ducked his head as I had.

"You two are new in town I'm guessing." She waited for Shawn and Jo to introduce themselves.

"I'm Shawn Ericson and this Jo Nicholson," Shawn said, for them both.

"Well it's nice to meet the new kids in town. Now what can I get you to drink?"

We ordered our drinks and Mrs. Baneberry shuffled off to get them.

"She seems nice," Jo commented.

"She's a snoop and one of the town gossips," Billy said, leaning back in his chair before remembering he was in a tux and sat up straight again.

"What town doesn't have a least two snoops and gossips?" Shawn asked, chuckling.

Mrs. Baneberry came back with our drinks and took our orders. After she left we all looked at each other.

"I feel like we should be having some very adult conversation since we are dressed up, but I cannot think of a thing," I said, before taking a sip of my soda.

"That is what I was thinking too," Jo said, looking around the room at the other prom goers. Most of them were laughing and talking, but there were a few who looked too uncomfortable to eat.

"I remember this one time about six years ago," Billy started, and my eyes grew huge. "Liz and I were hiking behind my house. We were only ten or eleven, so we couldn't go too far away from the house, but it was far enough. Liz's grandpa had given her some Black Cat firecrackers and there was this huge boulder. We were convinced if we could crack it in half it would be filled with gold and we would be rich."

"How big was the rock?" Shawn asked.

"About ten feet long and five feet high." Billy smiled. "Anyway, we had one of my mom's garden spades and dug a hole under the rock. Once the hole was dug we put one firecracker in the hole, lit it, and expected the rock to crack in half. Of course, it did no damage at all. We decided we needed more bang, so we took the rest of the package, dug further under the rock and lit them."

"Did you split the rock in half?" Jo asked, trying to hold in her laughter.

"No, but we both ended up with rock-shrapnel in our shins because we stood too close."

"I still have a scar," I said, about to pull my dress up to show them but thought better of it at the last second.

"Shawn and I got in big trouble about the same age, only it included BB guns," Jo said, looking over to Shawn.

"I still owe you for the doctor's visit," Shawn said, laughing, and rubbing his arm.

"You didn't shoot him in the eye, did you?" I asked, starting to laugh too.

"No, in the arm, but it got embedded. I think it was the last time my dad actually spanked me."

"I got a spanking out of it too, plus all the shots and stitches." Shawn laughed.

Mrs. Baneberry brought our food out at that moment and sat it down in front of us. We chatted about all the trouble we got into as kids while we ate and we all finally relaxed.

Shawn and Billy were dividing up the bill when Tiffany came over to the table dressed in a very short, dark pink, sequined dress.

The neckline dipped dangerously low, giving everyone a view of her cleavage.

"I hope everything was alright," she said, leaning over between Shawn and me, forcing him to look at her boobs.

"Everything was fine," Jo said, in a clipped voice.

"Good, what did you think, Shawn?"

"I was great until a few seconds ago." He pushed his chair back. "Are you guys ready to go?"

"Yeah," Billy said, standing up and offering his hand to Jo. "I'm ready to leave all of a sudden." Jo took his hand and stood.

I got to my feet. "I definitely lost my appetite."

Shawn stood, and Tiffany straightened but didn't move away, so she was practically pressing herself against him.

"Tiffany," Todd, another senior, called to her. He looked hurt she was flirting with my date.

"I better go. See you guys at the dance." She turned and strutted back to Todd.

"She doesn't know when to quit," Jo said, taking Billy's arm, and heading toward the door.

"No kidding," I murmured as Shawn took my hand and we went to the door. He jerked to a stop in front of Tiffany's table and pulled me into his arms.

He brought his lips down to meet mine and I wrapped my arms around him as he deepened the kiss. He pushed his tongue past my lips and I snuck mine through his. Shawn was letting me mark my territory and I loved him for it.

The sound of someone clearing their throat had us breaking the kiss, but not eye contact. After a second, he winked and pulled me toward the door.

"You should have seen the look on her face," Billy said, walking toward the Jeep.

"You guys saw?" I asked, blushing. I could kiss him in front of the whole town but Billy seeing it made me blush? What was wrong with me?

"Yeah, Tiffany just about fell out of her chair," Jo said, laughing.

"If her jaw was hanging open any wider she would have dislocated it." Billy laughed.

"I just hope she gets the picture," Shawn said quietly.

"It was worth a try," I said as we got to the Jeep and he opened the door for me. Billy did the same for Jo. Once we were all in, we made our way to the high school, where the prom was waiting for us.

CHAPTER 31

When we entered the gym, I was taken back by the decorations and the lights. The theme was a *Midsummer's Night Dream*, and everything looked like a forest, there were even little creatures from the play hidden in the trees. We did the picture thing, again, then entered the party.

As soon as we went into the gym it felt like everyone stopped what they were doing to stare at us. I wanted to shrink back, take Shawn, and run out of there, but Shawn pulled me forward, not giving me a chance to escape. I stood, pulled my shoulders back, then let Shawn guide me to a table. He took his jacket off and hung it on the back of a chair.

"Are you ready to dance?" he asked, tapping his foot to the upbeat song the DJ was playing.

"Dance?" I looked at him questioningly. "I don't know how to dance."

"Then now is a great time to learn." Shawn took my hand and led me onto the dance floor. He wrapped one arm around my waist and took my hand with the other one, before I knew what he was doing we were moving around the floor to the beat of the music. "See, you can dance. Just feel the beat and I'll show you where to go."

I laughed, hardly believing I was dancing with the best-looking guy in the room. The song ended and a slow one started. Shawn stopped, let go of my hand, and put it around my waist. "Put your hands behind my neck," he said, pulling me in until the only thing keeping us from touching everywhere were our clothes.

I rested my head against his shoulder and let him move us to the beat of the music. "This is perfect," I whispered in his ear, and he squeezed me tighter. In that moment nothing could bother me, not the mark on my wrist, the goblin trying to suck my soul out, or Tiffany trying to steal my boyfriend. Everything fell away except for the feeling of Shawn's strong arms around me.

When the song ended and a fast one started, he pulled away and looked down at me. "Do you want to keep dancing?"

I looked around at the other people who were already moving to the music. "Why not? It's a dance, right?"

We danced until they started to announce the royal court and I excused myself to go to the bathroom. It was blessedly empty when I walked in. I went into the stall and did my business. When I was done, I flushed the toilet, and was about to unlock the stall door when the outside door opened, and I froze.

"Did you see Liz Lawson?" someone whose voice I didn't recognize asked.

"Yes, I wonder how much she spent at the salon." I heard Tiffany say, recognizing her voice immediately.

"No kidding, I wonder how she got the oil out from under her nails."

"Her hands are disgusting; it looks like she never washes them. She must be a pretty good lay if she is here with Shawn. What else would he see in her?"

I looked down at my hands. They were clean now, the soap they gave me at the salon worked. My throat tightened, and I felt tears burn the back of my eyes. I never knew girls could be so mean, it made me glad I never hung out with them.

The door opened and someone else came in to join the girls. "Liz are you in here?" Jo asked, looking around.

Great, I thought, I was planning on waiting until they left to leave the stall, but now I had no choice. I took a breath, opened the stall door, and walked to the sink ignoring the now silent girls staring at me in disdain. I held my head high, washed my hands, dried them, and pretended to check my makeup before turning to Jo. "Sorry, are you ready?"

"Yeah," she said, looking confused. I walked out the door with Jo trailing behind me. I entered the gym and looked around for Shawn. "Hey, are you okay? What was going on in there?" Jo asked, taking ahold of my hand.

I pulled away from her wiping a tear off my cheek and turned to face her. "Tiffany was talking shit behind my back again. I need to find Shawn, I want to go home. This was a mistake." I turned and began searching the crowd for him.

"Don't go. She's just jealous because you look better without makeup than she does with it. Come on we can still have a good time." Jo rubbed her hand on my back.

"Hey, we got punch for you two," Billy said, coming up behind me.

I turned trying not to meet their eyes. "Thanks," I mumbled, taking the punch from Shawn, and swallowing the cup in one gulp. "Can we please go now?"

"What? What's wrong?" He gave his cup to Billy and pulled my chin up with his fingers. My eyes were filling with tears and I jerked away from him. "What happened?"

"I don't want to talk about it. This was a mistake. Can we please leave? Or you stay and have fun, I'll call my dad he'll come get me." I would not let myself fall apart in front of everyone. I turned, hurried out of the gym, down the hallway, and out into the cool night air. Tears streamed down my face as I walked to Shawn's Jeep where my phone and everything else I brought was. I pulled on the door handle and it didn't open. I slammed my palm into the door in frustration before I bent over and sobbed. There was no way I was going back into the gym. I would just sit here until someone came out. Then I would ask to borrow their phone.

Something was draped over my shoulders and I stood and sniffled.

"Do you want to talk about it?" Shawn asked, as he rubbed my arms up and down trying to warm them up.

I gasped trying to hold a sob in. Talking about it was going to make me cry even harder. "Can you unlock the car? I just need to get my stuff, then you can go back and enjoy yourself."

"Come on, Billy's truck is here. We don't have to wait for them." He unlocked the Jeep and opened the door for me.

I was trying to hold the tears in, but I couldn't. They came spilling out and my nose clogged up with snot. I sniffled wanting to wipe my nose on something, but I did not want to get Shawn's jacket dirty.

"You can wipe your nose on the jacket. It's a rental, they'll dry-clean it before the next guy wears it."

"Thanks." I wiped my nose on the sleeve as he started up the Jeep.

"Do you want me to take you home?" he asked, after he put his seat belt on.

"I'm sorry, Shawn. I didn't mean to ruin your night. You can go back in if you want. I know you were having a good time." I looked at my dark reflection in the side view mirror. I couldn't look at Shawn, I felt horrible for making him leave.

"I was only having a good time because I was there with you. I don't want to be there if you're not. Tell me what I can do to make you feel better."

I wiped the moisture from under my eyes and looked over at him. "I don't want to go home, but I can't go back in there. Is there anything you want to do?"

He smiled. "I had a plan in case you didn't want to stay the whole time. How about we go look at the stars for a while?" He put the Jeep in drive and we rolled toward the exit of the high school. "You are going to have to show me a good spot though."

"I know where we should go. Turn left at the end of the parking lot." I smiled, at least he wasn't mad he was leaving prom for me.

Twenty minutes later we were parked in a wide meadow, surrounded by twisted pine trees, and flattened grass from the year before. I changed out of my dress and into my jeans and hoodie in the back of the Jeep, while Shawn changed behind a rock. Feeling more like myself, I pulled my rune out of the bag, pulled it over my hair, then tucked it under my hoodie. I tied my Chucks and walked out to the meadow and looked up at the night sky. There wasn't a cloud in sight as I watched the stars lazily twinkle from the heavens.

Shawn came out from behind the rock and went to the back of the Jeep. He opened the rear hatch, pulled out two blankets, and a basket. He turned on a flashlight and came back to where I was standing.

"What's all that?" I asked.

"Can't a guy have a backup plan?" He spread out one blanket on the ground and motioned for me to move over to it, then he sat next to me, and spread the other blanket over our legs. He put the basket down in front of us and pulled out a bottle of champagne.

"Wow, is that for real? What's the occasion?" I watched as he pulled out two glasses and a small box about six inches by four inches.

"No, it's sparkling cider and it's prom, I think it's occasion enough." He thumbed the cork on the bottle and it went flying out into the night. He held the bottle away from the blanket as some of the liquid bubbled out. He filled up a glass and handed it to me then filled his own. "To us, one more year of high school and we are done." He clinked his glass with mine and we both took a sip.

I giggled as the bubbles exploded in my mouth, then smacked my lips together. "That's good."

"I'm glad you like it." He picked up the box, opened it and offered it to me. Inside were chocolate covered strawberries.

"Those look too good to eat," I said, picking one up, and biting the tip off. "But it won't stop me."

"They are so good." Shawn turned the flashlight off and picked one out then put the box down on the blanket. He moved closer to me and took a bite of the strawberry goodness then sipped his cider.

I took a sip of mine and finished off the strawberry. "Shawn, thanks this was a great idea." I sat my glass on the ground next to the blanket and I lay down to stare at the sky.

"I'm glad you're enjoying it." He lay down next to me. "Wow, the only time I've seen the sky like this was in the planetarium. It's amazing."

"We're pretty spoiled. I couldn't imagine living in a place where you couldn't see the stars." I found Shawn's hand and squeezed it. How did I get lucky enough to find a guy who knew exactly what I needed to feel better? "About earlier, I owe you an explanation."

"Don't worry about it. I'm just glad you didn't make me take you home." He brought our linked hands up to his mouth and kissed the back of my hand.

"No, I ruined it and you deserve to know why." I turned my head to look at him then back to look at the sky. "You know I'm a tomboy, I have never liked hanging out with girls, well except Jo and Heather, they're cool. Well, when I was in the bathroom, Tiffany and some other girl came in and they were talking crap about me."

"What were they saying?" I saw Shawn turn his head to look at me out of the corner of my eye.

"They were making fun of me because I was all dressed up, that my mom must have spent a ton of money on me for me to look this good. Then they said I must be a good lay since you were with me."

"Those bitches." I felt him tense up next to me.

"That's why I don't hang out with girls. They are always out for each other. Their drama is not worth my time. I feel like an idiot because I let them get to me and ruin our night. I'm sorry." I squeezed his hand and turned to look at him.

"Are you happy right now?"

"Yes."

"Then they didn't ruin our night." He leaned into me and kissed me softly, and heat that had nothing to do with the blankets began to burn through me. I didn't think kissing could get any better until he deepened the kiss, our mouths opened, and our tongues tangled together before breaking apart and coming together again. He moved without breaking contact until he was above me with half his body leaning against mine. His hand came around my waist and squeezed my side. I wrapped my arms around his back and tried to pull him closer without breaking the kiss.

We broke apart for a minute to catch our breath and he began kissing my neck, moving up to my ear and gently bit it. I let out a moan, found his neck then kissed and sucked at it. I wanted him closer, but there was only one way we could get closer and I was not ready for it.

"Shawn let's slow down for a minute," I said, with my chin resting on his shoulder.

He groaned but pulled away and lay down on his back pulling me with him, so my head rested on his chest. "You're right. I promised your dad no 'hanky-panky.' Can we just lay here for a while?"

"Okay." I kissed his chest through his hoodie.

We lay there looking up at the blanket of stars covering the night sky for a few minutes until a huge meteor streaked above us. "Wow," Shawn said, squeezing me. "Did you see that? I've never seen one that big before. "

"Yeah, neither have I. Make a wish." I told him, before wishing we could close the gate and remove my mark.

"I already did. What about you?"

"Me too." My eyes were starting to feel heavy, I closed them, telling myself it would only be for a second.

"Are you warm enough?" He wrapped his arms around me.

"Huh? Yeah, snug as a bug in a rug." I felt warm and safe. I let myself drift, knowing Shawn would wake me up if I fell asleep, and I'm sure he would have, if he had not fallen asleep too.

CHAPTER 32

I was standing at the mouth of the mineshaft and the voices were calling to me, inviting me to enter. I knew I was dreaming, but I didn't remember going to bed, then it hit me, I was sleeping under the stars with Shawn. I froze, I didn't have the protection of a dreamcatcher.

I was starting to panic. I wasn't ready to take on the mare. I closed my eyes and imagined my favorite Colt 1911 and a holster. I found the gun on my hip and smiled at the comfort it gave me, but I was going to need more than one gun. I thought of the machete I used when I trained, and it appeared in my hand.

I didn't want to be in the clearing, there was nothing I could do to help the voices calling to me yet. I needed to find Shawn, the goblin never showed up when I was with Shawn or Heather. I closed my eyes and thought of him. I opened my eyes, but I was still standing at the mouth of the shaft. Shawn must not have been asleep. I was about to look for Heather when something stopped me.

"Liz, help me," Shawn's voice called from the dark abyss in front of me. "I can't beat them on my own."

The mare was trying to lure me into the darkness. It wasn't Shawn, if he was sleeping I would have been able to go to him. I started to walk away from the shaft, but the wind began to blow in my face. With each step I took, it became harder and harder to move forward. I was losing ground. I needed help, and without Shawn, there was only one person I could think of.

Heather. The world shifted, and I was standing next to Heather in the diner. She was shooting at a mare ten feet away. I took my Colt from my holster and began to fire at the goblin. "What are you doing here?" Heather asked, between pulling the trigger on her gun.

"Shawn and I were looking at the stars and I fell asleep without my dreamcatcher. The goblin was after me. Shawn must not be asleep because I can't find him. I thought I would hang out with you until he wakes me up," I said, emptying my clip and reloading it without a thought. This mare was different than my stalker, he was tall and skinny like my stalker, but he was covered with a light dusting of coarse brown fur from head to toe. Now riddled with bullet holes, he fell to his knees a few feet from us.

Heather walked behind it, pulled its head back, took a knife from her boot and cut its head off, then threw the head to the other side of the room. "Well, since you are here you can help, it's been a busy night with prom and all. It seems like everyone in town is having a nightmare." She walked back over to me and took my hand. "Come on, let's get to the next one before it's too late."

We jumped and found ourselves in the high school gym. It was still decorated for prom, but the paper trees and animals were real, swaying and moving to a breeze only they could feel. We moved out of the trees as screams and moaning assaulted our ears.

The dance floor was littered with bodies. Blood pooled under most of them. People were kneeling over the bodies with their faces resting on the torsos of the fallen. I moved closer to one and bent a knee to comfort the mourning person. As soon as I touched her shoulder her face jerked up and she met my eyes.

"Heather, zombies," I yelled, jumping to my feet, and pulling my Colt from its holster. I aimed and pulled the trigger hitting the zombie in the head. I put the Colt back in the holster and manifested a shotgun as I ran back to Heather. "The movies were right, a shot to the head and they die," I yelled to Heather.

We began moving around the room shooting anything that wasn't human. I had to constantly think about reloading the gun, and the zombies were dropping like flies. Hopefully we would find the victim before it was too late.

Something grabbed me from behind. I whipped around to see the zombie version of Billy. His face was missing its skin on one side. One of his eyeballs had been pulled out of its socket and rested on his cheek. It rolled back and forth as if trying to understand what it was seeing. Only half his mouth would close while the other half hung on by tendons and swung back and forth as he moved his head.

He grabbed ahold of my shoulder and started to pull me toward him. I pulled up the machete up to stab him in his good eye, but his arms were in the way. I kicked and punched at him, but there was nothing I could do. "Heather," I yelled right before the zombie's head popped covering me in brains and blood.

Wiping the grey matter from my eyes, I looked around for Heather, but my eyes landed on Shawn. He ran up to me. "Are you okay?"

"Yeah, just helping Heather." I looked around for her but didn't see her.

"You fell asleep without the dreamcatcher." Shawn pulled a machete from the air.

"So, did you by the looks of it." I gave him a tight smile. "Behind you," I said, bringing my shotgun back up, but Shawn was quicker. He pulled up a

Glock and shot the zombie through the eye. "Let's stand back-to-back."

"Good idea." I turned and backed up to Shawn's back as we killed zombie after zombie. Some I recognized as students or teachers, others were so disfigured, I would never know who I was killing. When there was nothing but a pile of rotting flesh, I looked around.

"Where's Heather?" And with a thought we were standing beside the stage where the DJ booth was. There was a chunk of flesh missing from her shoulder and she was trying to stand. I bent down and put my arm around her to help her. "Heather you're hurt. Wake yourself up."

"No, I want to make sure you're safe," she said, taking a ragged breath after each word. Then she passed out, falling forward into us. We caught her and laid her on the ground.

I looked at Shawn. "What do we do? How can she wake herself up if she isn't conscious?"

"Fuck," he ripped off his shirt and pushed it against her wound. "Hold this and keep her safe. I'm going to look for help," he said before disappearing.

I took my hoodie off and wadded it up to make a pillow for her. "It's going to be alright, Heather. Shawn is going to get help." I stood and looked around the gym for anything that didn't belong. "Whose dream is this anyway?" I did not see anyone who needed help.

"Yours," the scratchy voice of my stalker said from behind me. "I knew you wouldn't be able to protect yourself forever. Now I can cross planes and eat until I am satisfied."

I whirled around to see my goblin, disguised as Tiffany. "Good luck with that," I said, before shooting him in the head. The bullet hit him between his eyes, he leaned back to absorb the recoil, almost lost his footing, but found it and smiled as the hole from the bullet disappeared.

The mare was stronger than last time Shawn fought him if a bullet didn't stop it. I wanted to think about it, but he launched himself at me. I shot him again, but it didn't slow him down. Before I had time to think of anything else I was on my back with the knees of the goblin on my chest making it hard to breathe. Panic took over my body and I was frozen as he brought his mouth to mine ready to give me the kiss of death.

This was it. Jon was right. I wasn't even going to make it a month with this mark, I thought as my stalker's mouth connected with mine. I thought of my friends and parents, of Shawn. He would be blamed for my death. He let me fall asleep without a dreamcatcher. I could not let him suffer for my death when it wasn't his fault. I had to fight, I closed my eyes and thought of my hunting knife. My hand curled around the hilt and I slammed the point into the goblin's ear canal. He reared back grabbing his head. I pushed him off me and jumped to my, feet never taking my eyes off him.

"Why?" he screamed at me, pulling the knife out of his head, and throwing it back at me.

I jumped out of the way as it passed by me. "Why what?"

"Why couldn't I suck out your soul?" he bellowed, starting to circle me. "As soon as I touched my lips to yours I should have been able to take over your mind and dine on your soul."

I moved as he did, confused as to why I was still alive. I felt the tug of the rune around my neck and smiled. It wasn't broken, I just didn't need it when I had my dreamcatcher. I picked up the machete I dropped when he got the jump on me. I ran toward him holding the primitive sword out as he ran towards me with a battle cry. I swung the blade across his neck and watched as his head fell to the ground. I waited for his body to crumble to the ground, but it still ran toward me. I brought up a can of hair spray and flicked a zippo in my other hand. I aimed before pushing down on the hairspray and a jet of fire engulfed him, but now a flaming body ran toward me, instead of just a headless one.

I thought of a running chainsaw and brought it up ready to dismember him. I waited until he was within striking range, then I cut into his body, starting at the neck, and working my way down. I felt the heat from the fire's flames and thought of a fireman's jacket. Protected from the burning corpse, I finished cutting the body in half. The halves fell to the ground, no longer having balance to stay upright it flopped across the floor in my direction. I went to one half and used the saw to cut off his leg then his arm. A hand grabbed my ankle and I jumped before seeing it was the other half of the goblin.

"This is not the end, little bitch. I'll be back before you know it," he said, somehow able to talk even though he did not have a voice box to talk through.

"Rot in hell," I yelled, using the chain saw to cut his head in half.

When I looked up, Jon was standing next to Heather, with his legs slightly spread and his arms crossed over his chest watching me.

"Is she going to be alright?" I asked.

"Yes, no thanks to you." He frowned while his foot tapped insistently on the hardwood floor.

"How is this my fault?" I asked, getting mad. "All I did was fall asleep and try to outrun my nightmare."

"Just because you are Victor's daughter doesn't give you the right to fight the mares. It takes years of training to be proficient at it."

"This is my dream. What was I supposed to do, let them kill me?" I crossed my arms over my chest, ignoring the blood and viscera covering them.

"No, you could have waited for someone to help you who

had more experience."

"Heather and Shawn are the only ones I know. Where is Shawn?" I asked, looking around.

"He was here?" Jon looked around searching for his son.

"Yeah, he went to get help after Heather passed out." I closed my eyes and thought of Shawn. When I opened them, I was back in the forest in front of the mineshaft. Shawn was standing just outside the opening, staring into the darkness.

"Shawn," I called, not wanting to get any closer to the entrance than I had to. He didn't move, it was almost like he didn't hear me. "Shawn." I ran up to him, took his hand, and started to pull him away from the opening. "Come on, we have to get away from here. There's something wrong with this place."

"They're begging me for help. I need to go in there and save them." He tried to pull away from me, but I held him back.

"No, Shawn, it's a trick. They have been trying to lure me down there every time I dream of this place. We need to find another way to save them." WIth my hand firmly holding his I thought of Heather and we were both back in the gym.

"Where were you?" Jon asked Shawn.

"In front of a mineshaft, there were people calling to me for help. I couldn't go down the shaft though, something was holding me back." He looked at me and squeezed my hand in thanks.

Jon looked at me then back to Shawn. "I'm going to get Heather home, you need to wake up and take her home."

"Yes, sir," Shawn said, before disappearing.

"Come to the house tomorrow, we need to talk," Jon said, putting a hand on Heather, and disappearing as Shawn had.

CHAPTER 33

"Liz are you alright?" Shawn asked, waking me up.

I blinked a few times and pulled the blanket tighter around me to keep the chill away. "That was the worst nightmare I have ever had, Shawn." I closed my eyes, found my rune on the outside of my hoodie, and rubbed it absently. "Heather?" I sat bolt upright. "Will she be okay?"

"She'll be fine. Remember what I said, as long as you don't die in the dream there is nothing to worry about." Shawn pulled me to him. "I'm sorry I left you to get help. What happened after I left?"

"It's okay, I'm alive, the rune saved me," I said out of the side of my mouth.

"What do you mean? Tell me what happened."

I told Shawn about the goblin and when I was done, tears of relief that I had survived were streaming down my cheeks, and I was shaking uncontrollably. It was the scariest thing that had ever happened to me. Shawn pulled me closer and rocked me, telling me everything was going to be okay. After I stopped shaking, he let go of me.

"I should get you home, it's late or early depending on how you look at it."

"Your dad wants me to come over to the house today. He said we needed to talk. Should I be worried?" I asked, watching the darkness turn to twilight as the sun got closer to peeking over the mountains.

"As long as you are not his son, you have nothing to worry about." Shawn pulled me to him and held me for a few seconds before I pulled away and started putting everything back in the basket.

"Thanks for the reassurance." I stood, pulled the blanket off him, and began folding it.

"He's very strict with me is all I'm saying. I'm sure it will be fine. I'll go start the Jeep." He stood, took the basket, went to the driver's side door and opened it.

I pulled the blanket off the ground and shook it out trying to dislodge anything stuck to it. "I'm sorry, Shawn. I hope you don't get in trouble because of me." I folded the blanket and put it to the back of the Jeep.

"I don't know why I would, it was your dream, it wasn't like you were trying to be a Knight or anything." He came around back and put the basket in. "I'm sure it will be fine." He took me in his arms and gave me a hug. "I'm sorry we fell asleep and ruined the night." He pulled me in tighter and kissed the top of my head.

"It's not your fault we fell asleep, and it didn't ruin the night. I had a great time." I kissed his chest through his shirt. "Why don't we grab some breakfast before we head home?"

"Is there anything open at," he brought his wrist up to check his watch. "Four-thirty in the morning?"

"When we get to town the café will be open." I let go of him and went to the passenger-side door.

"Sounds better than going home and dealing with my dad," Shawn said before I shut my door.

"Agreed," I said after he got in and buckled up.

Once we were back in town my phone started to go off. I dug

through my bag and pulled it out. It was a text message from my mom. **Billy said you and Shawn left prom early. Where are you? Are you alright?**

"Billy," I almost yelled, startling Shawn.

"What is it? Is something wrong with Billy?" Shawn asked, glancing at me from the corner of his eye.

"Not yet, but he's going to have a hard time dislodging my foot from his butt when I see him." I looked over to Shawn and he gave me an expectant look. "He told my mom we left early last night, and she wants to know where I am."

"Billy isn't going to have to worry about one foot, he is going to have to worry about two feet."

I dialed my house number and waited for it to ring. "Liz, where are you? Is everything okay?"

"Yes, Mom, Shawn and I went up to the meadow to watch the stars and we fell asleep. We're going to the café for breakfast then he will bring me home."

"You fell asleep without a dreamcatcher? Oh my God, sweetie I'm so glad you are alright."

"I had Victor's rune, Mom. I'm fine." I blew out a breath, at least I didn't have to keep it a secret from her anymore.

"Shawn didn't do anything you weren't comfortable with, did he?" I could feel the panic in her voice.

"No, Mom we fell asleep with all our clothes on and they were still on when we woke up."

"Okay, good. I'll see you when you get home," she said, ending the call.

I hit the end button on the phone and let out a breath. "That went better than I thought it would."

"She's not mad? Did you have a curfew?" he asked.

"She sounded more worried than anything. They said as long as there was no drinking I could stay out as long as I wanted."

"Well, we did have sparkling cider." He laughed and pulled the Jeep over in front of Twisted Café.

"Oh no, she won't like that at all." I laughed then undid my seat belt and opened the door.

"True," Shawn said when we met on the sidewalk. He looked at me for a second. "Please don't take this the wrong way, but there are some napkins in the glove box. You might want to clean your face up before we go in. You know how people talk."

I didn't understand what he was talking about until I got back in the Jeep, pulled the visor down, and opened the vanity mirror. I cringed at what I saw. I was wearing mascara halfway down my face, and there was eyeshadow on my cheek. My hair was sticking out all over the place. I opened the glove box and found something better than napkins: wet wipes. I pulled one out and got to work. When my face was makeup free, I pulled my bag out of the backseat and found my brush. I pulled the bobby pins out of my hair and dragged the brush through it then I found a hair tie and put it up in a ponytail. Finally, looking more like myself, I got out of the Jeep, put my hands on my hips, and glowered at Shawn.

"What?" he asked, holding his hands in the air.

"Next time I wake up looking like that tell me before I go anywhere." It was nice he did not seem to care how terrifying I looked though.

"I promise. Can we eat now?" He looked from me to the café.

"Yes." I went to the door of the café and held it for him.

We sat at a table near a window and waited for the waitress to get us our coffee. After I had my first sip I started with the questions. "What did you think of the mineshaft?"

Shawn looked around to make sure there was no one near

enough to hear us. "I have never seen anything like that in a dream before."

"I have dreamed of it at least four times. I think it means something." I took a sip of my coffee.

"You might be right, but it is too dangerous for us to investigate," Shawn said, pouring cream into his mug.

"Agreed but what about the people who need help?"

"I want to help them but I don't know how." He blew on his coffee and took a sip before continuing.

"Do you think Jo would help us?"

"Yeah, I'm sure she would." Shawn gave me a tight smile as our waitress came over with our food and put it down.

"Can I get you anything else?" she asked.

"I think we're good," I said, almost drooling over the pancakes sitting in front of me.

We dug into our food and enjoyed a comfortable silence.

After breakfast, Shawn took me home and helped me bring my bag inside, before kissing me goodbye chastely while my parents watched. "I'll see you later. Let me know before you leave?"

"I will." I watched him get in his Jeep and drive away.

"We need to talk young lady," Dad said, walking away from me and into the living room.

I looked to my mom, and she put her hands on her hips. "Now."

"Okay." I followed my dad into the living room and Mom followed me. He was standing in front of the fireplace with his arms crossed over his chest.

"Sit down." He pointed to the couch, and I went over and sat while my mom stood in front of me.

What was going on? I thought to myself while folding my hands and putting them in my lap.

"You told us you were going to stay at the high school all night. Billy called at ten last night wondering if Shawn had gotten you home safely," Mom said.

"We stayed up worrying all night after he called. We called the hospital, the sheriff, and all the hotels," Dad said, shaking his fist at me.

"I'm sorry. I should've called. Some girls were being really mean to me and I had to get out of there. Shawn and I went to look at the stars and we fell asleep."

They both stared at me while I talked looking for any indication I was lying. "Did he act like a gentleman?" Mom finally asked.

"Why wouldn't he? We lay on a blanket and watched the stars and fell asleep. It was way better than having to listen to a bunch of girls talk crap about me." I wanted to go up to my room and take a shower, but the look in my parents' eyes told me I wasn't out of this yet.

"What did they say?" Mom asked, looking concerned.

"I don't want to get into it, but it reminded me why I don't hang out with girls." I blinked back the tears threatening to fall.

"You're sure nothing happened with Shawn?" Dad uncrossed his arms and took a step toward me.

"The worst thing we did was French kiss," I said, feeling myself blush.

Dad took a step back, turning a shade of red.

"Then go get cleaned up. I'm sorry they picked on you. They were probably just jealous." Mom came over to me as I stood and gave me a hug. "You shouldn't have let them ruin your night."

"They didn't, we had a great time if you don't count the time I spent with them. Don't worry, Mom, I won't let them get to me again." I squeezed her tight, let go, grabbed my bag, and went upstairs.

When I came back downstairs an hour later my parents were arguing in the kitchen, I snuck to the door to listen when I heard my name.

"You can't trust her, Sandy, she's almost seventeen. We need to get her on birth control," Dad said.

"Burt, she has always been honest with me. I've never had a reason not to trust her, when she's ready she will ask," Mom said, sounding tired of the conversation.

"There is something about Shawn I don't trust. How can we stop her from seeing him?"

"We can't, and I don't know what you are talking about. He seems like a nice young man to me. Just because he hasn't spent his entire life here doesn't mean he is going to take advantage of Liz."

"He reminds me of *him*," Dad said, emphasizing the last word.

"Who? Victor? Are you out of your mind? He looks nothing like Victor." I heard my mom get up and walk away from the door. "Why would that matter anyway?"

"I don't know. It's just, I get a bad feeling about him. Like something bad is going to happen to Liz because of him."

I marched into the kitchen, I was done listening. "Dad, stop. You are being ridiculous." I almost said Shawn had saved me more than once in my dreams, but I caught myself. "Why do you hate him?"

He blew out a breath, unwrapped his arms, and rested them on his thighs. "I don't hate him. What I don't like is how you are falling head over heels for him. You've never had a boyfriend, and I don't want him to break your heart."

"Dad, how many times did you have your heart broken before you found Mom?" I sat in the chair across from him and folded my arms in front of my chest.

"It doesn't matter. I don't want your heart to ever be broken. You can break all the hearts of boys you want, but they can't break yours."

"Burt, I think that was the sweetest thing you've ever said." Mom went behind him and put a hand on his shoulder.

"I know you want to protect me, but getting your heart broken is part of growing up. I don't think Shawn will break my heart, but if he does then at least I can come home and cry on your shoulder. I won't be away at college on my own with no one to help me through it." I reached across the table and took his hand in mine giving it a squeeze. "I love you, Dad."

He sat silently for a minute before squeezing my hand back. "I love you too, sweetheart."

"I have to go. Shawn's dad needs to talk to me." I moved to stand.

"About what?" Mom asked, looking concerned.

"I don't know, he called Shawn this morning and asked me to stop by today. I shouldn't be long."

"Will you call me if you are going to be late?" Mom asked.

"Yes, but I won't be. I have school tomorrow and a ton of studying to do. I won't be long."

CHAPTER 34

I parked next to Shawn's Jeep in the parking lot of the mansion, I was more nervous than when I came to meet Shawn's parents. I had no idea why Jon wanted to see me, but I didn't think he was going to ask me to join the Knight Flyers.

A knock on my side window made me jump out of my seat. I looked over to see Shawn laughing at me. I flipped him off and opened the door. "You scared the crap out of me." I got out of the Jeep and mock-hit him.

"You looked stressed out, I thought it would relieve some of the tension." He grabbed my hand and closed the door of my Jeep for me. We walked toward the same door we used last time I was there.

"It worked for a second." My stomach was tightening up again.

"It will be fine. He can't do anything to hurt you," he said, holding the door for me.

"I know but promise you will go in with me." I looked over at him as we walked to the staircase.

"I will do everything I can to stay by your side, but you have to understand my dad runs this place like the military. If he tells me to leave, I will, or I'll be grounded for a month. I don't think I could survive not seeing you for a month." He brought our linked hands to his mouth and kissed the back of my hand. I think it was becoming one of his favorite places to kiss me.

"I will be a big girl, if I have to. I don't want to go a month without seeing you, either." I gave him a weak smile.

Shawn knocked on the door of his dad's office when we arrived. I heard a muffled voice call for us to come in.

"Liz, Shawn, please have a seat," he said, without looking up from his computer.

Once we were seated in front of his desk he swiveled his chair to look at us. "How long have you been able to manifest weapons in your dreams?" He cut right to the chase.

I thought for a minute. "I don't know; I never really thought about it like you do. I always thought it was the dream doing it not me."

"What about dream walking? How long have you been able to do that?" He put his elbows on the desk and rested his chin on his laced hands.

"You mean move from dream to dream?" He nodded his head. "Shawn showed me how. It's pretty easy."

"It appears you have inherited your father's talent even though you mother has none." He leaned back in his chair and looked at the ceiling as if in deep thought. "Shawn, leave us."

I jerked my eyes to Shawn pleading with him to stay. He mouthed 'sorry' to me and got up. "Dad, I was teaching her to protect herself, I wasn't trying to go behind your back," he said, backing to the door.

"That will be all, Shawn," Jon said, waiting for Shawn to leave. After the door shut, he brought his chair to my level and met my eyes. "What will it take for you to leave my son alone?"

"Why do you want me to leave him alone? What have I done to make you think I should?" I was confused, I thought he wanted to talk to me about what happened the night before.

"You are distracting him from his job. I don't want him to get attached to you. With your mark, you are not long for this world, and I can't let his pining for you distract him from his life's purpose."

"I am going to find a way to remove the mark, in the meantime I have all the protection I need. I will not let the mare get me, and I won't stop seeing Shawn because of you."

"What protection? You mean your dreamcatcher? It only works when you have it. Look what happened last night," he trailed off, leveling his gaze on me.

"I'm not talking about the dreamcatcher." I pulled the rune from under my shirt and showed it to him. "I'm talking about this."

Jon leaned forward to get a closer look at it. "Where did you get that?" he asked, almost growling the word out before lunging for it. I sat back in my chair and put the rune back under my shirt.

"It was Victor's, I found it with his things. It is the reason I survived last night, while you were standing by doing nothing." I didn't know how long Jon had been there while I was fighting the mare, and I didn't want to tell Shawn that his dad made no move to help me.

"I was protecting my daughter, besides, you had it under control," he lost the growl to his voice. "Did you tell Shawn I didn't help you?"

"No, I wanted to take it up with you first. I understand wanting to protect Heather, and I have no idea what she needed protecting from, but I know where I stand with you now, and I won't forget it."

"Are you trying to blackmail me?" he asked, using his growly voice.

"No, but I want to learn how to be a Knight Flyer. I want to save people and protect myself."

"No, you are marked as it is. You will be a magnet to mares, you will endanger more people than you'll save."

"I will draw them away from innocent people and kill them. I will make everyone's job easier."

"Like father like daughter," he paused for a second. "What if I could get you into the Air Force Academy?"

"You could do that?" My mouth gaped open. It was incredibly hard to get into the Air Force Academy.

"I wouldn't offer unless I could make it happen." He leaned forward and rested his forearms on the desk, lacing his fingers together.

I thought about it for half a second. If I was going to get into the Air Force Academy I wanted to get there on my own merits, not because I was bribed. "I don't need your help to get in. Train me, please."

"Train you so you can leave just like your father? I think not." He pushed back from his chair and stood.

"I won't stop until everyone is safe from the mares, I am not Victor."

"He left us when we needed him the most," he bellowed at me coming around the desk. "Do you know how many Knights we lost after he left?"

"No, and I'm sorry, but I'm not him. Why won't you give me a chance?"

"Every time I look at you, all I see is him," his voice softened before he shook his head. "You're too old to start the training."

"Shawn and Heather both said they are amazed with what I can do without any training. Give me a chance."

"No, before you know it you will take on a mare you can't beat. I can't afford to lose anyone else," he yelled at me.

"I am not my father. Give me a chance, give me and Shawn a chance. I won't disappoint you."

"If you joined us, you will have to reconsider all your future plans."

"You mean going to the Air Force Academy?" I swallowed hard.

"Yes, you will have to live near a command center and be available at all times." He laced his fingers together.

I had dreamed about going to the Academy since I was in fifth grade. I wanted to be a mechanical engineer and help NASA get to Mars but being a Knight Flyer was so much bigger than NASA would ever be. People needed to be saved, and I had the talent to help them. How could I say no? "I don't know if I could live with myself if I ignored a gift designed to save people's lives. It's a sacrifice I am willing to make."

"If we take you on you are going to have to quit your job and plan on spending your summer here. How are your parents going to feel about you spending the summer at your boyfriend's house?"

Crap, it was going to be a hard sell. "If you talk to them, there is a good chance they will agree." I had no idea if they would let me or not, but if he talked to them there would be a good chance they would go along with it.

"I'll draw up a contract. You will dedicate five years to our cause, then we can renegotiate."

"Are you going to pay me? In five years I will be twenty-two, I'll need to be making my own money."

"All trainees get a stipend, when you pass the training you will receive a salary based on your tenure. I'll include it all in the contract."

"Then we are in agreement?" I stood and offered my hand.

He stared at it for a moment then took my hand. "We are."

CHAPTER 35

Mom was waiting for me when I got home from Shawn's. I was nervous, I had no idea how she was going to take what I had to tell her about my new job. "What did Shawn's dad want to talk to you about, dear?" she asked, stirring a pot on the stove.

"Where's Dad?" I asked, looking around the room. He had no idea what was going on with my dreams, and I wasn't ready to tell him about them yet.

"He is watching hockey in the man cave, don't worry he won't hear us." She moved to lean against the counter.

"I don't know how much you know about what Victor did, or what he was trying to do, but Jon wants to train me to work for him." I didn't know if I was going to have to spell it out for her or not, but this was the best way to find out.

"I don't want you risking your life in dreams to help that man. Victor did not like him at all." She folded her arms across his chest.

"Mom, it's not just saving people, it's learning to protect myself too. This mark is like a homing beacon for the goblins. If I don't learn how to fight them, I don't know how long I will survive." My hands started to shake as I talked, and I shoved them into my pockets to hide it from Mom. She didn't need to know how scared I was.

"But, can you trust him?"

"No, but I trust Shawn, Heather, and Jo. They have been helping me, and I'm sure there are other people who will help me too."

"I don't like this, Elizabeth." She took a step toward me with her arms out and I fell into them trying to hold back the tears threatening to fall.

"I don't either, but what other choice do I have?" I squeezed her tighter.

"I don't know, but we are going to have to find a way to sell this to your dad."

I smiled and pulled away from her. "Thank you, Mom. I know this is the right thing to do."

"Me too, I just don't want you to end up like Victor."

"I'm going to do everything I can to find a way to remove this mark and live a long and happy life, Mom."

We told my dad I was going to be helping with a summer camp at the mansion over the summer. It took some convincing, but I was going to start my training as soon as school let out for the summer. After dinner I did my homework then went to sleep, hoping I would see Shawn in my dreams.

As soon as I entered my dream, I thought of Shawn and found myself in his padded room. I still didn't understand how it worked, but all I had to do was think of the person I wanted to see, and if they were asleep, I would end up in their dream.

Shawn was sitting on the floor of the room with a notebook in his hand. "What good is a notebook in your dreams? Can you bring it back whenever you need it?" I asked, sitting down in front of him.

"I don't know. I've never tried but it was worth a shot." He looked up at me and smiled. "So, your talk with your parents must have gone well."

"I told my mom since she already knew half of it. She is going to let me start training as soon as school is out. We told my dad I would be helping at a science summer camp your company puts on every summer. He hates the idea of me working with you, but we convinced him when we told him how good it would look on my college applications." I looked down at the notebook. *How we are going to close the gate and remove Liz's mark*? I smiled, he did not beat around the bush.

"I'm glad your mom understands what's at stake."

"She doesn't want to lose me like she lost Victor, it wasn't a hard sell." I was nervous to start training, and I worried Jon would try to take advantage of me and attempt to steal my rune, but I didn't want to tell Shawn about it. "Are Jo and Heather coming?"

Shawn looked at his watch. "They should both be here shortly. Heather is going off active duty for a while. She has to see a shrink after what happened to her last night."

I closed my eyes and grimaced. "Why? Is she okay?"

"She's fine, it's standard protocol. If you get hurt badly in a dream you must see a doctor to make sure it won't affect your fighting. PTSD is worse in dreams than it is in real life. Your subconscious is always reminding you of it, and when you dream, it's easier to relive it. If you change the outcome in your dream it can still kill you." Shawn reached out and took my hand in his. "How are you doing after last night?"

"I'm okay, but I have my moments. Sometimes I can't stop the tears or the shaking."

"Don't worry, it will get better with time and training." He squeezed my hand reassuringly.

"I'm here, but I'm leaving my eyes closed until I'm sure you guys aren't making out or anything," Jo said, from behind me. I turned around to see her standing in the middle of the room wearing a white tank top and loose-fitting army-green pants. Her hand was over her eyes and she was tapping her foot impatiently.

"We aren't making out and all our clothes are on," Shawn said, laughing.

"Thank God." She brought her hand down and opened her eyes. "Sounds like you had quite an adventure last night."

"I guess you could say that." I stood, not feeling comfortable enough to talk about it yet.

"Did your parents ground you for not coming home until this morning?" she asked, sitting down next to me.

"No, they never said I had to stay at the high school. It wouldn't have been such a big deal if Billy hadn't called them to make sure I made it home. I'm blaming him for getting yelled at."

"He knows he's in trouble with you." She laughed and put her hands in the back pockets of her pants. "Where's Heather?"

"Here," Heather said, popping into the padded room. Her blond hair was pulled into a high ponytail leaving the pale skin of her face looking sharp and angular. She was wearing a My Little Pony T-shirt and black yoga pants. "Let's get this meeting started before Dad finds out I'm not in my own dreamscape."

I thought of a table and four chairs then sat in one. "If we are going to get anything done I need a place to sit."

"Good idea," Shawn said, getting up from the floor and moving to a chair.

With everyone seated Shawn started. "As you know, Liz's biological father was Victor Robinson. She found a box full of his stuff and she found a journal. Liz why don't you tell them what was in it."

After I told them the gist of the information in the journal Jo said, "A normal life? I'm in, but why did it cause a fight? Isn't that what we all want?"

"Jon didn't want to close the gates. He thinks of them as job security. He does not want the mares to go away."

"You're telling me your dad found a way to get rid of the mares completely and my dad wanted nothing to do with it?" Heather asked in a tight voice. I was not sure if she was mad at her dad or mine.

"Yes, I can let you look at the journal if you don't believe me."

"I believe you. I just wish my dad wasn't such a dick. How could he put the lives of so many in jeopardy, so he could keep living his life the way he wants to?"

"I don't know, I'm disappointed in him too," Shawn said, running his fingers through his hair. "But we can't let Dad know that we know why they parted ways."

"Agreed," Heather said, looking over at Jo.

"The last thing I want to do is talk to your dad about something I have no right knowing. Don't worry about me." Jo leaned back in her chair and looked at the ceiling. "What are we going to do now we know what's going on?"

"We are going to figure out how to close the gate and get rid of Liz's mark," Shawn said, letting the statement sink in.

"How? From what you said it doesn't sound like the journal tells us how to do it, or even if your dad was able to close a gate," Heather said, looking frustrated.

"It is going to take a lot of research. I don't have any of my dad's notes, but you guys have a whole library full of information on mares." I looked over to Shawn who nodded his head. "We are going to spend all our free time looking for the gate, then we will figure out how to close it."

"What if Jon finds out?" Jo asked, bringing her chair down and leveling her gaze at Shawn.

"I don't think we should plan on telling him until we close it and notify the council."

"Alright, where do we start?" Jo asked, leaning over to look at Shawn's notebook.

"Research. We split up, two of us will dig up everything we can on places like Twisted Pines where there is a large number of mares. If we find out when they arrived maybe we can pinpoint what caused the gate to open. The other two will try and find any reference on how to close the gate," Shawn said, while making notes.

"Do you think Dad would keep any information on how to close the gates around? If he is so hellbent on leaving them open, I bet he burns any information about it," Heather said, putting her elbows on the table and resting her head in her hands.

"We might have to look somewhere besides our library. The council has a ton of information online, but there are other places to look. Native folklore, myths, legends. I bet we will come up with something," Shawn said.

"How are we going to do all this research and study?" Jo asked the question I was thinking.

"I will start on the research while you guys finish up the school year, but then I expect you to pull your own weight." Heather sat up and folded her hands on the table. "I am already done with my online classes, and since I'm off active duty for the near future, I have nothing else to do."

"Thanks, Heather. In the meantime, we need to find a place where we can meet and talk without Dad finding out." Shawn looked to me. "Liz, is there a place we could meet and not be overheard?"

I thought about it. "We could meet at my house. It is the only place I can think of where we will have privacy. My parents are never home before five. If we met after school, we could make it work."

"Sounds good to me. I don't trust my parents not to bug my

room." Jo got up.

"Let's meet next Tuesday at my house then?" I asked.

"We have one more thing we need to do," Shawn said, getting up.

"What?" I asked confused.

"We are going to pay Tiffany a visit," Jo said, standing up and closing her eyes. In the next instant she was wearing a long, black cloak with a hood that covered her face and she held a scythe in her hand.

"The grim reaper? What are you thinking?" I asked, looking over to Shawn who was now dressed like Jo.

"I want her to stay away from me and stop talking shit about you. What better way to make her stop than scare the crap out of her?"

"Come on, Liz, put your custom on, let's go get even," Heather said, joining Shawn and Jo.

I thought of the cloaks they were wearing and the scythes in their hands. I looked down and admired my own cloak and scythe. "Let's do this."

"Everyone hold hands," Heather said, taking one of mine while Shawn took my other one and Jo's. The padded room evaporated into the gym, still decorated for prom. It was empty except for one couple dancing to a sappy love song. I recognized Tiffany right away and wondered who she was dreaming about dancing with. They turned in a circle, and I saw Shawn in her arms. I whipped my head around and found Shawn still holding my hand with his hood up. "It's just a dream, I'm here with you not her," he whispered.

"Let's do this. I have training in ten minutes," Jo said.

We let go of each other's hands and walked as one, over to where Tiffany was dancing.

"Tiffany," Shawn's voice bellowed and echoed around the room.

She stopped dancing and looked at us with terror. Her dream Shawn disappeared, and she backed up a step. "Wh . . .What do you want?" She held her arms up as if they would save her from us.

"You have not been a good person, have you?" Shawn asked.

"Yes, yes, I have," she said as tears began to trail down her cheek.

"What about Liz Lawson?" Heather asked.

"Oh, well. I guess I've been mean to her, but she stole my boyfriend."

"Was he really your boyfriend?" Jo asked, trying to pitch her voice lower than normal.

"No, he wasn't, but I want him to be." She let out a sob.

"He is not yours," I said, wanting to rip her hair out.

"If you do not leave Shawn and Liz alone, we will come back for you and take you to the afterlife. Do you understand?" Shawn said, holding his scythe out menacingly.

"I promise, please don't kill me." Tiffany turned and ran from the gym.

Everyone started to laugh, and I pulled my hood back. "Do you think it will work?"

"I guess we will find out tomorrow at school," Shawn said, pulling me into his arms.

"Yeah, it was fun, but I've go get to training," Jo said, morphing back into her street clothes.

"I am going to leave too. There is no point in getting trouble with Dad yet." Heather got up and stood near Jo.

"See you at school," Jo said, then she was gone.

"See you Tuesday," Heather said, before she disappeared from the room.

Shawn pulled me into his arms and we moved to a boat in the middle of the lake. It was a beautiful day with no wind, and the sun was just warm enough.

"What are we doing here?" I asked, looking at the distant shore.

"I thought we could use some downtime. Your life is about to get crazy and I wanted to spend at least one more dream with you before our jobs got in the way." He took my hand and pulled me back, so I was leaning against his chest.

"It's all going to change isn't it?" I asked, looking up at the sky.

"Yes, but I will always be at your side."

"And I will be at yours." I turned my head and found Shawn's lips. Something told me Shawn was right, time was fleeting so we had better enjoy what we had while we still could.

Thank you for reading the first installment of Knight Flyers! I hope you enjoyed it. You, the reader are the reason I write. I hope this story took out of your everyday life and allowed you dream, because you can do anything if you dream big enough.

This book has been a year in the making and I could not have done without the help of some very special people. Jess, your input on this book gave me faith in the story, without you I don't know that I would have gotten this far with it. Leah, you always believed in me and helped make me who I am. Amy, you read this book twice and each time had the best insights and comments. Last but never least a huge thank you goes to my husband who lets me spend most of my free time writing and doesn't complain about it too much.

Look for the next Knight Flyer's book in late 2018

Ann McCune

I live on forty acres in Northwest Colorado with two dogs (Ajax and Achilles),

my amazing husband and an ever changing amount of barn cats.

I love to write about the Heroines Journey in the paranormal universe,

because writing about everyday life is boring for me. I love taking a character

who thinks she is weak and showing her how strong she really is.

When I am not staring at the monitor writing, I am staring at my Kindle

reading, or spending time with my husband and animals.

Check out my website: AnnMcCune.com
Follow me on Social Media!
Facebook: @KnightFlyers
Instagram: ann_mccune